ISBN-13: 978-1494231125
ISBN-10: 1494231123

Cover Illustration, Design & Typesetting
by James Tuomey

UNDONE

Daire O'Driscoll

CHAPTER 1

ALONG THE waterfront there was little to be heard but the centuries old cracking of wooden fishing vessels and the grating of rust devoured bodies of iron desperately struggling to stay afloat. A glowing moonlight was generously reflected atop the water's blackness, but the light emitted by this reflection seemed to lose all strength the instant it reached the cold stone of the waterfront. Despite a handful of lamps suspended along the pier at the water's edge, the surroundings that stood on solid ground were lost in shadow. An intimidating ennui of the dream-world hung about this spectral plane, a plateau perfectly suited to the persuasions of even the least learned scholar of subconscious solitude.

The small harbour was soaked with smells far more sinister than the usual aromas of the sea, perhaps as much a product of one's mind as of any sins hidden beyond the glow of the lamps. It was not immediately clear to the untrained eye whether the harbour had been used in the last decade or even century. It felt as though every surrounding object had ceased to function a long time ago, if indeed they had ever done so.

A lone figure navigated this landscape of decay, straddling the thin, lamp-lit line between the creaking, rusted monsters to its right and the point at which the lamplight faded to its left. Beyond this boundary, all that could be seen or heard was the odd flicker of light in one of the endless, deserted buildings, or gurgled sounds from which one could just as easily discern drunken laughter or screams of agony. The figure displayed no interest in the sounds or sights of the dock, but merely strode forward determinedly, omitting an air of confidence, yet also a desire to be free of its surroundings.

What seemed to be the frame of a tall, well-built man was concealed beneath a dark-brown coat which hung well below the knees, while the face protected its secrecy by means of both the coat's collar and a grey bowler hat. Underneath the coat all that was visible was a pair of black trousers which came to a halt atop a pair of shoes that shone a bright white against the darkness of the picture. Beneath these shoes, steady and heavy footsteps took hold of the surrounding quiet, and echoed between the water and the wasteland.

The frames of the seemingly defunct factories and fishing yards to the left of this man flew by as his own concerns drove him onward, instantly ending any intentions of satisfying what curiosities such surroundings naturally inspire in a person. His footsteps continued to echo with authoritative resonance as he marched along the pier, neither halting nor slowing for an instant.

Indeed it was curiosities of another sort that transfixed this character's thought, as his mind raced back over the events of the past few days. Just a short time ago he had been preparing to spend the foreseeable future with little of the usual exertion or danger involved in his life. Instead he had been roused from his slumber-like existence, partly by the substantial financial benefits, but also by the appeals to his ego, the need to explain the bizarre nature of the requests for his services and the sheer thrill he gained from completing his tasks. These urges fired him onwards down the dank and dingy promenade, his bright shoes carving through the darkness around him like flashing blades of steel, until they came to a sudden stop under a lamppost with an old and rusted sign swinging from it.

The sign displayed a crudely painted ship, seemingly centuries old, traversing a stretch of ocean. It was alive with sailors and deckhands all frantically engaged in their duties, which at present were concentrated on keeping the ship afloat. In the bottom left hand corner of this scene an enormous whirlpool threatened to engulf all the cohabitants of the picture. The whirlpool was presented in such a way as to be able to see down the proverbial eye, at the bottom of which a blazing fire burned, further dooming all that fell to the water's fierce wrath. Though the sign was clearly the work of an amateur, the artist had succeeded in capturing the fear of the ship's crew. The sailors screamed, at one another, at themselves and at whatever power they believed was in the darkened skies above them, all the while their faces fixed with grotesque expressions of pure terror.

The figure stared at this sign, taking in the disturbing scene, before turning left down an adjacent walkway he had clearly expected to be there. This shoddy road of rotted planks seemed barely strong enough to support a grown man and with every frequent gap in the wood the black water beneath was visible, bubbling menacingly under each step forward. This pathway led between several dark, abandoned buildings, some of which looked to have been lost to fire long ago, while others simply had the façade of places that no sane person would ever desire to discover. Their very appearance warned off potential interest, with an eeriness that could not be related to any particular aspect of the buildings themselves, but nonetheless seeped powerfully from the murky picture. None of these structures indicated, any more than the ones the figure had previously passed, any inhabitancy or use, and accordingly he proceeded past them until he came to a halt.

He stood before a large and grim looking building, placed upon solid foundations of concrete which began where the dilapidated walkway came to an end. It gave the appearance of being a two-storey construction until the figure came closer to it and realised that another floor was accessible at the bottom of a small flight of crude, stone steps, descending below ground level. Based on the glimpses he caught of the water between the boards, at high tide this floor could quite possibly be beneath sea level, with only a few layers of plaster and mortar separating whatever awaited inside, from what lay in the unforgiving depths of the sea.

The part of the structure that was above ground seemed little more than a dilapidated wreck, another empty frame succumbing to damp and decay and rotted far beyond salvation. No light or sound escaped its many dark orifices. Indeed its numerous vacant windows, crumbling chimneys and heavy wooden door impressed the idea upon the man that nothing had ever resided in this building, and that if anything had taken place there it had been of such a nature that its secret escaping the walls could not be beneficial to the world in any way.

The figure quickly took the wreck in with a glance before turning his attention to the unlit, stone staircase that took one below. He slowly began to descend the uneven, broken steps, gripping the walls tightly for want of any railing. Several times he almost lost his footing on a slippery substance that lay under his darkened feet. Slowly he made his way to the bottom, and about a dozen steps down he seemed to be on even ground once more.

The figure could see nothing before him but managed to feel out what his hands told him was a small, wooden door in his path. Despite its miniature size, it seemed strongly built and was covered in rounded, iron studs. As his eyes adjusted to the darkness he slowly became aware of a picture of sorts, attached to the slimy wall that lay on the left of this door. He was able to make out that it was a sign depicting the same haunting scene as the one that had previously guided him. The figure now knew he was at the right place. He lifted a fist wrapped in a tight, black, leather glove and pounded heavily upon the wooden door. Almost instantly a gruff voice, muffled by the apparent thickness of the door, scowled out a response to his knock:

"Who's there?"

"I'm expected by a Mister Albright."

"What's your business with him?" came the stern reply.

"That's something I'd rather discuss with Mister Albright. I'd appreciate it if you let me enter before I do so of my own will."

This seemed to satisfy the voice on the other side of the door. There was a clanging of chains and the door was pulled back to allow access to the visitor. The figure took one last breath of fresh air, glanced back up the staircase at the angry night he was departing from, ducked his head and stepped through the doorway.

Chapter 2

Once inside the door there was an immediate waft of aromas, and the figure entered a short passageway, surrounded on all sides by stone walls and capped with a stone ceiling. At the end of the corridor a dull, glowing light was visible. In many parts the brickwork of the walls was hidden by dense masses of moss and a variety of other anonymous substances. This made the newcomer to the passageway wary, contemplating to what extent this growth may have been attributed to the constant raging of the sea that took place on the other side of these walls. Miniature empires of insects spanned these stone and moss bases, engaged in their own duties and undisturbed by the two visitors to their realm, seemingly accustomed to such passings by.

The smells that attacked the man's senses comprised of a multitude of generally indistinguishable ingredients. At first there was the immediate force of the damp and the growth upon the walls. It had a revolting effect that at once summoned images of both sea and sewer to mind. The twosome continued down this darkened, stone hallway and upon coming closer to the light than the door from which they had entered, the figure noticed a shift in the aromas. The offensive, salty air was displaced by something new. It was a sweet, pungent smell which gave the impression of something that had once been soothing having gone sour. Its vapours were strong and thick, sending a challenge to the senses. The lack of air in the small tunnel made the first encounter with it almost overpowering and the man's lungs felt as though they were being squeezed by iron fists from within, while his eyes struggled to hold back tears from the sheer sting in the air. These vapours possessed the agonising whisper of unaccountable familiarity; an odour that strikes suddenly and immediately states that it has been smelt before, but the remembrance of where disappears before it allows itself to be recalled, leaving a hideously frustrating sense of déjà vu.

The footsteps of the two men echoed resoundingly in this confined space with neither uttering a word until they emerged out of the corridor into an open space from which the light was coming. It was a low-ceilinged room, deceptively large due to the weak nature of the light that glowed from lamps and candles at various points upon the walls, failing to illuminate its many dark corners and crevices. At regular intervals there were crumbling stone pillars, so ancient they looked exhausted from the mere act of running from floor to ceiling. The figure had entered into the south-east corner of this enclosure and on the opposite wall was amassed a large quantity of barrels, while further along this same wall was a wooden counter which appeared to function as a bar, currently unattended.

If one was not given ample opportunity to stop and examine the surroundings, but was merely brought through this area, the pillars and lack of light combined to obstruct any opportunity of looking deeper into the gloomy recesses of the room. Wooden tables were dotted around this squalid tabernacle, mostly concentrated in these dimly lit areas. The short, stout man who had opened the door gestured to the figure to follow him across this scene. As he walked upon the outlines of the man's fleeting footprints, all the figure could distinguish in the shadows were minor details of what lay within them. At one table a glance of a dark tattoo against sun scorched skin. A ringed hand clutching a lit cigar passing quickly between two pillars. Between the bar and barrels a clutch of shadows gathered round a table, an innumerable amount of recluses from the world conducting the basest of business in this dank and stinking dungeon. The only audible sound from any of the figure's fellow inhabitants of the room was a low murmuring that all melded together to lend the place a soundtrack somewhat akin to the violent, simultaneous buzzing of a beehive.

The guide led the figure to another heavy, iron-studded door on the left hand side of the bar and knocked heavily upon its wooden body. A muffled sound of frustration was the knock's only echo. The guide opened the door slightly and quietly mumbled something to whoever waited inside. After a few more words the man brought his head back out of the doorway, held the door open for the figure to pass through and muttered that Mr. Albright was ready to see him.

The figure now ventured into an arena far more finely furnished than the previous space, yet just as strange in its own manner. The room was not particularly wide but stretched upwards to an impressively high ceiling. This effect caused one to wonder, upon entering, whether the room occupied the two stories of the building above water level as well. However, between the corridor and the gloomy bar area the figure had lost track of what part of the building they were under, if indeed they were still below it at all.

The floor of the room was graced by a thick, soft and richly-coloured purple carpet, which allowed feet to lightly sink into its folds with every step. The walls were adorned their entire length with dark, crimson curtains, so that none of the crude architecture of the other rooms was visible. On each of these four walls, a large oil painting covered part of the curtain, just a little above eye level. Each depicted scenes upon the seas, not dissimilar to the one the figure had hitherto twice encountered, but none held the blazing fire within their frame. All depicted great vessels engaged in various activities, one struggling violently with an enormous harpooned whale, another nervously anticipating a foreign ship which appeared upon the horizon. The next painting had the boat braving the slope of a wave's monstrous jaws, while the fourth showed a sun-scorched ship upon a motionless sea, the eyes of the crew all fixed upon a giant bird of prey circling overhead.

In each corner of the room a lamp sat upon a small table, flanked on either side by plush, black, leather couches, giving the room an almost complete walled seating apart from the break where the door lay. The only other light in the room came from a lamp that sat atop a wide, oaken desk. A single leather armchair lay on either side of this desk.

"Please make yourself comfortable Mr. Mason," said the man who stood waiting on the opposite side.

The voice was full of social grace and class, but reeked power. It seemed soft without being gentle, but each word still echoed through the chamber as loudly as possible short of being threatening or shouting. It was like the tolling of an iron church bell, the familiarities of society mixed with a gargantuan volume that rung around the tower of that high-ceilinged arena. To the figure, his words seemed tinged with an unidentifiable, foreign accent. It was so subtle, however, that he believed he may have merely created it in the workings of his own imagination, due to the exotic nature of this man's surroundings.

Alan Mason decided against sitting for the time being. Instead he slowly surveyed the man in front of him.

"I'm not getting comfortable until you make a few things clear Albright," he spat, "I'm not in the habit of being threatened by clients before I take on a case and I'm definitely not accustomed to being on good terms with them afterwards."

Mr. Albright assumed a reclined, yet dignified and defensive, position within the thick, leather chair on his side of the desk. He was a man clearly comfortable enough to not be concerned with whether those he dealt with liked him or not, and who seemed satisfied to ponder for a significant period how he would meet Mason's spirited greeting.

Mason guessed from the way Albright presented himself and responded to others, that he was a man of at least fifty years, probably older, and if not was merely accustomed to being listened to and obeyed without question. His features and manners, though matured by age, seemed almost timeless, as though they could have been born of any civilised society from the preceding five hundred years. He wore an elegant suit of the plushest, black velvet, as if it were designed for the sole purpose of lying beneath diamonds in a shop front window. Underneath lay a white shirt, but this was rendered almost invisible by the depths of the suit's darkness.

The man's face was clearly aged, with wrinkles and undesirable lines creasing his countenance here and there. However it still maintained its original shape and proportions, and, besides these dents upon his skin, his face resonated with the physical power of a much younger man. The hair atop his head was almost entirely grey but precisely cropped. His face was clean shaven but his thick eyebrows were of a black akin to his suit, fiercely striking atop his features and looking so heavy as to almost drag his face to earth at any moment. Below these masses of darkness lay his eyes. They were eyes that defied satisfactory description due to their constant assumption of different forms. The pupils appeared to be ever changing in size and depth.

They were simultaneously blue, brown and green, all battling for dominance, sometimes all and sometimes none. When Albright would become even slightly interested they became inflamed and swelled to prodigious proportions, almost threatening to swallow the rest of his face, marauding around his sockets, defying the weaker eyes of others to meet his stare. When seemingly placid or merely calm, his pupils were minimal almost to the point of disappearing altogether. They would recede back and disappear in the swirl of blue, brown and green, but Mason was still always aware of their gaze. He may not have been able to determine what exactly Albright's eyes gazed upon but he could feel them almost penetrating his person when Albright looked in his direction, the pupils like invisible needles, testing his body for points of weakness.

"There is absolutely nothing to fear here in my chamber Mr. Mason," said Albright, "and I apologise for what you may have perceived as my rough handling of your appointment. However, this is a matter of great importance and the security of its privacy is almost as dear to me as the conclusion of the task at hand. So please, be seated, and we shall discuss your duties."

Mason disliked what may have been interpreted as a patronising tone in Albright's voice but nonetheless decided to hear him out. He would remain on guard and ensure not to become entirely relaxed, but his curiosity and driven ego fuelled his desire to hear the statement of the case. He sat upon the edge of the armchair and sullenly invited Albright to proceed. Albright began to speak.

CHAPTER 3

"I want you to find a man," Albright began. "This man has taken something of great value from me and I wish you to return the item in question. To me. Here. And to bring the culprit too. Thus it is a simple enough assignment for one in your line of work Mr. Mason, but the reward shall be substantially greater than that associated with your average case."

"And what's the reason for this substantial bonus to my wage?" inquired Mason, always eager to straighten out any grey areas in his cases and to immediately establish their true nature.

Albright smiled a little, revealing a perfect set of teeth, dazzlingly white.

"The job in question requires absolute secrecy towards the uninvolved world, and a certain amount of discretion on your part," he said. "You will be given your instructions and you will follow them without question. You are merely the factor that ensures this affair proceeds according to plan – it is none of your concern to become interested in the causes of those involved. I will pay you a princely sum because I believe you are a man whose loyalty can easily be bought. I want you to carry out the task I assign you and I am paying you a handsome amount to do so without questioning my methods or motive. Needless to say I have been wronged by the party in question and you will see to it that I am righted. With the amount of money involved there will be little for you to think about besides following orders and completing your assignment, regardless of what that entails."

"Sounds like you're paying me to either ignore some particularly important details or do something illegal," Mason replied.

"It certainly would not be the first time, would it?"

Mason chose to remain silent, merely maintaining contact with Albright's eyes.

"Your reputation as a man who is willing to do anything to attain his goal is what grasped my attention to begin with. There are plenty more of your kind out there, willing to work, I would wager, for a prize of significantly lesser value, whom I could just as easily have contacted. However, I have been told that you are a man who always successfully completes his task, and who has occasionally blurred the lines of the law in doing so."

This irritated Mason somewhat.

"Yeah, there's been occasions when situations arose that required certain actions of an unwholesome nature on my part, sure, when no other avenues of progress were open to me and I did what I had to do. I'm not, however, used to it being insinuated at the outset of a case that my job will almost certainly involve illegal actions and that I'm expected to blindly dive into it without knowing anything as to its actualities. This is what worries me and makes me instantly apprehensive, or should I say more apprehensive than before, about doing business with you."

Albright let out a quiet laugh, the mirth of a powerful individual secretly aware of surrounding events and finding great revelry in the misinformed fools about them. It was a deep sound, not clearly audible but noticeable, like the reverb of a bass or the purring of some ferocious jungle-cat. He struck Mason as a man who never laughed any other way.

"Yes I know, Mr. Mason, and I suspected that this would be your initial attitude. However, I also know of both your love for money and, more importantly, of your ecstatic curiosity and thrill in such cases, along with your egotistical leanings. That is why I hired you in such a rough-handed manner, as I knew you would come to me regardless, offended and angry or not. That is why I am offering you such a considerable payment for your job, because I know as well as you do that you are intrigued, and that by the end of our conversation you will have agreed to accept it."

Mason did not like being discussed in this petulant manner as though he were not present, being referred to as some mechanical creature that always followed the same course of action, the few parlour tricks it had managed to master. He tried to remain calm and not allow it show that Albright had got under his skin.

Albright purred a heavy laugh once more.

"Ha, I see I have already ignited fires of contempt in your eyes.

And despite your urges to perhaps strike me or cause humiliation by other means, I am the one in the position of power and I can tell those fires also burn with your desire to hear the particulars of this affair. Therefore I shall explain and you will be on your way."

Mason clenched the rests of the armchair to restrain his rising aggravation, as he struggled not to respond to Albright's taunting.

Albright continued to speak.

"The man you will find for me is named Raymond Sadler. He is a pathetic, low-rent journalist and photographer that used to frequent this establishment. My business associates and I often use these rooms for our own private functions, to discuss important matters away from the prying eyes and pricking ears of a suspicious world. Due to the small clientele of this place you tend to encounter the same rabble time and again. Sadler and I got into a slight altercation when I accused him of eavesdropping on my business affairs. He was removed from the premises swearing revenge. The next day my security box in this building had been wrenched open, the lock destroyed and my private belongings removed. A small brooch of significant monetary and sentimental value was stolen and nobody has seen Sadler since. I know it was Sadler and I want it back. Now I would like you to go and find him."

Mason leaned slightly back in the comforting chair for the first time. It was so deep that it felt as though there was no back to it, that one would merely sink back further into its recesses until extricated, like a black and beautiful pool of quicksand.

"Are you absolutely positive this is the man who took the item?"

"Mr. Mason, do not for one instant take me for a fool, or indeed second guess the information I give you. Sadler stole it. I know this. I want it back. Now you know this. You may leave and return both him and the brooch to me."

"Listen Albright, I'm a professional and there are certain details that I'd like to know, whether this fits in with your delusions of grandeur and the spooky atmosphere you've orchestrated here or not. What's the significance of this brooch? What business did the argument with Sadler concern? And what exactly do you intend to do with him if I decide to bring him to you?"

"The continuous run of zeros marking the cheque on the table will ensure that you will sleep tight, Mr. Mason, without having to worry yourself over such trivial matters. As I have explained this is a matter of immense personal importance, one which I demand the unknowing world remains detached from and oblivious to. Think of this job merely as transport to your retirement. You will receive more money than you will be able to spend for the rest of your natural life. So long as you keep your mouth closed and follow my instructions, you will be sufficiently furnished to fulfil whatever fantasies you desire."

Mason intensely disliked the job already. He had thus far come to the conclusion that there were a number of unlawful reasons for Albright's demand for secrecy, and suspected that the plethora of details omitted from Albright's summary of the matter at hand would come to light in a nasty fashion, possibly with unpleasant consequences.

However, this apprehension was matched, if not bettered, by his thirst to find these facts out for himself, both to satiate his ignorance of the case and, now, almost to spite Albright. The thrill of such a mysterious hunt also fired up his pride. He leaned over and picked up the cheque. For the first time his outward demeanour of coldness, nerve and a certain suave was shattered, albeit only for an instant, by the monumental figure scratched out upon the document in dark ink. He could not deny that Albright spoke the truth about the potentials of the cheque's figure.

His shock must have been noticeable to the older man.

"I gather you will accept the job then?"

Albright opened a small drawer on his side of the desk and brought out an envelope of a fine, dark, red paper and placed it in front of Mason.

"Any further information at my disposal that may be of use to you is contained within. I am a busy man and it is imperative that this matter be resolved as soon as possible. It is now the 24th of the month. You will have brought Sadler and the brooch to me by the night of the 29th and not a moment later."

"That's not a whole lot of time."

"It places five days at your disposal. Not much perhaps, but sufficient for someone of your experience to find a simple reporter, especially at such a price. Now, Mr. Mason, I intend to spend my evening involved in more frivolous matters with significantly improved company. I trust we will speak with each other soon."

Mason ventured one last question.

"How can I get in touch with you?"

"You will not," Albright replied simply. "If any need should arise, I will make sure to contact you myself. I know how"

Albright promptly turned and left the room by an almost invisible door in the wall behind his desk, opposite that which Mason had entered by.

"Come on" was muttered abruptly and Mason turned to see the overweight doorman standing beside their own point of entry. He was unaware whether he had been present for the entire conversation. He stood up, pocketed the envelope and followed the loathsome man out of the room.

As he walked through the filthy bar area once more he pondered the recent scene, running its minutiae through his mind. Albright had said that he only frequented the establishment for certain business meetings but Mason sensed that Albright was extremely comfortable in these surroundings, so much so that he may have even played a role in designing the place. It also seemed unlikely that a man like Albright stored valuables in a security box in a place he only went to for discussions with his business partners, particularly one of such contrasting natures of squalor and splendour, if indeed it even had such a facility. He wondered what kind of business was discussed in such a foul, secluded dwelling...

However, in truth Mason did not particularly care what Albright did or what purposes this dive served for him. He could stretch the creativity of his imagination sufficiently far so as to see Albright and his business associates all dressed up in devil worshipping robes or circled round a table at some twisted séance, but it was of little interest to him. So long as he solved the case and got his money such details did not especially matter. He was going to find this Raymond Sadler and he was going to deliver him to Albright without question. The sturdy gatekeeper opened the way to the night outside and Mason swiftly crossed the threshold to return to the world from which he had come.

CHAPTER 4

Alan Mason had been contemplating giving up his business for a considerable time. However his aforementioned mental attributes, or detriments depending upon how one viewed them, had ensured that every now and then someone managed to secure his services for another job. Often this feat was accomplished without a great deal of effort required on the part of the paying party.

He was financially secure enough to enjoy the rest of his life in relative comfort and, if necessary, he could easily have pursued a number of other less demanding and dangerous career paths. He was at the age in a man's life where his heartbeat entitles him to the same amount of exercise and capacity for living, but sometimes at a slightly less efficient level. In his line of work scuffles and full out brawls were not infrequent and, although Mason could still hold his own against most men, he could not ruffle a room of muscle like he had in bygone times. Standing at almost six foot three, he was a towering figure and a youth shaped and formed by strict service in the army before assuming his life as a bounty hunter had smouldered him into cast iron. It had also provided him with an early growing disdain for much of humanity.

Mason disliked the way the world worked. He considered it a mostly hopeless, hypocritical collection of the very worst life had to offer, a place where one could expect to achieve virtually nothing beyond making enough money to survive by any means. The thought of contributing anything to the restructuring of society or even the helping of an individual struck him as little more than a pointless waste of time in a land where everything and everybody was already far beyond rescue. The best way to handle life was simply to look after his own interests. He had always considered most of the people he caught as less than scum, entirely deserving of whatever punishment they received. He was merely a soldier for justice, justice that could not be purchased in courts, at least certainly not as easily or cheaply. At the outset of his career this had been an easy role to assume as most of his cases were on a small scale, family related matters where the results would often be the mere returning of a runaway teenager to their parents or the admission of an affair by an unfaithful spouse.

However, as his stature had risen, naturally, so had that of his employers and thus his cases. He quickly found himself being employed by successful companies and wealthy prospectors. The consequences of his finding missing people became more and more extreme, while the lines between just punishment and vigilantism, whether out of court or not, began to become less clear.

Originally he had been turned on by the job due to the mysteries it presented, along with his distaste for the way civilised society supposedly operated and the advantages of his brutish size. He felt adrenaline coursing through his veins like lava through the lines of a volcano, waiting to erupt, as he embarked on a new case, and hunted down another sinner. He was excited by the rush he felt when tracking someone, and was overrun by his pride, proud of the fact that he always found and delivered his target. This thrill was too much to turn down and he embraced it time and again, believing himself to be a bottomless bottle of bleach in a world of germs and parasites.

Over time though, the mystery that had once enticed him had been further veiled as he was unable to predict the fate of the people he brought in. His clients had become even more powerful. Rich businessmen with fortunes of questionable origin and high profile lawyers with ties to organised crime demanded he hunt down names on sheets of paper without inquiring as to who they were or what their sentences might be. In some cases he would not even be informed of their names. However, days later he would often read of the disappearance of such and such a witness or property development regulator, occasionally related in some vague and suspicious, but untraceable way, to his client.

Mason considered himself a man who merely reversed the results of some of the misdeeds in this world and, with his lack of a soft spot for humanity, regarded his actions as not entirely unjust, even as something of a necessity. However, despite deluding himself into subscribing to his own brand of outlaw justice, he did not consider murder to be an acceptable form of punishment and grew increasingly concerned that he was delivering his targets to a fate proportionally worse than the crimes they had committed.

The rise in priority and underground infamy of his work had also resulted in more dangerous jobs and he had made himself a hate figure for several large companies and local criminal figures. Being a sizeable, physical threat that could stand toe to toe with almost any opponent had served him exceedingly well thus far and made him comfortably wealthy, but as he began to come closer to reaching half a century of life, he had started to think that this line of work was becoming unsuited to a man of his lessening abilities. Of late Mason had found it difficult to sleep as soundly as usual, his thoughts often becoming twisted in unpleasant fashions by his subconscious and submitting him to nightly mental tortures, of which he would have little recollection upon waking. He often awoke in the midst of a terrible nightmare which he immediately forgot, but from which he would still feel physically shaken.

In the rare cases that he had accepted in the last few months, however, the thrills and pride had overridden these sensibilities, with employers praising his reputation and presenting him with challenges they almost dared him to complete. Most of the time his brief moments of concern for the well-being of the hunted were quickly dashed, replaced by his driven determination and desire for superiority. Besides, Mason reasoned, if you tangled with rich, powerful crime bosses and unscrupulous businessmen, the chances were you either wanted to be one or were simply outright foolish. They deserved everything they got. This was the state of mind he was in as he entered the employment of Mr. Albright.

Two days earlier the envelope that would bring so much turbulence to Mason's world had slipped under the door of his small but elegant apartment, on the third floor of a charming building. It retained much of the beauty of a house of antiquity, but offered the utmost comfort available in the modern abode of the well to do. Mason lived in a respectable and safe neighbourhood, a rarity in the wretched city, but still just a short distance from the grime and filth of the centre.

Outside the city was suffering beneath an inexhaustible heat-wave. Between the hours when the sun rose and set, it held an unchallenged dominance over the skies, with no clouds daring to drift even so far as the fringes of the horizon. The sun scorched the streets of the city, turning plants into charred, smouldering ruins and people into drowsy, inactive corpses. Even during the dark of night the humidity denied respite from the oppressive heat. The air, thick and heavy, refused to be drawn into the lungs, and held a tight grip on the body. Mason would frequently be woken due to his bed having become a dripping pool of his own sweat. Despite expensive air conditioning, he rose in the morning more exhausted than when he had gone to sleep the night before as a result of these nights of intense, constant sweating. The weather forecast had said it was the highest temperature recorded in the city for over seventy years and that it was only going to get hotter.

The message did not arrive until sometime in the afternoon, hours after the regular post had been received. It had hence been delivered in person and was devoid of stamp or address. It was a pure white envelope, but with an impressive detail of swirling spirals upon the finest paper. It immediately embedded itself in Mason's brain, complete with the exciting enticement that is occasioned by the prospect of something unknown. It was sealed by the traditional wax method, a rich, ruby-red wax, with the single letter 'A' engraved into the dried shell. 'Mr Mason' were the only words to be found upon it, written in lavish handwriting of elegant lines and loops.

Mason was used to potential clients attempting to impress themselves upon him and playing to his pride, although he was probably less aware of how effectively these methods worked, and he opened the envelope immediately without giving further consideration to the extravagant presentation. However, it did not escape his vexation that he had been contacted at his home, as opposed to the office he rented deeper within the city, the place where he usually conducted all of his business. This invasion of his home was unprofessional, provocative and undeniably mysterious to Mason. This person had obviously wanted to send this message directly to him and strike a nerve while doing so.

Inside was a single slip of paper, comprised of the same luxurious qualities. It presented a single paragraph of words, scribed in the same sublime scrawl.

Mr. Mason, I am willing to offer you a job which requires your particular talents and a certain degree of disclosure. Your payment will be far more substantial than any previously received for your employment. It is a job where secrecy is of profound importance and once you commit to it you must be willing to complete your task no matter what it entails. Once you are made aware of the circumstances you will not be permitted to refuse this employment. If you are not interested forget this business now and burn this letter. If you wish to pursue this case deliver this letter to room 57 in the Osbourne Arms Hotel opposite the Central Train Station tomorrow. Under either circumstance you will not mention this letter to anybody, and under either circumstance you may expect a visit, the nature of which will be dependent upon your actions.

Mason immediately disliked the tone of the letter. He abhorred the opening sentence, the statement that the client was willing to offer him a job, as though it were an act of pity, a gain-less sacrifice for the mercy of a man stretched upon the rack. He also disliked the thinly masked threat in the final sentence. However, he was not shaken by this manner and assumed it to be another client playing up their own grandness. He would bring the letter to the hotel the following day. He would discover the terms, conditions and particulars of payment from this prospective employer and, although he was not overly disturbed by the warnings, would not mention it to anybody until he had acquired a vague grasp of the situation at hand.

He was not afraid of these overblown businessmen, idolising themselves and their own stabs at power, one of which his current potential employer undoubtedly was, wasting his time on such frivolous trivialities as envelope presentation. He would learn the details of the affair and felt comfortable that he could easily detach himself from it if necessary, without this person following up on their threats.

The following day Mason carried out the instructions as planned and afterwards sat in his apartment, doing little other than awaiting further notice. He had brought the letter to the hotel early in the morning. Upon entering the busy and beautifully decorated lobby he had crossed the marble floor to the reception. Mason told the chirpy, young lady behind the desk that he had stayed there previously and asked whether his favourite room, number 57, was available that evening. The receptionist informed Mason that it was unoccupied that night and for the foreseeable future, but eyed him suspiciously, mentioning that there were far nicer rooms than number 57. He excused himself to find his way upstairs and arrived at the room in question on the third floor of the building.

Mason knocked upon the door to the room several times but was answered only by silence. Thoughts crawled their way into his mind of forcing his way inside, now that his interest had been aroused, but he decided against it. Regardless of who this strange, and now seemingly non-existent, client was, it was still possible that this case would be a profitable one. It was not wise to destroy a potentially beneficial relationship at the first opportunity by disregarding instructions. Despite his curiosity being piqued and an urge to catch the conspirators unawares, he slipped the letter under the door as ordered and returned home.

By six o'clock that evening there had been no response of any kind, nor had there been any indication that one was to follow. Mason began to wonder whether the prospective client had merely been an over-enthusiast, or indeed whether the letter was an elaborate hoax for some unknown person's benefit or amusement.

He continued to wait, growing ever more impatient with inactivity and now feeling idle, having already entered the mind-state required for an eventful, working day. As late afternoon turned to dusk, and dusk darkened to night, Mason sat, solitary in his living room, becoming invisible in the blackness, having sat waiting stationary without even turning on a lamp. Eventually, close to eleven o'clock, as his eyes began sinking heavily, he was shaken into life by a crisp rapping upon his front door.

Mason pulled the blockade back to come face to face with a short, stocky man with dark hair stretched back over his scalp almost to the point of uprooting itself with his neck's next motion. He wore what appeared an expensive, cream suit and his eyes were decorated with sunglasses despite the lateness of the hour. The skin surrounding these decorations was unnaturally pale, indicating to Mason that the man rarely braved the outside world during daylight hours, and that the sunglasses were most likely a necessary addition to his wardrobe. He was holding another small, white envelope by his side in a hand blighted by numerous dark-red and purple veins disgustingly running up and down its fingers. It looked as though most of them had been recently burst, perhaps by a steamroller or a stampede. Mason stared at this disfigured limb-ending for a moment until his distraction was interrupted.

"Mason," the visitor abruptly began in a dry, crackling voice. It sounded as though his mouth had been devoid of saliva for decades. "Follow the instructions in this envelope to arrange your employment. We trust you are as yet the only person involved?"

Mason went to take the envelope but the man's hand drew it out of reach.

"Relax," Mason said, "no-one knows about our delightful correspondence. How's your hand?"

"That is good for your own sake," croaked the little man, ignoring the question. "If you have brought the situation to the attention of other persons you can trust that you will be reprehended accordingly."

Mason eyed him unflinchingly – "Listen, don't come to bother me in my home throwing threats around or I'll make sure you'll leave this building on your hands and knees. Next time contact me at my office and, while you're at it, try and do so in a professional manner."

The man hissed a low sinister sound, crackling loudly inside the dry hollow of his mouth.

"It is not me who is concerned with your actions. Rather my employer, who has now also become your employer. I repeat, you will be punished accordingly if you disobey us."

Mason scowled at him and, deciding to remove this unwelcome visitor from his door as quickly as was possible, grabbed the envelope from his hand.

"You certainly have a tendency towards the dramatic. Trust me; I haven't sold out your little circus."

The man looked at him from behind his dark glasses and hissed some inaudible words. The two stood staring at each other for several seconds, Mason wondering what was going on in the mind of his unwanted guest. The man then slowly turned and departed, making his way down the stairs at the end of the hall. Mason took the envelope inside and opened it. It solely contained a note written in the same writing as before.

Come to the address provided tomorrow night at 11pm. Look out for the sign. I trust my messenger has already made your commitment to this case clear.

Underneath was an address situated somewhere in the docklands. A small picture on a piece of card was also inside, depicting a ship battling a raging inferno on the seas.

Mason sat in his home two days later and opened the red envelope that Albright had given him. It contained several documents and photographs. The first three photographs all had writing scribbled in their corners identifying the man who occupied a similar space in each of them as Sadler. In the pictures the target was not involved in any particularly interesting activities – Sadler crossing at traffic lights, sitting drinking a coffee, and a close up of him talking on a payphone. They had most likely been taken by somebody who had been secretly observing his actions, assumedly before his disappearance. He was a short, thin, slight man, in his mid-twenties perhaps, or, if older, graced with that particular charm of looks that signifies youthfulness, appearing as though he would always look younger than he actually was. Based on these images alone, Sadler did not impress Mason as a particularly threatening individual. Sadler struck him as a wholly unremarkable, young photographer, possibly having recently finished his education, a regular person with an eye for detail and no better means of earning money in his life to date. If he had crossed swords with Albright, he did not look like someone who would, or even could, cause any harm, unless he had somehow fortuitously found himself with the upper hand over the businessman, having stolen the brooch, or perhaps even being in possession of some deleterious secret of Albright's. Even then, he seemed to Mason as one who would not use such an advantage unless he was in a desperate crisis, financial or otherwise. However, if Mason had learned anything from years spent in his business, it was that appearances were unreliable, that anyone, even with the seemingly youthful normality of Sadler, could potentially be evil incarnate, or at the least a skilful and dangerous opponent.

The next photographs he examined were of an attractive, young woman with reddish-fair hair, certainly no older than thirty. In one picture she was at a bar with Sadler and in another she was jogging in clothing of a material that left little to the imagination. She possessed a strikingly attractive face and immediately appeared a more singular, noticeable character than Sadler. These pictures had been marked as containing Sadler's girlfriend, Rachel Gaines. She appeared athletic and struck Mason as a very driven, most likely successful, woman.

Also provided in the package were the addresses of both Sadler's and Gaines' homes, along with a pile of bank notes, a considerably large sum of money compared to what he was usually offered as an advance. At the bottom of the pile there sat a slip of paper, written in familiar handwriting.

Do not forget that you are working with a deadline. Your employment will be terminated if this deadline is not met. Do not fail to remember your commitment to this job and that withdrawal is at this point unacceptable

Mason briefly scanned through this collection once more. It struck him as peculiar that there was neither picture of, nor information regarding, the brooch in question. Essentially it was not of enormous significance, as once he caught up with Sadler the man would surely hand over whatever he had taken. Regardless, it was odd that the package was devoid of mention of the brooch at all. Mason shook his head to clear his thoughts and decided to get into bed. It was now several hours after midnight and he was eager to get to work the next morning. He let the kitchen tap run for several minutes but the water running through the building's warm pipes refused to cool. He nonetheless filled a glass, placed it on his bedside table and slipped under the sheets into slumber.

CHAPTER 5

Mason pulled his car up opposite 73 Oakfield Drive, removed the scribbled address from his coat pocket and made sure that it matched the number of the building in question. The house was a two-storey, single-standing structure that appeared at first glance to have been abandoned for some time. The building itself displayed no strikingly decrepit signs on its exterior, but rather emanated an aura of disrepair, deterioration and, ultimately, desertion. The light-blue, wooden slats that comprised its walls seemed to Mason to be the house's breathing apparatus, like the gills of an enormous fish that had been stranded upon land, gasping to draw breath in a final, futile attempt to live. Despite the bright, warm day outside, the house windows were impenetrable from a distance. All one could see was black dirt. These were the eyes of the beast, and their closed top halves constantly threatened to come crashing down to the sill's bottoms and shatter the filthy glass, as though these eyelids were blinking. Mason pondered whether he perceived this sense of destitution merely because he was so unsure as to the fate of the house's owner. Raymond Sadler was most likely not to be found here, if indeed he was to be found at all. However, it was the best place to start his investigations.

After a half-hearted attempt to summon somebody with the doorbell, a light knock sent the door swinging open. It had been left unlocked. Mason reminded himself to be on his guard. He pushed the door further open to step inside. The hinges did not so much creak as crack, snapping backwards, holding their burden open wide as though they challenged any visitor to enter. Once through the doorway, Mason was thrust into a moderately sized living area, although such a term was inappropriate at present unless referring to the miniature kingdoms of subhuman creatures that infested its foul, fume-emanating contents. The space had clearly once been planned as a spacious family room, but decay and ruin had been the most recent designers to spread their wares across the interior. The rotting furniture stank and every movement Mason made seemed to cause another billowing of rank dust, as if by merely entering this quarter every pocket of his clothes themselves had become saturated with the stuff. The floor was covered in piles of loosely stacked newspapers, at any moment ready to topple over and supported only by other piles falling against them. The room was very dark and attempts at exerting some influence upon the place by means of the light-switch went unrewarded. At the windowsill the forces of shadow were holding their fortress secure from the siege that daylight laid upon them. Mason listened carefully but heard no sounds and saw nothing to indicate that anybody was there, or had been anytime recently. He decided to look around the house. Perhaps there was something here to indicate Sadler's whereabouts.

Mason began his search in this living room but initially came across little of interest. There seemed to be nothing that offered any information, other than the general state of uncleanliness indicating the absence of any recent occupants. A quick search of a bedroom, that lay through an open archway in one wall, revealed a large wardrobe full of clothes and shoes, of a significantly high quality. The condition of the house and the area in which it was located indicated to Mason that Sadler was not overly wealthy. However, based solely on the presence of some expensive possessions he came across in the bedroom, Sadler nonetheless seemed to have been doing well. Mason suspected that dealings with people such as Albright would bring an abundance of untaxable profit. Regardless, the only reason for goods of such quality to be left to rot in a wardrobe, unless money was not an issue to the party in question, was if the person had left in an unexpected hurry. The current state of the house also caused Mason to ponder exactly how long ago Sadler had fled and whether Albright had already employed other means in bringing about his return.

Mason returned to the living room and noticed a much smaller mound of newspapers sitting atop a crumbling chest of wooden drawers, stacked in a noticeably neater manner than those around it. The top three newspapers were from three consecutive days four months previously, and the front pages had little in common other than general economics, sports headlines and information on a company called Rovkrand buying majority shares in a lot of smaller, disgruntled companies. Mason was about to turn away from the pile when something caught his eye. On the front of the most recent edition that sat atop this printed throne was a photograph of several businessmen standing in a circle outside one of these smaller company's buildings, decorated with a sign that displayed the name Farrow Enterprises. Two of them wore matching, dark-brown suits and matching anger had been captured on the features of their furious faces, flashing from their eyes. To the front of the picture were two other men shaking hands. The print beneath the photograph identified the man on the left as the politician Michael Roach, a significant figure in the running for the upcoming mayoral election. The other man, referred to simply as "a Rovkrand shareholder", smiling a shark-like smile, was Albright.

"Good Evening, and welcome to Havan-ha-ha-ha!" boomed out from another room.

Mason spun round and instinctively placed his back against the wall, his ears alert for any further outbursts. He deemed it safe to assume from the semi-comical, foreign accent of this intruder upon the silence, along with the generally bizarre nature of the sudden outburst, that the sound had come from a television or radio. However, the fact remained that this sound now occupied a space that had previously been silent. Someone had caused this sound to be heard and now lurked somewhere in this desolate house, waiting, their movements drowned out by the cackle of Cuban sailors.

Mason tensed himself and prepared for confrontation. A rush had released itself, shooting along his spine towards his brain, apprehension mixed with excitement, driven by the desire to overcome whatever force shared occupation of this building with him. His muscles began to tighten and his whole body crackled with tension, waiting for the fellow intruder to make a move. His right-hand swiftly flicked open the sharp, steel blade in his pocket and tightly clenched itself around its black, rubber handle.

"You want to go to Liverpool? Ay, we'll toss for it. Your ticket or your blood!"

The voice shattered the quiet once more, relieving the tense pressure in Mason's chest for an all-too-brief moment, though it flooded back immediately afterwards with a doubled sense of conviction. The Cuban accent had come from the same general direction as before – an open door on the far side of the living area that seemed to lead onto a jaded hallway. Mason slowly crept across the room, keeping his back to the wall, his eyes constantly shifting to take in all corners. He reached the hallway and crossed the faded, green, dust-drenched carpet before ascending the stairs, at the top of which the voice continued its cacophonous chatter. The patterns on the staircase carpet intermingled large, red spots with a deeper green, and automatically sent thoughts of bloodstains flashing through Mason's mind, firing up his adrenaline further. As he reached the top of the stairs the voice grew louder. It seemed to be coming from around a corner which turned into a passageway off to the left of the landing. Mason took a deep breath, gripped his weapon tightly in his hand and sprung around the corner.

Nothing and nobody waited for him there other than an old, empty wardrobe with its doors ajar at the end of the passage, the sound seeming to blare from somewhere within its walls. Then Mason realised that the sound was not coming from the house at all but rather the building next door. The walls were clearly paper-thin in this crumbling abode. One could listen to all the evil deeds the neighbour committed with complete discretion.

Suddenly Mason heard a noise from behind and swung round into the blow of an unidentified but solid object. It struck him across the right side of his forehead and he fell to the floor from the force as a figure flew down the wretched staircase four steps at a time. Mason rolled backwards across the carpet, reeling from the blow. It had been a heavy weapon, but the attacker could not have been particularly strong as the damage did not seem, for the time being, to be as serious as it may have at the hands of a more ferocious assailant. Mason wiped his brow and recognised the broad spread of burgundy painted upon his fingers, just as it began trickling its warm way down the front of his face. Despite the weight of concussion he felt grappling for rulership within his head and the drowsiness spreading quickly across his brain, he picked himself up and awkwardly stumbled down the stairs as quickly as he could manage. With each step Mason took, he used the banister or wall for support, leaving upon them deep bloodstains, like a man cursed by plague spreading it throughout his doomed fellow townspeople. Mason splattered his way through the downstairs living room, splashing the furniture with his indelible stains. The urge to pursue his assailant mingled with the loss of the proper functioning of his senses to result in his flailing across the room wildly like a whirling dervish. He burst through the front door and almost rolled down the small set of steps onto the lawn, just barely in time to see a figure running down the street and turning out of sight behind a neighbour's hedge. He could only make out a shade of slight height and build, as his eyesight gradually became more and more seduced by the influence of the oncoming sanguine shadows.

He lurched forward, his brain overheating, feeling as though it may explode with a ferocious force at any moment. The blow now appeared significantly more serious than he had first considered. Mason remembered the first aid kit stored in his glove compartment and figured that he could at least use the filthy rags in his boot to wrap around his throbbing head, to halt the pulsing flow. The dizziness was heightening. He had to stop the bleeding before something serious resulted from the attack. He stumbled forward, adrenaline alone driving him onwards. He slapped his bloody hand upon the car window. Inside a man stared back at him.

He rapidly realised that in his semi-blindness he had targeted the wrong vehicle. He also managed to recall that when he had pulled up in front of Sadler's house there had been no other cars parked on that side of the street. The car had parked directly in front of his, at some point in the last fifteen minutes.

From behind his blood-soaked eyes, Mason could only vaguely acknowledge the features of the man inside the car. The man stared through the window with a face that Mason could barely map out but which he recognised was remarkably pale. He wore what seemed a black, wide-brimmed hat and, to the extent that Mason could observe any aspect of his appearance, the man's head was completely devoid of hair, lacking any under the sides of his hat or even above his eyes. The only thing Mason could determine for sure was that the man held a look of utter disdain upon his face. Mason was unsure of whether he could clearly see this or whether he simply sensed it, but he could feel the stranger fixing him with a stare of absolute contempt. The man continued this glare which, perhaps due only to his current extreme condition, shot piercingly through Mason, with an air of impending tragedy, and struck him with inexplicable force.

Mason heard a loud, metallic crunching noise, a mechanical tiger growled, hungry to devour its prey. He felt the support of the steel frame slowly start to slide out from beneath him. The creature inside turned its evil gaze to the road ahead and Mason slumped to the ground, struggling to maintain consciousness for several seconds before succumbing to a battle-induced blackness.

CHAPTER 6

"Stand back, he's coming to!"

Mason's head beat and throbbed as though it contained a second heart within, and as sight returned to his pained eyes, the wrinkled, worried face of an elderly lady leaning over him came into view. As his senses became clearer he realised that this woman was cupping his head in her arms and he noticed that a crowd of several concerned bystanders, curious onlookers and neighbours with nothing better to do had gathered around him. He wiped his hand across his forehead confirming to himself that he was still drenched in blood, though he could tell that he had stopped bleeding. He must have been knocked-out for merely minutes at most

"You poor dear," said the woman who held his limp body, "just stay still, an ambulance should be here any minute. It looks as though you've suffered something awful."

Mason instantly switched from his comatose state to one of alert when he heard this sentence. He did not like becoming involved with the health or legal services on his cases and, despite his being assaulted, he had no good excuse for breaking and entering, for being in Sadler's to begin with. He could still feel the pain picking away at what felt like a shattered skull with a selection of vicious tools, but gathered from his estimation of the attacker's strength that it looked and felt more severe than it truly was. He had probably suffered a mild concussion at worst. Nothing that he could not recover from by his own means.

"And that awful, awful man, driving away, leaving you in this horrible state."

"What man?" Mason immediately demanded.

"Why the monster that must have seen you, covered in all this blood, and drove away the moment you leant upon his car for help."

Mason asked the lady which way the car had driven and noted that it was the same general direction in which he had seen his attacker flee. He lifted himself off the ground and, despite the urges, protests and, in some cases, angry demands from neighbourhood residents for an explanation as to this disturbance, slumped into his car, making a promise to himself that he would not pass out again until he had reached his office.

Mason arrived at the building that contained his office and took the lift directly to his rooms. It was an unremarkable, high-rise building consisting of hundreds of other offices, of which Mason knew very little. Its grey, limestone exterior crawled higher than the surrounding buildings, blackened in parts by the filth and the fumes of the city centre. The iron box rumbled through the building, delivering the hunter to his lair. His office itself was merely a waiting room, not furnished with anything more exciting than a coat stand and several dusty, filing cabinets, which lead into his consulting room. It was a small but comfortable space with a large window taking up almost an entire wall, giving Mason a bird's eye view of the fraying fibres that attempted to hold this town together as it fell apart. He sat on the chair behind his desk, put a damp towel against his temple to restrict any bleeding that might decide to renew its duty and let his mind wander.

So Sadler had been observing, or at least following the news of, several business deals that had taken place a few months ago, deals that had involved Albright. It would be too bizarre for his appearance in those newspapers to have been a coincidence. Clearly Albright had not told him everything. Mason flirted with the thought that the story about the stolen brooch was merely what his employer had considered a believable tale with which to entice Mason into hunting the man down. Perhaps Sadler had discovered that this Rovkrand Corporation, which Albright was at least a shareholder of if not directly involved in, had seized these properties in an illegal manner. Perhaps he was a law-abiding citizen who had procured evidence and was going to the police, or perhaps he was involved with one of the minor companies being bought out. Then again he may have been hired by another party to spy on Albright. Perhaps he was even personally blackmailing him.

Whatever the reason, the chances were that Sadler probably had what was coming to him.

Mason's mind drifted back to thoughts of his two strange encounters in and around Sadler's home. Who had his attacker been? As the person had come from upstairs, then they must have been there for the entirety of Mason's visit. Otherwise he surely would have seen or heard them entering. In that case, what had they been doing in the upstairs of that damp, collapsing building? Prowling its upper halls in search of something substantially more interesting than the stagnant contents below? Mason figured that it had quite likely been Sadler, returning to find some essential he had left behind, perhaps having left Albright's brooch in the house. This was quite a risk though. It was unlikely Sadler was stupid enough to return to his home and, if so, why seemingly so long after he had originally abandoned it? Then again, it could have been any number of other as-of-yet unidentified characters, unknown to Mason, who were involved in the matter – other bounty hunters? A friend of Sadler's? It could even simply have been a thief gifted with bad timing.

The man in the car also intrigued him. Of course it was entirely possible, likely even, that this man was simply a local resident or a passer-by who had pulled over to see two men fleeing a house, one covered in blood. However, Mason still sensed the power of the stare he had received, the unbridled sensation of loathing that the man's look had sent shrieking through his bones...

Mason decided not to overthink mysteries that could not be immediately explained. He would continue with the case and hope that all of these details would become clear with time. Despite his inherent courage, arrogance and disdain for the threats against him, he suspected that it would be a foolish move to back out now. He lay back in his office chair, deciding to relax for the evening until his head was fully healed, and closed his eyes.

CHAPTER 7

Mason opened his eyes. A thumping noise was resonating in the back of his skull. The noise was difficult to make out but most definitely existed, akin to music coming from another room, distinctive yet muffled by thick walls. With every thump the sound grew louder as though it were coming closer.

He was lying face down in the middle of a road paved by cobblestones. Mason stood hesitantly and looked around him to take in a familiar street but one that he was sure he had never graced before. It contained several multi-storied, red-brick buildings on either side, built up high enough and badly enough so that their third and fourth floors seemed to lean forward, lurching over the street and only maintaining their balance by supporting themselves against the floors from their counterparts on the opposite side, forming a sort of concrete canopy above the road, through the cracks of which the black and red sky of sundown was still visible. Several nondescript people, slumped forward from the heat, walked along the footpaths on either side of the road, going to and fro without paying Mason the slightest bit of attention. They walked quickly, without hesitation, as if hurrying home before something dreadful they knew of could take place. The thumping noise seemed to be getting closer still.

How had he arrived here? Mason could not remember. He barely remembered the moment of waking. Had he been drugged? Or knocked out and brought here? Had Sadler arranged this? Or was Albright still doubtful as to his commitment? Either way, it seemed a bizarre method by which to rid oneself of somebody who was causing trouble. Unless danger existed within the thumping, which continued to grow louder. Except it was no longer simply a noise. Now there was a throbbing surge in the ground. Wherever it was coming from, it pulsated through the street like a monstrous earthquake about to surge through the concrete beneath and pulverise all that walked. The thumping noise was louder now. The physical force of the shudder underneath his feet grew more powerful.

... and now the street was empty. People no longer scampered past Mason. He was alone. Whatever was happening, or had happened, the others knew better and had left him to fend for himself. The noise had become almost deafening. The rise and fall of the hard concrete started to throw him off balance until, eventually, the climax of each swell of the ground threw him several feet into the air, before he fell back down when the stones receded.

Mason grabbed for a nearby lamppost. He held onto it with as much strength as he could muster but his arms felt feeble and seemed to move much slower than his mind willed, as though gravity had ceased to have any influence over them. The terrible thumping was now a pounding, the sound of steel being flexed in and out of shape by an intense heat. Mason could feel this heat burning in his mouth, causing his eyes to water and flooding his brain until he found it impossible to concentrate on any single thought other than the thunderous, deafening roar in his ears. Now it was as though someone drummed on a flat piece of iron with what sounded like a stone hammer or a giant cinder block.

And just as suddenly the swelling had stopped. The throbbing still reverberated through the stones with each bang upon the iron, but now, instead of scooping him up, it merely coursed through the cracks between the cobbles of the street, like a snake slithering across the surface of a desolate marsh.

The noise and the surge had now congregated in one specific part of the street and Mason could establish where they were coming from. A manhole in the centre of the road continued slightly rising and falling with each bang, the iron lid itself twisting above this strange, subterranean force. He tentatively took several steps closer, but when he wished his legs to stop at a safe distance they continued to slowly keep steering him, against his will, steadily towards the beating manhole.

As he came closer he could see that the banging, and the deafening thuds, had changed from their heartbeat-like, perfectly rhythmical pace to a more random thumping. There would be some seconds between the swells in the iron before another seismic smash would raise the metal once more.

And he suddenly realised that it was someone trying to get out. The bangs became more rapid, less focused and more frantic. They were still agonisingly loud but in between the bangs Mason was sure voices were audible from beneath the streets, at first too quiet to hear, then rising until he could be sure that somebody down below was begging for help, for escape. The voice was unidentifiable, but sounded weak, feeble, exhausted and helpless.

"Please," he made out, "you have to help me."

Mason flung himself to the ground and began clawing at the cover. It was slippery, covered in a disgusting, black, greasy substance. He tried to twist the bolts that fastened it to the ground and frantically scraped the iron shield until his fingertips began to bleed from beneath his nails, the blood mixing with the oil that greased the manhole lid to form a revolting mucus upon the ground.

The metal suddenly shot upwards, spraying Mason with his own blood and sending him sprawling backwards. He could see the bending metal shell of the manhole cover swell and then sink back below street level as if some enormous creature were sucking and blowing the air through the city's sewers or as though the cover were the beating heart of the street itself. The sounds became louder, the swelling grew more rapid. The voice begging for mercy grew more desperate until there was a terrible shriek of metal being torn in two. The helpless screaming and the hole in the street burst into a fountain of the oil, the liquids of the city's sewers and the blood of the person beneath, and this flood crashed down upon Mason, drowning him until he could no longer breathe...

Mason woke in a sweat with his throat parched, his temples burning and his muscles racked by a powerful pain. He had been lying unconscious, reclined on his office chair. Perhaps he had unwillingly blacked out once more from the force of the blow to his head earlier in the day. However, he felt that the hurt that now ravaged his body was the result of contortions, of his whole frame being twisted in agony from the force of the nightmare. It was an unusual sort of pain – his body was not merely suffering from the exertions placed upon it by the force of a powerful dream, but actually feeling the pains that he had felt during the surreal vision, and the panic and sheer horror that had gripped his mind were unlike those resulting from any assaults on the world of his sleep that he had previously experienced. He felt as though the events of the dream had truly taken place and he had only now fallen into a deep sleep.

Mason shook his head, wiped his face with his filthy blood-stained shirt and, after staring, deliberating, at a bottle of rum in his desk drawer for several minutes, filled a cup of water from the cooler in the hallway outside. He drank three quick cups before the intense feeling of dehydration left him. He craved the bite of alcohol. Its strong, acidic burn would vanquish all memories of the nightmare, but thought better of it after giving due consideration to the agony of his body and the state of his pulped head. He filled another cup, returned to his office and stumbled slowly across to the window, supporting his sluggish, hulking frame on the pale-lime, plastered walls.

In the night outside the city was at the stage of an in-between ebb. It neither slept nor operated to the full capacities of consciousness, rather it just lulled on by. It was foul, drenched by its own corruption, which rose from the streets like the filth from an open yet diseased pore, obliterating the senses of sight and smell, or any other bodily functions one could use to distinguish decay. Down on the street there were few signs of life. Mason glanced at the rows of parked cars lining the opposite footpaths, as though in his own mind arranging an enclosure for a duel to take place between two oncoming vehicles.

As his gaze crept across these still creatures, lying, waiting, neither alive nor dead, he felt a disturbance somewhere in his person. The presence of one of them caused his mind discomfort. The dark, purple car across the street awoke something within him, a vague familiarity perhaps – but then it was not familiarity. He did not recall seeing the car before and there was nothing unusual about its appearance, but an ominous sensation drifted across his senses, which foretold of terrible events that were destined to happen.

Due to the darkness and the car's positioning out of the streetlamps' reach, Mason could not describe anything of the car's interior, or whether there was even anybody sitting inside. After he had stared for a longer period than he may have intended, pondering, allowing his mind to wander, the car's headlights unexpectedly blinked on as the engine growled into life. The car pulled out and drove slowly down the darkened street until it crawled around the next available corner and out of sight.

Mason peeled himself from the wall and returned to the chair behind his desk. After finishing his water and crumpling the paper cup in his fist, he decided to sleep once more.

CHAPTER 8

The next morning Mason felt refreshed. The aching in his head had numbed and a more peaceful sleep subsequent to his nightmare had helped place him in a better mental state. In the scorching light of a summer morning, the evils of the previous night's visions were washed away. He began to wonder whether he had simply entered this case in a bad state of mind and allowed its early mysteries and dramatics, combined with a painful crash to his head, to seize control of his imagination. The horrific nightmare was just that and the ensuing sight of a car eerily lurking outside his office was most likely the creation of an assaulted, overworked brain. Mason even toyed with the idea that he had not woken up at all until the morning.

He walked through the front door of his building, ignoring a homeless man lying out of his mind in a nearby doorway, face dripping with saliva and other substances. The sight was a flashback to yesterday's exploits and their results, but he disregarded it, wishing to embrace the reinvigorating power of the new day to its fullest. The air came in short, sharp gasps to his lungs, the closeness and mustiness of the day compounded by the sheer heat. A blue sky was reflected in the roofs of the cars. Mason opened the door to his car, the glare reflecting off its metal almost blinding him, and drove towards his home.

Several hours later, the car came to a halt outside a four-storey, pebble-dash building and Mason leaned back in the front seat while he took it in. This area had once been the pride of the city but when casinos, drugs and organised crime had moved in it had slowly been reduced to another dismal, melting collection of streets struggling to survive the carnivorous consumption of civilisation. The building had clearly once reflected the grandeur that had surrounded it but now looked as though several large chunks had been blown out of its sides. The exterior appeared as though it were constructed of paper, paper that had been soaked through with water, only managing to stay stable and upright thanks to the heat of the sun baking it solid once more.

Mason had driven home, showered and breakfasted, before scanning the newspapers that sat patiently outside his front door. He was pleasantly surprised to see that nothing of the incident at Sadler's house had made it as far as the press. He guessed that none of the locals had known what course of action to follow, or else had assumed that he would report it himself. Feeling more alert than the previous day, Mason's thoughts ran clearly through his mind once more. He had been attacked by somebody, in a manner that could have left a serious injury. Whoever it had been, they were clearly unconcerned with Mason's well-being and did not wait to ask questions before attempting to shatter his skull. Thoughts of Sadler's potential innocence, along with Mason's concerns over Albright's questionable motives, had been washed away by the blood that had poured forth from his forehead. Now the matter involved getting even.

Mason had decided to further his enquiries by paying Rachel Gaines, Sadler's love interest, a visit. He sat outside the building for a few more minutes wiping the sweat off his forehead, not wanting to appear uncomposed for their first meeting. The intense heat of the red sun had almost transformed the car into a sacrificial altar, and even with all the windows rolled down he still had to gasp for air. He took the blade from the pocket of his heavy, brown overcoat that lay across the backseat of the car and played with it in his fingers, telling himself that he would not allow anyone the opportunity of landing the first blow again. Mason stepped out of the car and crossed the street towards Gaines' building, trying to ignore the smell of rotting rubbish that harassed him from several different directions.

After entering the open front door and strolling through the lobby, Mason climbed the crumbling staircase to the third floor and walked to the apartment marked D. He knocked loudly upon the door. There was no answer. After waiting a while he rapped upon it once more but again received no response. The wood wore an air of age and weakness and, after making sure the hallway was deserted, Mason leant his entire weight heavily upon it with a dull thud. After several attempts the door's weak lock gave way.

Mason entered a large, darkened sitting room, thick with an unpleasant scent. Two windows, some ten feet tall, that ran along one wall, allowed some little, subdued streaks of sunrays into the place through their drawn curtains, revealing a mess of old magazines, faded clothes and cigarette butts scattered haphazardly across the patchy, yellow carpet and mustard-green furniture. The place was in a state of chaos, the smell of the cigarettes was overpowering. Piles of rubbish from indeterminate sources lay at various spots along the sides of the room. Wardrobes hung open, their belongings, wildly on display, forming a never-ending waterfall of slovenly possessions slowly slipping out. The room desperately struggled to maintain a former glory with its high ceiling and impressively adorned mirror placed above an enormous, elaborate marble fireplace. However the cracks had begun to appear in the walls a long time ago, the carpet had been worn down, barely more than tufts of material sprouting up between the wide stretches of wood, and the mirror had not been cleaned in months. Mason crossed the room and flung the curtains open, letting the light stream in despite the best efforts of the grubby windowpanes. As he felt the overwhelming flood of the sun penetrating his skin once more, Mason wondered whether the fireplace had been strictly for show.

A high-backed, purple sofa divided the room into two sections. Its rear was to Mason, while it faced a doorway into what looked, from where he stood, to be a kitchen. Like everything else in the building, the sofa emitted an aura of ancient prestige but was now reduced to a few bits of bare thread struggling to slide off pieces of insect-infested mahogany. Walking past it to investigate the room beyond, Mason became aware of another presence in the room. He turned quickly to see a woman's body sprawled across the sofa, previously hidden by its raised back. His first reaction was to bury his fist in his pocket and grasp the knife in case there was another assailant about, but after quickly checking the small kitchen and a bedroom, which seemed to constitute the rest of the apartment, and satisfying himself that they were alone, he went back to examine her.

She was the young woman from Albright's photographs, wearing a pair of miniscule, red shorts and a filthy, once-white vest. She had managed to cling to something of the striking, visual attractiveness she had portrayed in the photographs, but only just. The well-formed features of her face could still be identified but they had been corrupted. Her hair was dishevelled. Her face looked darker. Sunken cheeks sat under purple blotches beneath her eyes, due to substance or physical abuse – it was difficult to determine exactly which. In fact it was difficult to tell if she was even breathing.

Mason felt a cold chill shiver through his body. Had he broken into a home where a murder had been committed? His every instinct told him to leave the room immediately but the small piece of humanity that he still possessed forced him to lean in closer to the woman. She remained motionless. Mason tapped her lightly on the cheek. With that a repulsive trail of white foam bubbled from her mouth and ran down the side of her face. She choked herself awake, wiped her mouth and turned to face Mason with bloodshot eyes, consumed by hatred. Without taking her eyes from him, and with an agility that was surprising considering the state he had found her in, she bounded to the other side of the room and grabbed a sizeable kitchen knife lying on one of the cluttered desks.

"Who the hell are you?" she screeched at Mason, ferocity emanating from every pore of her body.

Her face was frantic but determined, as if this woman was used to strangers bursting into her world and had decided that it was time to defend herself. She advanced across the room, waving the knife in Mason's direction.

"Hold it there Miss, I'm only here to help," Mason tried in his friendliest voice, hoping to undermine his large, threatening presence.

"Why are you in my apartment? The door was locked!" she raged.

She had stopped just a few feet from him, knife in outstretched arm, its tip twitching as though she relished the thought of slicing Mason no matter what response he offered.

"Listen Miss, I'm a friend of Ray's from way back. I only came here to try and get some news on him. We haven't been the best at keeping in touch but I'd always hear from him now and then. I tried calling his home, several times, but no answer, until a message eventually told me it'd been disconnected. I called over yesterday and the place was deserted, looked like no-one had been there in years. Sorry I startled you but the door was hanging open when I got here and I decided to just let myself in, to make sure everything was okay, that nobody'd broken in or anything, you know?"

Mason reckoned she had passed out in a state that was not conducive to the possession of a clear memory of having secured her home. He saw a brief glimmer of confusion in her eyes, before they reset themselves in their aggressive, animalistic approach.

"The door was locked!"

"Honestly it wasn't," Mason stammered, just hoping to calm her down. "I got your address from the editor in one of the papers he worked for. Ray had told me he'd been seeing a girl for a while now and I just came here to find out whether you'd talked to him at all lately. I'm just worried about him."

Mason had taken a gamble with this answer. There were too many variables that he was uninformed on tied up in it but nonetheless it seemed to satiate something in her psyche as he noticed her tensed muscles relax slightly. Then, as she collapsed back onto the sofa, Mason became unsure whether it was actually satisfaction, or merely carelessness, a tired resignation regarding her own safety.

She snatched up an unmarked, clear, glass bottle lying on a stained coffee-table beside the sofa and swallowed a considerable amount of the liquid inside, before laying back and lighting what appeared, for all intents and purposes, to be a hand-rolled cigarette. She stared at Mason.

"Listen, I know *Raymond* hasn't had any friends for a while but I don't have the energy to do this anymore. I'll answer any questions I can, as long as you people leave me alone. I just want you to know that I'm not stupid enough to believe your bullshit stories."

Despite this interesting statement Mason decided it was best not to retire his supposed identity, regardless of whether she believed him or not.

"Well Ray and I haven't been in contact for quite a while but I'd been thinking about him a lot recently and I felt I should get in touch again. After I discovered that his home phone was out of service, I got his work number off an old mutual friend. There they told me that nobody'd seen him in weeks, so I've just been looking into it. After asking a few questions around town, I was led here."

As he sat down on the sofa beside the woman he instantly smelled a warm, repugnant odour coming from her direction. He could not precisely identify it but it was almost certainly an intoxicant of some kind, possibly mixed into her cigarette. It seemed obvious to him in hindsight that the reason the woman had displayed no signs of life as she had slept on the couch was because whatever she was taking had almost reduced her breathing and general reflexes to nil. Now her breath reeked and her bloodshot eyes darted rapidly here and there, constantly scanning all exits and entrances. With a closer look one could more clearly make out the nets of bloated and ruptured veins on her face, running from chin to temple, lending it that repulsive purple shade. There was little left of the radiant woman from the photographs. She had been replaced by a shivering, drug-addicted wreck. Fear and anger vied for mastery of her eyes.

"I know you're lying but I don't really care anymore," she laughed scornfully and took a drag on her cigarette. "Just tell me what it is you want to know.

"When was the last time you saw Ray?"

"I saw him three weeks ago today. The bastard told me he was going to the bar to sort out something about money. He went out the door and didn't come back. I didn't hear anything from or about him until three days later, when other men started coming around asking questions. Soon they stopped bothering to even ask."

The woman laughed nervously and took another drag.

"What bar was this?"

"I don't know. Some hole down in the docklands. He'd started going there three or four times a week for the few months before. As far as I could tell he was doing a lot of gambling down there. My best guess was that he owed somebody a lot of money and didn't deliver. I figure they were the wrong people. Though I suppose you already know that..."

She seemed to recite these words from memory, as though she had previously performed them multiple times and had already told her version of Sadler's story on numerous occasions, often against her will.

A heavy, wooden fan hung motionless from the ceiling, making Mason feel uncomfortably warmer with its ineffective presence. He was finding it difficult to breathe with the rank smells coming from the woman's mouth and cigarette.

"Could we turn that on?" he asked nodding towards the fan.

"No," she sharply snapped back. "Listen, I don't have any money. Sadler didn't have any money and you can tell Douglas or Max or Albright, or whoever you work for, that this kind of false friendly approach won't force any money out of me if beating it out didn't work before. There simply is no money. Now please just leave me alone."

She took another swig from her bottle.

"I really don't know anything about any of these people. Who are they and was it simply money they were into Ray for?"

"I don't know, I think so. Except for Albright. Raymond seemed to have an obsession with him, going beyond gambling and debt. In the last few weeks before he disappeared he'd started acting real strange. He'd sleep most of the day and go out to work close to sundown. When I asked him where he was going he'd generally mumble something about having to fix things with Albright. He'd come home with reams of photographs he'd spent all night taking. I rarely saw any of these pictures 'cause he'd develop them over at his work lab, but from time to time I'd manage to sneak a look in his bag and find some of the developed ones."

"What did you see?"

"They were pretty mundane things. Groups of wealthy looking guys getting in and out of limousines, going into bars and clubs, having drinks, that general kind of thing. I eventually came to recognise one of them as this *Albright* Ray would constantly go on about, 'cause I noticed him in group photographs from business magazines Raymond would leave lying around. Albright's face would often be circled or meaningless lines in the articles would be underlined."

Mason allowed this speech to nestle in his mind, wondering once more how much of what Albright had told him was true. The contents of the bottle and cigarette seemed to be wearing down the walls of her aggression, towards Mason at least.

"And you say men have been here to get money out of you?"

"Yeah, they've roughed me up a bit too. Most of them just shouted, demanded money, slapped me around a little."

"What about Albright? Did he send any men?"

"His guys would come and always say they were from Albright, as if that was supposed to mean something to me. It was funny though because they'd never demand money. They'd come every day or two insisting on talking to Raymond and ransack the place without saying they were searching for anything in particular. One time they had this really big guy with them. He stood out in the hall all the time so I didn't get a proper look at him. He didn't say anything until after they had trashed the apartment. When they demanded to know where Raymond was and again I didn't have an answer, he came inside. His face was funny looking..." Rachel's voice began to waver. "H-he ... I didn't always look ... like this ... he did ... things to me."

She drank another mouthful of the liquid and turned her face away.

Mason felt pangs of sympathy for the woman but it was not his job to look after her and he could not assume that everything she said was true, no matter how much support her convincing condition lent her story.

"And you haven't heard a thing from Sad ... Ray since then?"

She laughed dryly, both of them aware of his mistake but beyond the point of caring.

"He disappeared that night three weeks ago and that's all I know. I loved him at one point but I was an idiot. He abandoned me, left all his problems and his debts dangling above my head. I've suffered terribly for his mistakes. I honestly hope he's fucking dead."

With the force of this statement, the substances took a final hold and Rachel slid slowly down the couch, back to the position she had been in when Mason arrived.

Mason searched the rest of the apartment. He found little more than further tools of personal abuse and countless gossip magazines, although whilst searching a desk in one corner of the bedroom, he came across an address book with Rachel's name scrawled on the inside. Under Raymond there was the address he had previously visited along with another one on the other side of the city. He speculated that this could be Sadler's workplace, or possibly his development laboratory, and wrote the address inside a small notebook which he kept in his trouser pocket. The intense smell of the woman, the heat, the fumes, the flat, the building, began to become overpowering and Mason decided it was time to leave.

He took one last look at Rachel. He guessed that she was most likely more involved in these events than she claimed. However, in the grand scheme of things he reckoned she was probably still one of the victims rather than an aggressor. He took a pink pillow, embroidered with a small, red candle, from the foot of the couch and lifted her head to place it underneath. He thought she might choke on her vomit, or else the disgusting white foam he had already been witness to, if left lying completely flat and at the moment he did not need that on his conscience. As he closed the front door behind him he remembered that he had broken the lock on his way in. He could not deny that he felt guilty about leaving the door open with dangerous people around. However, the kind of people who were likely to come looking for Sadler sounded as though they would manage to make their way in, flimsy lock or not. He shrugged to himself, pulled the door over, walked back downstairs and out the front door of the building. Outside the sun was keeping its tireless vigil.

CHAPTER 9

Mason drove back towards the city's simmering, stone centre with his windows rolled down in vain, the air entering the car as stagnant as that already inside, smelling from the roasting of the sins of the city outside. He crawled through the streets, deserted in the stifling sun, and parked outside a grotty café, the only establishment nearby making any visible attempt to do business.

The counter of the place was wrapped in old, clear contact, with dead flies buried beneath. With the slightest of motion the door shrieked for attention on the rare occasions that someone wandered in. Fans twirled above his head, screaming like rodents in a trap with every rotation. Mason decided that he would hole up here until the outdoors cooled down somewhat. Afterwards he would go to the address he had found in Rachel's house. For the time being he would gather his thoughts here and, if there was access to a telephone, call Walt. Walt was one of the few friends Mason possessed and he still could not go so far as to say he knew him well. In fact, all of those Mason counted amongst his friends could be better described as acquaintances, mostly of a business kind. However, they all had their uses and Walt was useful for information.

After drinking several waters, then several coffees and scouring a discarded newspaper without really taking any of it in, or indeed noticing that it was days old, Mason's mind eventually returned to his conversation with Rachel. He was particularly distressed at the thought of these other people who were conducting searches on behalf of Albright. Were they also solely looking for Sadler? Was Mason merely replicating the motions that they had already run through? If so, then what need was there for Mason? Was Sadler so difficult to locate that it was deemed necessary for Albright to hire a private bounty hunter in addition to his own bunch of thugs? Perhaps Rachel had invented much of her story, but what were her reasons for doing so? Regardless of the answers to these questions, things were undoubtedly beginning to become more complicated than Mason would have liked and he decided that he too could benefit from some outside help, to try and resolve this affair before any further surprises reared their heads.

Mason asked for a telephone and followed the instructions of the sweaty barman's curt pointed finger. He stepped into the grubby, glass booth, slipped a coin into the machine and dialled Walt's number. The phone rang to its conclusion. Mason tried twice more before, as he was about to put the receiver down, an angry voice shouted abruptly down the line.

"What do you bloody want this time?"

Mason recognised the raw, emotional rasp of the voice, the sound obstructed by thick walls of flab upon the face, as Walt's.

"Good afternoon Walt."

"Mason? Oh, I'm sorry. It's these damned reporters hounding me all the time. If I try to offer my own opinion on the matter they just argue and dredge up countless sources who say this or that about me. If I don't answer the phone then I have to listen to the damn thing ringing all day and accept the likelihood that my name will be plastered all over the papers tomorrow. I just can't get anyone to listen to my own bloody point of view in this thing."

"Right Walt. You know I didn't call to discuss your personal life and I'm not really interested in what you did or didn't do, though for the record I'm sure you probably did it. I need information."

"That's a pleasant way to get reacquainted. Not so much as a 'how are you Walt?' before accusing me of things you clearly know nothing about! Anyway, I thought you had decided to retire?"

"Not for the moment. Now are you available for work or not?"

Mason was in no mood for small talk.

"Alright my friend, relax. I was just enquiring. After all, why would I want you to retire? You're my best customer! So, if you need information about someone I'm going to have to charge you double the regular price due to all this interminable scrutiny I'm coming under from the press. I can't afford to be taking chances prying into people's personal lives for any less. And if it happens to be somebody of note I may have to charge even more."

Mason considered the figures for a moment. The information Walt provided him with was usually reliable and quite often proved extremely useful, or even essential. He had frequently contemplated how phenomenal a bounty hunter Walt would be, due to his knack for uncovering dirty, little slivers of gossip and hearsay concerning secretive people, were it not for him being practically terminally overweight and lacking in any social refinements. Expensive as the cost was, it was still nothing in comparison to the figure that Albright was offering and would be money well spent if it helped bring him closer to his prey. Besides, Walt's services were never available for anything less than extortionate sums of money. He was constantly working in what he would deem unusual circumstances. Mason was not sure if he had ever actually paid the 'regular price'.

"Fine Walt, but you better make it worth my money."

"Don't I always?" Walt responded exuberantly.

Mason could see him in his mind, grinning his fat, drooling grin over the phone.

"What would you like to know?"

"I need you to find out anything you can about a young journalist named Raymond Sadler. Tell me whatever you can about his personal life and any friends or family you hear about along the way. I want to know everything possible about him."

"Sure, sounds straightforward enough. I pity the guy if you're going after him – he'll probably end up face down in a ditch somewhere!"

"That's not funny Walt!" Mason growled.

"Yeah, yeah, I know. I'm just having some fun with you Mason. Anyway, they probably all deserve it. Anything else I can do for you while I'm at it?"

Mason wiped beads of sweat, along with any brief pangs of guilt that Walt had induced, from his forehead using the back of his hand. The heat within the boxed telephone booth was becoming overwhelming. His hand smacked the damp glass of the booth, pulverising a particularly bulky mosquito that had been irritating him. Its collection of blood for the day splashed across the side of the booth, its body sticking in the one spot while sweat and blood ran slowly down along the glass. Through the pane, Mason now saw the café with a dingy, red filter, a world drenched in blood. It simply made the booth seem warmer.

"Yeah, actually there is Walt. You can also tell me everything you know about a businessman called Albright."

Mason immediately felt the life being drained from the line. The silence following his sentence was glaringly out of character for Walt.

"Walt, are you still there?"

When Walt's voice returned to the receiver, it had changed somehow. Gone was the happy-go-lucky haggling and casual conversation. He now sounded jaded and occupied by matters elsewhere.

"Yes Mason, sorry I was just thinking about something. Did you say Albright?"

"Yeah Albright, you know something about him?"

"No, nothing really ... I just ... well, I've heard some stories floating around about this guy ... it's," Walt paused for breath for what seemed like minutes. "It's nothing really. I'll do what I can, within reason, and that information is going to be at least triple price, whether it's useful or not."

"Fine Walt, but tell me whatever it is you've heard about him."

"Listen Mason, I've got to go ... I ... I have a lot to do. I'll be in touch soon."

"No Walt, wait! Tell me what it is!"

"Just ... just be careful Mason, ok?"

Walt did not wait for a response before hanging up. Mason slammed the receiver down in frustration and cursed him. He wondered what could have sent Walt into such a sudden state of confusion and unease. Albright may have been more of a power mover around town than he had originally suspected, but surely there was no life-threatening danger in speaking about him. It was possible that Albright had already used Walt as a source, as he was well known in certain circles as a useful contact, and that he had already played his part in this Sadler drama. Possible but unlikely. It was not uncommon for Walt to make a scene simply to justify his increase in price. However, this time he had seemed genuinely distressed.

A loud rapping sounded behind him, breaking his concentration, and Mason turned to see a face smeared in blood leering through the glass, a disgusting grin, with foul bleeding, red, rotten gums. The demon was cackling and tapping on the phone booth with a silver coin, examining Mason through heavily veined eyeballs. Mason recoiled in horror but found his escape blocked by the opposite side of the booth behind him.

The man stumbled away still laughing his maniacal laugh, without getting to make his phone call. Mason breathed deeply. He realised that the disgusting figure had merely been a drunk waiting to use the booth, knocking impatiently, his profile filtered a vile red through the mosquito's remains. Similar to how the blood gathered by a mosquito causes it to swell; it was not the man's own blood, but that from elsewhere that had created the gruesome apparition. The repellent, flying minion is merely a much smaller creature on the brink of collapse, much like the pathetic drunk, until it drinks the life of another.

Through the stained pane Mason now saw the whole café had descended into apocalypse. The beers being consumed were now glass vials of red froth, the bar carried giant crushed wings, the lady working behind the counter now wore two shades of red on her apron, and the meat being consumed on customers' plates looked fresh and raw. The heat of the booth brought the sensation of this grotesque scene to life. An extremely attractive woman in what could only be discerned as a lavish, red dress with elegantly-styled, reddish-black hair, sat at a table by the front window that looked out upon the street, but her gaze, with its blood red pupils, was directed at Mason alone. There was something disturbingly bewitching in the way her darkened eyes intently observed him, with no regard for anything else in the café. He returned her intense stare for a matter of seconds before she quickly rose from her seat and pushed her way out through the front door. Mason stepped out of the phone-box. With the ring of the bell above the booth's entrance the vision seemed to dissipate and a grimy café returned. The woman had most likely been peering at what she perceived to be a deranged man, one who had been staring into space, at nothing in particular, from inside of glass box.

Mason was not sure whether Walt's tone had simply put him in a
bad state of mind or whether the blow to his head was still making him
groggy. He now felt idiotic for succumbing to terror at the sight of a
fool waiting for the phone. At least he had been asleep when previously
disturbed by visions. He had difficulty in accounting for why he found
himself fearing things that he should not be afraid of and why he found
it so difficult to shake the thought of these two visions from his head.
Once more something had seemed so intense, so of the very moment,
about this projection of the mind. He quickly paid for his drinks and
went outside to his car.

"Got any change for a phone call mister?" implored the drunk
outside, stumbling into Mason's arms.

Mason shoved him away in disgust, sending the man reeling back
onto a pile of black rubbish bags and cardboard boxes. He withdrew
his car keys from his pocket and pulled out into the road to get on with
his work.

CHAPTER 10

Mason swung his car around onto the avenue he was looking for and stopped a few buildings down from number 1365. He stepped outside into the oven of the streets, slammed the door shut and walked towards the address that he had come to discover. It was an old, tall and thin brick building of maybe twenty floors, each looking feebler the higher they rose. The top half appeared to be slightly swaying from side to side, like a jester popped from a jack-in-the-box, as though the next breath of a breeze would send it crashing down, if indeed there was ever to be even the mildest gust of wind in the midst of the overbearing heat-wave. Mason took out his notebook. The entry under Sadler's name in Rachel's address book lay on the ninth floor.

Mason entered the lobby. The lifts in this part of the city rarely worked. They had all been installed at least a decade previously and buildings generally kept hold of them merely to attempt adding an aura of glitz to their interior. He saw the door to the stairs and climbed nine flights, carrying the stifling heat upon his sweat-drenched back every step of the way. He turned onto the dilapidated, violet corridor and approached the wall at the far end until he stood outside number 7, the faux-gold numbering reflecting the dim light, mocking the attempts at decadence in the dullness of the reflected image. Mason banged firmly upon the door.

"Hey sugar," said a sensual, throaty voice behind him, "nobody's home today."

Mason turned to see a tall, abnormally skinny, black man, leaning against the open doorpost of number 8, wearing a denim miniskirt, and completely bare-chested. His ears were adorned with gold earrings the size of dinner plates, while his thin arms and ankles were wrapped with chunky bracelets. His braided hair was mixed with several small, imaginatively-coloured feathers. His appearance seemed a cross between an ancient, Incan thunder god and a crack-addled transvestite living inside a bizarre, drug-induced dream world.

"How do you know?" Mason asked, watching the slow, crawling motions of the hazy pupils.

"Nobody's been home for, I'd say, two weeks now daddy," was the reply in a voice so unnaturally high pitched and effeminate, it must have hurt the man to put it on.

"How do you know? Do you know Mr. Sadler well?"

"Mr. Sadler? Oh honey, please, that guy deserved the title mister about as much as my pretty self. Raymond has not been into his apartment in quite some time and left without even a kiss goodbye."

The man slowly and gracefully twisted his fingers to his lips and blew a kiss at Mason, who tried his best not to offer any reaction.

"Poor you. Listen, it's very important that I find Mr. Sadler, so could you simply tell me anything you know about him?"

"I don't know much sugar. I just observe people's comings and goings in my own little way, that's all. He was a strange guy. Cute but strange. I wouldn't say he had it all going on upstairs!" the man cackled mischievously.

Mason tried his best not to wince at the man's voice or words.

"Well some people are just unlucky I guess. What do you mean exactly by strange?"

A deeper voice bellowed out something muffled from within the Inca's apartment and he shouted something back in a foreign tongue, but in that same unnatural voice.

"Listen sugar, I've got company here so you'll have to excuse me. I just came out to tell you that nobody's home. You take care now and don't go getting yourself into trouble."

The man blew him another kiss before twirling around and prancing off, the bracelets around his limbs ringing as they struck each other and glinting in the festering rays of light that dared to penetrate his apartment, before the door swung closed. Mason could just hear her words trailing off – "some people are just strange, they just don't have it all upstairs."

Mason turned his attention to number 7 once more and decided to investigate behind the door, with or without permission. He figured that if the police were going to be looking for Sadler they would have already come around by now so there was probably little harm in forcing entry, though it did not escape his attention that it would be the third building he had entered of his own accord in the last two days, as he fulfilled his role of following the ghost of Sadler through the places it had once passed. He tried the handle and it clicked open without the slightest resistance. Another unlocked door into the world of Sadler, another portal deeper into the labyrinth of this man's mysteries. Mason took a step into the darkness beyond.

The room he entered was black as a beetle's back, but warm and stuffy. Mason slapped his palm against the wall to the left and right of the doorway until he found a switch. The dull lighting helped the room stutter into after-life, the discomforting, red glowing of a photograph development laboratory. Ahead of him, on either side, canvases smeared with thousands, hundreds of thousands, of dried-up pictures formed the walls for a walkway through the middle. They hung, dried-up black and white monuments to moments captured in the past, to people Mason would never know nor care for. Innumerable testaments to the stories of other lives, to mere seconds suspended in time that belonged to the worlds of strangers. In the deep, red glare of the laboratory they took on unsettling overtones that subtly implied the worst for all the unknowing models of these forgotten frames.

Mason slowly began to move along this walkway between the images, which continued for about twenty feet before it turned one-hundred and eighty degrees around a corner at its end and began another photograph dotted passage that ran in the opposite direction. Mason stood on his toes and thought he could see another fifteen or sixteen of such rows snaking their way back and forth across the room to the dim gloom of the far wall.

He crept slowly through this discarded waste of foreign lives, glancing left and right to see whether he recognised any of the images. He continued up and down the rows, his eyes moving rapidly across the faces, their features, the buildings, the landscapes, the despair of the city, all accentuated by the dark, red glow of the lights. The shadows in the corners of the room moved with Mason's, and the red and black of the light and dark decided to resign their battle, settling on drenching the room with a disquieting mixture of both shades. The pictures seemed to have grabbed hold of the filth of the city and its decline, and beaten it onto these sheets, splattering it violently upon them so that no viewer could possibly avoid or ignore it. Even photographs of picturesque landscapes, of a small girl playing with a dog in the park, were corrupted by the lighting and mingled with some suppressed secret of the mind to exhume rage from the hanging snapshots of life.

However, none of these desperate images intrigued Mason for any particular aside from their mutual horror. He continued his trek through the jungle of photographs, along the twisting passageway, until the giant snake reached its end at a desk with nothing upon it save for a few stacked columns consisting of further frozen frames of the world. Mason sighed and readied himself to retrace his steps towards the front door. It had been a waste of time coming here, only providing him with more disturbing images for his addled slumber, more visuals with which a tortured mind could easily work its destructive craft.

Then something on the desk caught his eye. It was a small scattering of photographs, precisely piled in a fashion that would have required deliberate attention, to the rear of the table. They displayed two businessmen having lunch together outside a restaurant on a busy street. Two men wearing matching brown suits and familiar looks of anger. Familiar from a newspaper cover he had seen before, from the picture he had seen in Sadler's house, of these men photographed with Albright. Mason removed the picture on top to reveal countless more continuous images, all of the two men, seemingly on the same day. Sadler must have been practically stalking them – in fact it would take a man of considerable talents to get this close for any substantial period of time without detection. Mason pulled back more pictures from the summit of the pile, taken in quick succession, and watched the men leave the restaurant and get into a black limousine. He watched the car turning through city streets, pausing at traffic lights, prowling through the lanes of traffic seemingly unaware of the camera following its progress just behind. Mason flicked through the pictures quickly, lending them the pretence of being a moving image, a film being played between his hands. The car pulled up outside a house in a pleasant suburb of the city. Mason watched the men get out of the car and enter the building through the front door. He observed, now through a window, the two men sitting down at a table opposite another man. Mason watched as the conversation became heated and he could hear their voices becoming raised in his head. Mason watched as the unnoticed eavesdropper shifted his position to another window with a better view. He saw the camera focus on the interior of the house again, continuing to document this intriguing argument. The camera showed the man who had originally been in the room strike one of the newcomers. Then the show came to an end. Nevertheless, in the last picture the third man was clearly visible for the first time. It was Albright. Beneath this picture of Mason's employer there lay only the bare, scarred wood of the table's surface.

Mason frantically swept his arms about the top of the desk, desperate to discover what had happened next. The photographs surely could not have simply stopped at this crucial point. He turned over the other piles of pictures, flipping through them manically, tossing them around the room in his search for anything that resembled a continuation. As he flung another pile of random city shots against the wall his eye fell upon a small, shiny object sticking out from beneath the left flank of the desk, settled against its leg. Mason bent down and saw that it was a short length of camera film. As he picked it up more film began to roll into his hands, out from underneath the desk, until he had drawn out several metres of film, the opposite end of which sat in a dusty envelope from another photograph development company.

Mason's eyes scanned the undeveloped images, only barely managing to recognise the frames of the pictures he had just examined in their original, minute form. He got as far as the men entering the car until he could distinguish little more of the roll's contents. The roll continued on for what seemed like several hundred photographs but, alas, they had been severely damaged, beyond any hope of examination, appearing to the untrained eye as though they had been singed or burned. Mason cursed his luck. He needed to know what had happened to these men. He felt sure that the case revolved around these remaining photographs, ones that were not present with the rest of their brethren.

Most likely something undesirable had come to pass, that Sadler had been aware of, and he had decided to threaten or blackmail Albright. Albright wanted Sadler scared, and possibly more.

If that was the case, then it made sense to Mason why Albright had offered such a high price. The money his company would make from assuming ownership of these smaller companies was probably monumental when sized with the fee he was paying Mason. It was worth hiring the best, at an exorbitant price, to make sure such transactions went ahead without fuss, especially if somebody had photographed occurrences that might jeopardise their progression. Mason gave up examining the end of the roll of film. It was too distorted to even begin hazarding a guess at what was happening in the frames. He needed the developed pictures. Mason finished his search of the desk but failed to discover any further continuation to the story he had followed thus far.

In one of the drawers, however, there sat a small, worn notebook, its pages curled from use. He scanned through it quickly. It seemed little more than a work journal, as most of the writings inside were just technical figures related to photography, along with the names and numbers of employers. Every now and then he would come across a more personal entry, but these were little more than thoughts running through Sadler's mind, from half a year beforehand, until one of the most recent writings, from only two months ago, caught his attention. It seemed to be nothing more than the random scribbling of Sadler's ideas at a given time, but interested Mason due to the presence of a familiar name.

"It's time to decide what to do about Albright. Different people suggest different solutions. According to Brian Cornell I'll have to sacrifice everything, which is ridiculous. Samuel Walters says it's the place I have to destroy. I don't know. These guys are probably all just madmen. Maybe I'm going mad myself. Another person would probably call me crazy. I guess it wouldn't do any harm to bring the place down anyway."

The rest of the notebook was filled with more work-related entries. There was nothing further to be learned here. Mason pocketed the book and hurriedly snaked his way back through the maze of pictures, turned off the light and closed the door behind him. Back in the hallway he could hear a loud, thumping music reverberating from the apartment opposite. The neighbour had obviously resumed his entertainment.

Once outside, Mason walked the short distance along the footpath to his car, his mind absorbed in contemplation, in the implications these images had presented to him. As he took the keys from his pocket he realised that the car door was already an inch ajar. He carefully opened it the rest of the way and looked inside. Nothing seemed to be missing, there was not much to take, but the glove compartment and his coat on the backseat had definitely been rummaged through. Scraps of paper, rubbish and the pages of an old newspaper were now strewn across the faded upholstery. Mason looked up and down the busy street. Nobody exhibited any manners indicative of suspicion, though if the intruder had not even closed the door fully they must have seen Mason exit the building and left in a hurry only moments before. Or perhaps they had wanted their presence there to be known. The people who were on the street merely shuffled drowsily by, their bodies drained and stooped, struggling to remain upright in the heat of the setting sun.

The following afternoon Mason rode the train to the outskirts of the city. From his stop he had walked a short distance and now approached his intended destination – the estate of potential mayor, Michael Roach. His home was situated in the hills that rose above the west side of the city, an area shared by many other politicians, businessmen, celebrities and those who had amassed their fortunes under more questionable circumstances.

The train had run slowly along the coast for several dozen miles before opening into the beautiful bay lying beneath the landscape of this neighbourhood. The hills played a pivotal role in keeping the probing rays of the sun somewhat hidden, while the harbour usually brought a slight breeze in towards the land from across the water. Today the air was completely still, and the greenery that flowed across the hills was succumbing to a rusty, brown tinge, the heat sucking out the very forces that animated the earth. Mason had chosen this form of transport due to the state in which he had found his car the day before. He did not want anonymous trespassers returning and decided that without the vehicle it would be simpler to disappear from anyone who was picking up his trail.

The ancient train had rumbled out from the station in the city's centre, boiling its passengers alive as it meandered slowly through the aching metropolis. The archaic air-conditioning system struggled to breathe its way into life, and the travellers inside fought for the spaces close to the small windows, gasping for the air that would drift in slowly, offering the slightest of relief.

After leaving Sadler's laboratory, Mason had busied himself with some research into the nature of Rovkrand's deals, along with the cast of sinister characters who had been involved in them. He had telephoned several offices and administrative organisations but came up empty-handed. Anybody he spoke to who was in any way related to the company was too busy to talk properly or simply refused to discuss the Farrow Enterprises takeover. As for Farrow Enterprises itself, there was little record of it having ever existed. The only sign that it had previously been a company was the number listed in his old phonebook, and that was now disconnected. The very fact that it had once operated as a business seemed to have been completely swallowed up by the larger company. Mason noted the location of the Rovkrand headquarters, but was in no rush to pay them a visit anytime soon. He was far more interested in the fate of the two men in the photographs than the internal dynamics of the company. He decided to visit Roach instead, the fourth character in the photograph of the deal taking place that he had seen in Sadler's faded newspaper. He had arranged an appointment with the man under the guise of a reporter from a local newspaper, interested in an interview concerning the upcoming election, knowing that the publicity was too good to turn down. Mason had some contacts in the local media. It had simply been a matter of finding out which reporters were abroad at any given time, and assuming their name.

Mason's knowledge of Roach did not go far beyond the odd newspaper article, overheard snippets of gossip and a small bit of research he had done that morning. Roach seemed to be little more than another addition to the already teeming population of businessmen turned politicians in the city. He was a self-made man who had encountered huge profit in the aggressive, and often dubious, purchases and sales of companies who, after achieving about all that was possible in his field, had turned his hand towards running the city. Mason reckoned that a man who undoubtedly mingled in the most powerful of circles may have something interesting to say about the takeover, or even about Albright himself. It was just a question of getting him to open up.

Mason reached the large, iron gates of Roach's address without noticing any characters lingering in his wake. He pressed a button on the pillar to their right and, moments later, a whiny voice crackled out onto the street from a small, speaker above.

"Who is it?"

"Hi, it's Ralph Crayton from Newstand. I've got an appointment with Mr. Roach for 3.30."

Mason waited for a long period of silence, broken only by the fuzzy crackle of the intercom. It buzzed like fresh meat sizzling upon a grill in the sun.

"Wait where you are."

He did as instructed and spent five minutes pacing the small strip of pavement in front of the gates. Mason took a handkerchief from his pocket to wipe away the thick layers of sweat that enveloped his forehead. A heavy dust drifted up from the beach and hung in the air, making the suffocation that bit more intolerable. He wondered whether Roach left all of his visitors waiting this long. Perhaps it was a method of making meddling journalists uncomfortable, hot and sweaty, to take the edge off their prying and often personal questions. Mason was certainly starting to feel like a drink.

The gates slid apart with a loud, slow grating, and on the other side stood an extremely large, intimidating looking man. Despite the aspect of the day in question he wore a heavy, black suit, but his face remained devoid of any sign of discomfort. His eyes were masked behind a pair of sunglasses.

"Wow, you guys are quick! Why don't you give me a few more minutes out here?" Mason joked in what he reckoned was the manner most becoming of an irritating journalist.

The man pretended he had not heard Mason's comment.

"Lift up your arms."

Mason did as he was instructed and the man conducted a brief search of his person, though there was nothing to be found.

"Follow me. Do not touch anything or stray from the path."

He spoke in a voice that sounded like an answering machine message, one that had replayed its limited speech countless times, that was now oblivious as to its significance. The man turned and started walking without waiting for a response, and Mason followed.

The dusty path immediately turned a bend, around which Roach's residency came into view. It was a colossal, bright, white mansion, spread out behind a spectacularly kept lawn which the path ran along the right hand side of. Two tall towers formed the ivory centre-points of the house, between which was the front of an enormous room facing out onto the garden, its walls consisting mostly of large windows that ran their entire length. The building continued to stretch out on either side of these towers and Mason could only imagine just how deep the house went on behind this dazzling facade. Directly in front of the towers were countless rows of small but immaculate rose-gardens, the eager, lush aroma of which captured Mason just moments after they came into sight. They were surrounded by sets of elegantly shaped bushes and shrubs that had been precisely pruned into a series of perfectly even cones and spheres. The roses were of a startlingly beautiful red, which contrasted powerfully with the blinding white of the mansion, and the gentle shades of green that made up the remainder of the front garden. Small lanes for playing bowls were engraved into the lawn and despite the overbearing force of the roses, the scent of freshly mowed grass was still unmistakably present. Mason guessed that it was cut every day in accordance with strict measurements. A row of elm trees ran along the inside track of the outer walls, safeguarding the stunning view from curious neighbours and passers-by. In the corner formed where this wall met the east wing of the house, someone had installed a swimming pool, with several deckchairs laid out alongside it. As the two men passed by, a lone and strikingly beautiful young woman stood up from one of these chairs and removed a towel from around her body, revealing a light-blue swimsuit beneath. Mason hesitated for a moment to observe her. The other man grunted.

"Come on, there's nothing to see."

"On the contrary," Mason burst out. "Who's that?"

"That's not important. Let's go."

"Ah c'mon," Mason whined, "just gimme her name."

"It's Mrs. Roach."

"Wow, Mr. Roach hasn't done too badly for himself has he?"

The man stared at him silently for a moment. Although he still wore his sunglasses, Mason could feel the look of dismay being thrown at him from behind the tinted lenses.

"Okay, I'll behave. Let's go."

The two of them resumed their march along the path, until they entered the fantastic house by one of the smaller side doors.

Mason was brought down several passages and corridors, constantly turning off in different directions, through the servants quarters and then through the back of the kitchen, all bustling with hordes of people busily rushing to and fro, their flesh looking as though it would begin peeling from them like layers of dough in the confined, baking air at any given moment. A final respite from the heat came when they turned into what Mason reckoned was the main hallway, though he had all but lost his sense of place due to their confusing route thus far, and a blast of fresh air from the fans set into the walls blew against his skin. He was brought across this elaborate opening, complete with enormous, marble staircase and pillars, and through a door on the opposite side of the hallway. This led into the room between the two towers that Mason had observed from the outside, constituting, it would seem, the centrepiece of the house. As he stepped into the room he heard his guide abruptly state "Wait here" before the door was silently closed behind him.

The room was large and spacious, running along some hundred feet of the building, and Mason could not decide exactly what function it assumed, resembling in equal measure a breakfast room, an office and a library. The numerous lengthy windows set into the left hand wall, that rose from floor to ceiling, let the light come flowing inside in glorious waves, immaculately illuminating the room, and turning its creamy coloured walls into something closer to a divine but rustic gold. In front of these were placed several small but select coffee tables, surrounded by a large variety of thickly cushioned armchairs, settees and recliners. The other half of the room was decidedly different in its nature, with the widow's counterparts on the far wall constituting a number of large filing cabinets and steel shelves, bursting with books, folders and loose documents. In front of these were placed a number of large writing desks, each complete with a wide array of drawers and reading lamps. It certainly seemed an interesting choice of room in which to greet a visitor in such a stunning residence, but Mason again considered the idea that he was not necessarily regarded as a desired guest, that perhaps it was another tactic designed to prevent reporters or other potentially unwelcome visitors from feeling entirely at ease.

Mason scanned the bookshelves for a short time, but finding it full of little other than political journals and economic reports, crossed the room and stood looking out through the glamorous walls of glass. A haze of heat shimmered above the impeccably even lawn outside, dancing above the exact, pristine blades as though they were sharp enough to slice it to pieces. Several grounds-men were now wandering its perimeters tending to its edges with delicate instruments. Mason heard a splash and his attention was again drawn to the swimming pool where Roach's wife was busy doing very little. He watched her for a time, backstroking her way with ease through lengths of the water. Mason wondered exactly what Roach had gone through to acquire such a staggering wealth, what secret crimes lay behind this vast fortune, what acts it was necessary to commit in order to achieve this illustrious prosperity. He could not prevent the thought from playing upon his mind that once he finished this case and cashed the promised cheque, he would not be very far removed from a similar life himself. His eyes continued to examine the curves of the young woman's body, working their way through her routine, while dreams of a luxurious retirement assembled themselves somewhere in his mind.

"Ahem!"

A throat clearing sharply shook Mason from his thoughts and he turned to see the man who had led him here standing in the doorway, once again eyeing him disapprovingly from behind his tinted glasses.

"Mr. Roach," he simply stated and stepped to the side, leaving the doorway open for his superior.

Roach entered the room. He was a burly, heavy-set but tall man, similar to Mason in height. Though appearing older than he did in photographs, and perhaps being in his mid-sixties, he still looked as though he were in very good shape. His thick, ebony-black hair, which impressed nothing upon Mason other than an extensive dyeing schedule, still maintained shades of grey around the temples and with each movement of his face a new set of wrinkles was displayed. However, he was dressed with an ever-present smile that Mason reckoned served to automatically flatter countless voters and fellow businessmen, while he immediately struck Mason as having that quality present in all successful politicians, the presence to fill a room and to attract all the attention at any event he attended. The large windows and bookcases seemed to shrivel and shrink in the presence of this mountain of exquisitely practiced manners. He spoke in a deep, rich baritone, a hearty, reassuring voice, which constantly indicated that all was well.

Roach walked forward and shook Mason's hand with a meaty palm that smothered even the latter's large fists.

"Mr Crayton, so good to have you with us."

Then looking back over his shoulder towards the door he instructed, "You can leave us now Parker."

The man hesitated a moment.

"Are you quite sure sir?"

This elicited a brief glance of anger in Parker's direction from Roach, which was enough to send him briskly from the room without any further questions, before Roach's more pleasant features arrested his face once more.

"Please forgive my shabby appearance Mr. Crayton, but I have been rather busy this morning with a number of matters, and have only recently arrived in from the burn of this infernal sun. I'm sure you know how busy it gets around election time."

Roach said this with his smile gleaming at Mason, who double-checked this shabby appearance. He was dressed in an exquisite, black tuxedo, and Mason judged that the cufflinks of his silk shirt probably cost more than his own car.

"Please take a seat and let's get started."

The two men sat facing each other on opposite sides of one of the low coffee tables. The rays of the sun came beaming down from the windows that loomed high above their heads, and left the men basking in the glow of an otherworldly light, as everything about them became touched by an amber hue and tinted with a heavenly aspect. Mason had brought an office dictaphone along with him and he placed it upon the table between them.

"Well Mr. Roach, let me begin by saying thank you for allowing me to conduct this interview and what a great pleasure it is, of course, to meet you."

"But of course my good man."

"We are running a series of these interviews, with yourself and also your competitors in the coming election. We'd like our readers to get a complete outline of each of the candidates' policies, but more than just an overview or precise points. Rather we wish to present a comprehensive summary of the candidates' positions based upon their own words"

Roach remained silent, simply nodding his understanding.

"So I guess I'll ask you to start by clearly stating what it is you hope to bring to this election, what the voters can expect from you and what exactly you can offer them."

Roach readied himself by removing a silver cigarette case from the inside pocket of his suit, gesturing towards Mason, who refused with a wave of his hand, and lighting one of the small, white sticks. He breathed in deeply before exhaling in a most satisfied manner, his giant smile a constant upon his face.

"Well, I don't remember seeing you smoking in any of your newspaper pictures Mr. Roach? Is this a new habit, just for the election?" Mason taunted.

"I suppose we all have secret, private sides to our character. Don't you agree Mr... Crayton?"

Roach's pause before uttering the surname, along with the questioning nature of how he pronounced it, made Mason feel a little uneasy. However he managed to prevent this unease from protruding through his relaxed demeanour.

"I guess so sir, I guess so. Now can you start explaining your policies?"

Roach took another enjoyable breath from his cigarette and began an extremely long-winded monologue. For the following half hour Mason barely managed to fit in a complete sentence, merely interjecting here and there with a "really?" or "can you elaborate a little please?" Roach poured forth an eternally flowing stream of information, all presented in the most lavish, political lexicon. He promised to clean up the environment, to solve the smog problems in the city while cleansing the rivers. He spoke about lowering both crime and taxes. He effortlessly enunciated his way through a speech about how change cannot be immediate, how this was all but a stepping stone across dangerous waters, of how he would not guarantee instant results like his fellow candidates, but rather would build a harmonious city up from the current festering wreck by working together with the people to create a brighter future. Roach interspersed all of this with numerous supposedly amusing anecdotes, off-topic remarks and light-hearted jokes. His speech reminded Mason of Parker's, in that it was blatantly rehearsed and being repeated for the thousandth time, having lost all of its meaning long before, if indeed meaning had ever truly been there. However, it was a much more refined effort than Parker's, spoken with eloquence and charm, using his guile and natural wit to win the listener's interest. Mason could see quite clearly that Roach had been keeping his eyes open for a gateway into the world of politics for a long time, and had spent much of that time preparing himself.

The rays of the sun, magnified by the glass of the windows, burned themselves upon Mason's forehead, and he found himself constantly raising his hand to his face in order to shield his eyes, an annoyance which Roach surely perceived but chose to ignore. When his winding dialogue seemed to be coming close to a conclusion, Mason asked whether he could have something to drink.

"But of course, my good man," replied Roach. "How thoughtless of me to overlook the offer in the first place. Where are my manners? What would you like? Water or something stronger?"

"Water will be just fine for now, thanks."

A small telephone stood upon a stand beside the armchair in which Roach was sitting. After the manipulation of a number of buttons, Mason heard him order –

"Bring some water for Mr. Crayton, and some whiskies too."

What seemed to Mason a deliberate lack of hospitality in the afternoon's proceedings had left him feeling somewhat wary. He quickly decided to fix the conversation upon the subject of business, asking Roach whether he could expound a little upon his life before politics. Another long speech followed, during which time a servant arrived with two iced whiskies. Both the servant and Roach overlooked the fact that the water had been forgotten, as the latter continued relating chapters of his life story which were entirely of no interest to Mason. The sound of another refreshing splash from the pool outside convinced Mason's mind that any drink would do for the time being.

"I think I'll have one of those whiskies after all."

"Splendid," smiled Roach.

They clinked their glasses together. Mason took a long gulp of the auburn liquid, which ran smoothly through him in a momentarily satisfying manner.

"Delicious stuff isn't it?" Roach mused.

"Certainly. So what can you tell me about some of the more, how should I say... well I suppose what some media outlets are describing as 'questionable' takeovers of other companies that you have been involved in?"

A flicker of an expression, that was as-of-yet foreign to Mason's knowledge of the man, slightly contorted Roach's features at the statement of this sentence, before giving way once more to the dependable smile.

"Questionable?"

"Not my choice of words remember, but yes questionable. Say for instance... for example the deal between Rovkrand and Farrow Enterprises. That was an aggressive purchase that you gave your backing to, wasn't it?"

The unknown expression returned to Roach's face and this time chose to linger there a while. He looked puzzled, as though trying to determine the answer to a question he had silently asked himself. After a minute of muted brooding, he seemed to have made up his mind about whatever matter troubled him, and smiled once more at Mason. During this time, the heat seemed to Mason to have developed a greater potency, despite the oncoming approach of evening and the lengthening of the shadows cast by the trees that guarded the edges of the estate. He loosened the collar of his shirt in an attempt to make himself more comfortable.

"It has been some time since that particular deal went though, has it not? What caused that to spring so suddenly to your mind?"

Mason took time to think before replying.

"Alright, I'll admit it's a deal that I've done particular research into. However, it is true, isn't it, that all traces of the Farrow company seem to have completely vanished?"

"As is quite often the case in a large takeover, is it not?"

Mason decided it was time to take a gamble with his questions.

"Perhaps. However there are a number of minor details of the purchase that I've tried, in vain, to inform myself of. It seems that several of the shareholders in Farrow, even the owners themselves, have also vanished, along with the company. Particularly evident is the impossibility of getting in touch with those who were opposed to the deal taking place. They seem to have disappeared, despite them being a fixture in the media at the time of the deal. Now they simply can't be found."

"Really? And what exactly is it that you are getting at here, Mr. Crayton?"

Roach reclined slightly in his chair, scrutinising Mason with a more fixed stare than the latter had become accustomed to.

"What's more I have called..."

Mason broke off mid-speech as a desert-like sense of dehydration suddenly overcame him, and he felt the sentence burn up in his throat before it could proceed any further in its voyage towards the outside world. He loosened his collar even more and drained the remains of the melted ice in his glass.

Roach again perceived Mason's discomfort, but this time made no attempt to conceal his observations. The politician's smile had been wiped from his face and was now replaced by a natural one, of a wholeheartedly suspicious nature. He removed another cigarette from his case and, after inhaling deeply, blew the smoke across the table towards Mason, who was now breathing and perspiring extremely heavily, and swaying in his chair with a pair of glazed, red eyeballs. As he exhaled, Roach leaned across the table and pressed the stop button on the dictaphone.

"Powerful whiskey, eh?" he gently murmured, smiling all the while as Mason's state deteriorated with every breath.

He once again picked up the receiver of the telephone and spoke into it, this time too quietly for Mason to make out the words.

"You know, I find it very interesting. We hosted a Ralph Crayton here just a few weeks ago. If I recall he too was from Newstand. You do not resemble each other in the slightest though, neither in manners nor appearance. Don't you find that strange?"

Mason was now finding it difficult to breathe at all. He felt himself slipping dangerously close to the edge of consciousness. Something had evidently been put in his glass. He attempted to stand up, but found his balance failed him, and merely stumbled across the room into another chair. He turned to look at Roach who was gradually becoming a shape shifting image, assuming different forms as though placed before a revolving set of circus mirrors. He heard the door of the room open and several heavy footsteps reverberating off the wooden floor. Mason felt himself dizzyingly fall upon the ground in a failed final attempt to stand up, and could just manage to make out three or four pairs of legs circling him as he lay there. He felt breath upon his face, close to his ear, and heard Roach laughing a menacing cackle, before he whispered.

"Ha, you must think we're pretty stupid around here, mustn't you? Well listen here my man – I don't care who you work for, what you know or what you want. Maybe you're from Rovkrand, you want more money? Maybe you know something about the Farrow guys going missing? I don't care! You think we don't get scum like you in here almost every second day? Listen closely for your own good, or else tell your boss or whoever it is that dreamt up this scheme, that I won't be intimidated and I won't be blackmailed. You think I'm running an election campaign without protecting myself, my interests and investments, without the backing of the most powerful people in the city? Nobody here can touch me. I could kill you or anybody else I wanted right in the middle of a main street in broad daylight and nobody'd give a damn, got that? Now you're going out by the same door you came in. And you won't be coming back."

Mason felt two light slaps on his face before the power of a fully formed fist crunched into his jaw.

Before he blacked out he heard Roach laugh and say "Goodbye Mr. Crayton."

It took Mason a long time, after regaining his senses, to realise where he was. His head was throbbing and dizzy, most likely from a concoction of whatever substance he had accidentally ingested and the beating he had received while he was under its influence. As his vision slowly realigned itself, he found that he was lying on a grassy roadside, down at the base of the rising hills. Evening had certainly arrived and the sky had begun to assume its reddish tint along the horizon, which battled the failing resolve of the calming blue of the coast. It took him several minutes, and numerous failed attempts, to get to his feet, his legs and arms aching and covered in newly formed bruises. He staggered down to a remote spot on the beach and used the water to wash his face free of the blood he had tasted when he had painfully licked his dry lips. He saw a swollen and bruised face looking back at him in the water's quivering reflection. Mason spent a few moments gathering himself, sitting on a wall looking out upon the clash of colours, before he figured the effects of the drugs had worn off, at least as much as they were going to in the immediate future. He then began making his way back to the train station. The clerk behind the ticket desk almost fainted at the sight of Mason's face when he stepped forward to the front of the queue.

CHAPTER 12

Mason reclined in his office chair, organising the day's events in his head and contemplating what his next move might be. Judging by what he recalled of Roach's farewell comments, there was little to be gained from tangling with him further. He was undoubtedly involved in a number of nefarious activities, but Mason was of the opinion that he was probably not directly involved in Rovkrand, let alone Sadler's disappearance. He was most likely only using the Rovkrand deal for another minor slice of publicity and the chances were he had not involved himself in the aftermath. His thugs had given Mason a considerable beating and the drug was still causing a spinning in his head. Mason would have liked nothing more than to dig up some dirt on the politician and begin getting even, but he decided there were more important issues to be dealt with than personal grievances. Roach was clearly a dangerous man, one whom Mason had made a mistake in underestimating, but he was likely to be of little use in this case for the time being.

What he really needed was the rest of the developed photographs from the roll of damaged film. He picked up the envelope from which the film had come. It bore the stamp of a larger photograph development company, which indicated that Sadler had developed them in another work place. Or possibly he had been too scared to develop or collect them in person and so paid somebody else to do the work and send the finished product to him. He turned over the envelope and read the printed posting address – 73 Oakfield Drive. The scene of his assault. Sadler's house. That was where the developed pictures had been sent. Was that why Sadler, if it really had been him, had returned to the house. It was possible that Mason had interrupted Sadler before he had managed to retrieve them. Perhaps they were still in the house. If Albright's men were watching, it would prevent Sadler from returning frequently without serious risk. Whatever the answer, Mason would have to brave the house again to see if he could find the crucial pictures.

Mason reckoned he was more likely to find something the sooner he went. However, it had been a long day – the sun had exhausted his body and the various blows he had suffered had burdened his brain – and he was unsure whether he was in a condition to put up much of a fight if there happened to be another incident at Sadler's. He decided that he would wait until he had slept properly and then go to the house in the morning, feeling refreshed, in a state of readiness to tackle any waiting monsters. He sat back in his chair and gently shut his eyes. Then the telephone rang.

"Hello, Mason's office," he answered.

"Good evening Mr. Mason."

It was that thundering, soft voice again, slowly and violently pulsating through the wire into the receiver, causing it to tremble almost to the point of explosion.

"Albright. What do you want? Make it quick, I've had a busy day."

"How is the job coming along? Have you located Sadler?"

"Not yet, but you'll be the first to know when I do."

Albright did not respond.

"Is that the only reason you're calling Albright? Because I've a lot of work to do and you're just taking up my time. Besides I might have a few questions for you myself. Have you got people watching me? Have you hired other people on this case? Or just some thugs to trail around after me and keep me on my toes?"

Albright's voice maintained its menacing tone but seemed to increase its intimidating intent as he spoke his next sentence.

"Mr. Mason, the day after tomorrow is the 29th. I am sure I do not have to remind you of our arrangement. It is imperative that the job is completed by that night. Otherwise the contract will be cancelled, and someone will have to be held accountable for its failings."

"What are you getting at?"

"Remember, Mr. Mason, that you are being extraordinarily compensated for the completion of this job. Likewise, you will be the victim of severe punishment should you fail me."

"Are you threatening me?"

"Do not fail me. Bring me Sadler by the evening of the 29th."

Mason paused for a moment.

"You mean Sadler and the brooch, don't you?"

Albright remained silent for several seconds before very forcefully repeating himself, emphasising every word precisely.

"Do not fail me. Bring me Sadler by the evening of the 29th."

The line went dead. Mason stood up and walked to the window, pondering what to do next. As he stood gazing out upon the street he saw a familiar looking parked car pull out from amongst the others and drive down the road until it took a left turn out of sight. Who were these mysterious visitors, he wondered? Were they actually Albright's men? Or was it possibly a person Sadler had hired? Or somebody else entirely? Or was it all simply the raving of an unhinged, paranoid, beaten and drug-influenced mind, exhausted and excited from the preceding days, finding suspicion in the most routine of events, casting doubt upon matters as everyday as the movements of a car?

Mason did not like being threatened and was not afraid of Albright. However, he was beginning to realise that the possibility of Albright being a very powerful man, a man who had potentially washed his hands of many crimes in his past and eliminated a lot of his enemies, was becoming ever more likely a reality. Mason did not like being pressured or intimidated but still preferred to have this troublesome business taken care of and to remove Albright from his life altogether. He was also eager to resolve the case before these mysterious cars and break-ins intruded any further into his life. He would get some rest and then go to Sadler's. Tonight.

Outside Sadler's all was quiet. The lights of the other homes along the street had all been extinguished, as was to be expected at this hour of the night, but their absence gave Mason the impression that the world was actively preparing for his visit to the house. All the cars parked outside were similarly darkened. Mason examined them closely but could not make out any phantoms waiting inside these deserted, ghostly carriages.

Even Sadler's house, which gave off its nauseatingly, aberrant appearance of respiration in daylight, now seemed to be lost in slumber. It seemed so fragile in appearance, so constantly close to collapsing in on itself. The occasional breath of wind fluttered through its wooden slats, causing them to rise and fall, furthering the sensation that this was no structure, but a living, breathing life form.

Mason crept to the front of the house and gently pushed the unlocked door out of his path. There had probably been such an incredible amount of uninvited guests to the place that nobody bothered to lock, or even close, the door anymore, knowing that another visitor would be following in their footsteps before long. Inside it was as dark as a mine shaft. Mason did not want to try the lights in case they alerted any sentries who sat outside, waiting for intruders. Instead he hesitated in the doorway a few moments, allowing his eyes to adjust to the darkness. However, the black within was virtually impenetrable by natural means. He took out a lighter and closed the door behind him.

Mason began his search for the missing photographs in the main room but came across nothing more than the mess he had encountered during his first visit to this abode. He remembered that the person who struck him had been upstairs, quite likely due to the presence of something valuable up there. Mason slowly and silently crept to the hallway and began scaling the dark staircase. His lighter only provided a small ring of light, about a foot on either side of the outstretched hand that held it aloft, beyond which was complete darkness. It extended just far enough to see the wall that ran alongside the stairs, on which was still plastered the trail of blood he had deposited during his previous voyage along these steps. Despite the exterior indication of some sort of a life within, the former home now felt completely soulless. No figures stalked the corridors waiting for Mason. No sudden surprises enlightened the edges of the circle spread by his flame as he ascended further into this silent mayhem. It felt as though nobody had dared to trespass upon this abandoned no man's land for decades and Mason struggled to remind himself that he had been here just days before. The wholehearted lack of life played tricks upon his mind, more so, even, than the thought of his attacker revealing himself again. The complete and utter lifelessness of the place seemed in that moment more terrifying to Mason than anything else could be, as he was left alone with nothing for company other than his own nightmare tinged imagination.

As he reached the landing, he turned to his right and walked down the bleak, blackened corridor in the direction from which his assailant must have emerged. At the end of the passageway were two doors. The one on the right led to an old bathroom fallen into disrepair, while the opposite door opened into what appeared to be Sadler's study.

It was similarly black inside and Mason slowly began to follow a path around the walls of the room, trying to get a sense of the size and shape of it. The walls were scaled by strong, wooden bookcases, packed to the point of bursting with thick, hard-backed volumes that gave off an air of having eternally existed, of being older than their very authors. These bookcases covered the entirety of the room's walls, from which a window was absent. As he cast a glance over some of the titles he quickly realised that the majority of them were some form of documentation on the occult and the supernatural. There were books dealing with certain dubious cults and sects, others regarding particular spiritual rituals, and others concerning unnatural methods of profitably progressing through life, attaining immortality or inflicting revenge. There must have been several thousand books crammed into this miniature library and at least half of them dealt with these unusual topics. The subject matter, along with the memories of his last violent visit to the building, mingled with the darkness to create an uneasiness in Mason, and he decided it would be best to try finding what he was looking for and get out of there as quickly as possible.

Mason moved hesitantly into the centre of the room, barely able to distinguish what lay beyond the length of his arm, until he bumped into a sizeable, flat topped, wooden desk. Sadler had clearly spent more time and money on furnishing this room than the rest of the house put together. Scenes of medieval attacks upon castles, religious massacres and foul forms of torture were masterfully carved about the desk's edges The majority of its top consisted of a soft padding, upon which were scattered countless papers, along with notebooks and what seemed to be piles of address books or diaries.

Mason began to sift through the pile, hoping that the set of photographs might emerge. Despite his desire to free himself of his eerie surroundings, he could not prevent his eyes from being diverted by the titles of several documents or newspaper headlines that functioned as a window into the kind of disturbing world that Sadler had been submerging himself in. One newspaper article he saw was clearly an excerpt from a thesis or essay of some sort, with the title "The realistic hopes of interaction with the deceased". A brief passage of the text was underlined by black ink.

"When questioning what methods one uses in attempting to contact the departed, the primary question is – what are one's' motives for making this contact? When this has been firmly and honestly established, it is only then possible to determine which method is the most suitable, whilst also going some length as to ensure the safety of those involved in the ritual."

Mason knew that he should not be giving serious consideration to these writings, but the atmosphere of darkness, destitution, silence and solitude, which so pervaded the library and all of its contents, served to continually unnerve him. He felt his imagination conjuring up other beings in the room, as though by reading these verses he was invoking evil spirits to enter. Mason lifted the lighter to examine the other end of the large desk. The light fell upon several more volumes and papers, until it touched the edges of something else. A high-backed chair was positioned on the opposite side of the desk and sitting in this chair sat a figure, with a wicked, wretched grin of contempt smeared across its face. Mason drew back in shock for a moment, letting the light slide off the figure. Then he felt it lunge at him, powerfully striking him out of its path and knocking the lighter from his grasp, before bolting through the door to the house beyond. Mason stood stunned, and alone again in the darkness, hearing the front door being thrown open, startled, wondering how long the figure had been sitting there, watching, observing him as he had gone through his investigations.

Mason felt a coldness come over him, his body lightly twitching in a nervous fashion, and suddenly he could think of nowhere else he would less like to be. There was something of ill omen in this house and he wanted to escape, photographs or no photographs. He hurriedly gathered as large a pile of books, papers and newspaper clippings as he could carry from the desk, constituting about three quarters of its contents, and left the building quickly, frantically dropping a considerable amount as he went, before any more ghastly figures could appear. Outside all was as deathly silent as when he had first entered the house. He wasted no time getting into his car and driving towards his office once more.

Back in his office Mason crumpled into his chair. He was exhausted. Partially from the long day of bruises and the drugs, but mostly from the shock he had received on seeing the figure sitting behind the desk, staring at him maliciously, with its evil smirk plastered upon its face. His lighter had only brightened the scene for a moment so brief it was virtually immeasurable, but in that moment he was sure it had shone upon the same figure he had previously seen in the car outside Sadler's. His mind desperately struggled to formulate any semblance of a theory as to who this man might be, but it felt splintered and damaged inside his skull, it felt confused as though it lacked any of the proper, necessary components for the processing of formulated thoughts. This time the face had not looked as smooth and devoid of features. It had been contorted and disfigured, and the smile seemed almost unimaginable sitting upon the face of the person whom he had seen the first time. It was entirely possible that they were two completely separate people but something in the expression upon the figure's face told Mason otherwise.

He decided to attempt organising the writings he had managed to carry from the room in his frenzied scramble, if only to momentarily rid his thoughts of the disturbing sight of this fiend. He knew that he would not be able to give this task the full attention it required, but he felt as though an aneurysm would erupt before long if he did not set his mind to more regular thoughts, to something that had at least once seemed straightforward – finding Sadler. He began to sort through the material, making separate piles of newspapers, books and what appeared to be Sadler's personal writings. As he identified the individual writings and ravings, Mason's eye eventually came to rest upon a small, indistinct, brown book that had the appearance of having passed through many pairs of hands down the years before arriving on his desk. It was titled "Diary of Sir Samuel Walters". He remembered the strange entry he had seen in Sadler's work journal the day before, the one that had mentioned this man's name. As Mason turned the volume over in his hands, the silence of his office was suddenly shredded by the shrill ring of the telephone.

CHAPTER 13

Mason hesitated before answering the telephone. He did not particularly wish to speak to anyone at that moment, and the chances were that somebody calling this late at night was not doing so to simply send their regards. Nonetheless, after seven or eight tones had reverberated in his ears, Mason begrudgingly picked up the receiver and mumbled an exhausted greeting.

"Hello?"

"Mason, we need to talk."

The voice on the other end did not belong to any of the suspects that had immediately sprung to Mason's mind. In fact it was possibly the one person he was relatively happy to hear from given the circumstances.

"Walt. It's a little late don't you think? I've had a pretty rough day. Couldn't this wait until tomorrow?

Walt had no desire to dissect this information in his mind and ignored Mason's protests.

"It can't wait. I don't give a damn about your rough day – you're the one who got me into this. I need to see you tonight. I need to see you now!"

"Hey Walt, hold on a minute will you? You've no idea what I'm going through myself. Anyway, once you got the price fixed in your favour I didn't exactly have to apply thumbscrews to get you on board, did I?"

"I think there are ... I'm not sure but ... I'm not safe Mason, we have to talk. I have your information but we can't do this over the telephone. You understand. You know more than you let on, I'd wager. Once I give you what you want I'll be washing my hands of this ... this case, alright? I need to see you to get back to my normal life. I'll see you at La Catedral in an hour. Bring all of my money or I'm disappearing for good."

Walt said nothing more and the connection ended.

Mason had little choice other than to meet as Walt wished. He had not exaggerated his difficult day and felt like little more than hiding himself from the world, hibernating in a comfortable place without any possibilities of surprise visions or visitors. However the information Walt had was very likely valuable and Mason had to admit that his time was starting to run out. Walt had proved extremely useful in the past and it would be foolish to risk losing his help. Indeed, the fact that he felt that his life was in danger, if true, though typical of Walt's dramatic, reactionary behaviour and very likely imagined, indicated that he was getting close to something interesting. Surely hunting Sadler would not set anyone directly upon Walt's trail, but if he had gone looking for dirt concerning Albright on Mason's behalf then who knows what strange or dangerous characters he would have come face to face with. Mason had certainly been allocated his own personal share of them. Another part of him, a part that was growing stronger with every moment this case went on, produced a feeling that was difficult to ignore, the fear that something unpleasant might befall another person due to his actions. Walt was right – Mason had got him mixed up in this affair, perhaps without informing him of, not entirely facts, but intuitions that he had been privy to that things could become volatile. Regardless, Mason decided it was time to erase these thoughts from his head. Due to the possibility of danger he was paying Walt extra and the slovenly man knew better than anyone that the higher the price, the higher the risks that followed.

Mason drove to his home, the hour now progressing to the heart of night's dark grip upon the world. Once inside, he opened the safe which lay behind a mirror hanging from the wall in his living room. Inside he had kept the advance that Albright had given him, along with some of the proceeds from other work, mostly for the purpose of such instances where immediate cash in hand was required. He took out Walt's payment and, before closing it back up, found himself staring at the piles of ill-gotten gains secretly stashed before him. The thought struck him that he would have no need to conceal the money were he not ashamed of it, of how he had procured it. He wondered how many other people had made phone calls like Walt's, scared for their lives or the lives of those they were close to, because of his threatening figure tracking them? Mason dismissed this unproductive speculation. He locked up the safe and the apartment, and got into his car to drive to meet Walt.

La Catedral was a popular club in the rotten depths of the city. The city centre, with its strip filled by depraved clubs and delinquent bars, was about the closest the Neolithic complex came to having living, beating internal organs, to any indication that life was to be found there, and that it could possibly be enjoyed or, if not, at least drowned and forgotten. The roads that wound through it were populated by brightly lit, cinema-style marquees, proclaiming the greatest act in town on any given night, next door to run down bars, with no indications of any business taking place inside other than kicked-in screen doors and trails of vomit running from their entrances towards the gutters in the street. Shadows of human beings drifted in and out of this demonic reality, transient shades merely filling their time until death, something which was not so far away for most. The aristocracy exited their limousines outside esteemed restaurants as policemen brutally beat nearby drunks with their batons. In this concoction of existence, consisting of every aspect of the malignance of the human condition, all had one common ground – that nobody seemed young, that even the beautiful betrayed a biting, dying cold, an end to dreaming and a hopelessness that the world was beyond a saviour's fickle powers

Mason's current destination lay within the midst of this mess of madness. Centuries prior it had been a real cathedral, serving its function by hosting daily Christian rituals. It had been abandoned for reasons that nobody seemed to have on good authority but which were the source of new rumours in the city with every passing week. Individual theories ran from devil-worship to religious figures becoming problematic close to particular election times. Whatever had come to pass, the fact remained that the building had stood unused for years, crumbling away while empires of decadence and sin grew up around its hallowed halls of supposed sanctity. However, recently a wealthy member of the city's elite had bought the site as a pet project, as a way to ensure he possessed diversions akin to his other entrepreneurial cohorts. The place now functioned as a music-club and bar. The design of the building had been kept mostly the same, aside from necessary renovations to essentials such as louse-ridden floorboards and shattered or stolen stained-glass windows.

The building preserved its original shape and general layout within, with the stage for performers having been set atop what was once the altar. The clientele could sit beneath the high-vaulted, slanted ceiling that rose upwards towards a triangular dome, with vast beams of wood running along it to support its titanic body. The bar, from which far more than alcohol could easily be purchased, took up one of the side walls, replacing the confession booths that had lain there long ago, once absolving or condemning the faithful for their actions.

The club usually held nightly jazz performances on the stage. Local musicians gathered in this sombre hall to provide further atmosphere to what was already a disastrous venue in which to be God-fearing and an intimidating place to be hedonistic. The sounds of a twanging guitar-string approached Mason as he pulled his car up out front. A sign beside the entrance announced that it was 'Tango Night' this particular evening, and the tones of some broken-hearted tenor caterwauling his pain away came to Mason's ears as he stepped outside. He gave his keys to the waiting valet, paid his entrance fee at the office window and entered La Catedral.

The interior was lit by a chorus of candles placed strategically throughout the emporium. Row upon row lay running along either side of the central aisle, where of a time the priest would have proceeded, frankincense in hand. On either side of this aisle, behind the rows of candles were round tables for over a hundred guests, and all walks of inhuman life sat here drinking in their fineries. Behind the tables on the left were the high arches that frequently decorate the edges of Christian churches, like a series of small, identical hills rising and falling one after the other, and beyond these the bar. Past the tables and arches on the right-hand side of this symmetrical temple lay an area with fewer candles, darkened so that more particular customers could enjoy themselves with some level of privacy while the rest of the guests could pretend that they had not yet noticed these questionable activities.

At the end of the aisle lay several rows of what were presented as the original pews of the church, though they were most certainly more modern creations. This was where one could sit and watch the music or dancing taking place on the altar-stage that lay before them. The band playing that night consisted of a foreign looking rabble, shabbily dressed in time-wearied suits, performing what one could only assume were a number of their native standards. Two guitarists accompanied an ancient, accordion player who squeezed the miniature organ between his fists with such force as to suggest that through it he was taking revenge on the world for all his of his own crushed aspirations. The singer was another elderly man, who sang to and gazed upon the crowd gathered before him with an air of eternal melancholy. His eyes seemed to be constantly welling with tears, droplets of water just waiting to run over the edge of his cheeks and drip from his chin to dampen the aged, ivy-green, tweed suit beneath. He prowled the stage in private agony, searching the church, scanning the crowd with his heavy eyes, for one long lost who was never going to arrive. The music grumbled and growled beneath his incurable sorrow, and, twirling around in the air, the sounds raced one another to the peak of the high-vaulted pinnacle of the church, to settle atop the great blackened bell that still waited there, hanging above the room to strike fear into the hearts of men with its damning toll.

The club was extremely busy for such a late hour. Mason observed that almost all of the tables were occupied, and the loud noises of large crowds of people whispering, talking and fighting served to compete with the music for selection of the soundtrack to this sacred site. Amongst this din of singing, smoking and plotting, Mason saw the figure of Walt, almost lying in a seat at a table by himself, oblivious to the proceedings going on about him.

Mason pulled out a chair and sat down facing Walt, without noticing any signs of acknowledgement in the man's eyes that his presence had been affirmed. His pupils wore a hazy demeanour and gazed out upon the room with a concentrated lack of focus. He was dressed in an unimpressive grey-suit with a white shirt beneath that appeared to be drenched with sweat. His clothes loosely fit his indulgent figure, draping themselves over inanimate limbs. The wicked smile of the man, usually the first sight one was graced with in his presence, was nowhere to be seen. The thin lips, frequently curled at the corners in a grin of glee or barely-masked derision, were pressed tightly together. Walt seemed to be conscientiously squeezing them shut, as though through such perseverance he could not be pressed into elaborating upon any of the mysteries that he may have unravelled.

Mason observed him for some time before Walt visibly recognised that somebody had joined him. His frozen glare was shaken into some semblance of life and he made eye contact. His flabby frame, an exemplar of a misspent life, was stripped of all its usual joviality. He met Mason in a silent stare for some time. The echoing rowdiness of the club circulated their small cavern of quiet. The music from the band and the sorrow of the singer's voice had begun to rouse revellers about them. However, in this static space between Mason and Walt nothing was allowed to intervene, as though they had been sealed off in their own chasm, surrounded by transparent walls to watch the merrymaking about them while they waited, trapped in this strange exchange. Slight refrains of sung Spanish words floated in and out of Mason's consciousness, the heartfelt failures of another wasted life. He finally gathered the required momentum in his mind to transcend the hopefully surmountable sanctitude of Walt's table, to bring them out of their void and into tandem with the rest of the teeming Catedral.

"I've got all your money here. Tell me what it is you found and we can both go home."

Walt continued to blankly scrutinise nothing for several moments. Then his voice stuttered slowly into life, the sweaty rolls of fat beneath his chin adding further tragic nuances to the defeated resonance of his timbre.

"Raymond Sadler is staying at the Fayes Hotel, on the crest of the hill behind the eastern road out of town. He is under the name William Bradbury and is in Room 417."

The precise, mechanical manner in which Walt had spoken left Mason with the impression that this speech was merely a formality, for the sole purpose of relating the necessary information as quickly and painlessly as possible. Usually, the man would delight in the revelation of such secrets, forcing his listener to beggingly tease each intricate aspect of every detail from his grasp, enjoying the delicious moments of power, of unshared knowledge. As he had spoken however, Walt had still radiated his air of measured quietude, leaving Mason sure that a well of filth and fury lay bubbling behind those tightly pressed lips, threatening to overflow and run pouring down his shaking jowls. Mason reckoned that with a little push all of the mysteries that pandered themselves to Walt's mind would unfurl to the outside world. A young waiter dared to encroach upon the solitude of the group, asking if the gentlemen would like a drink, seemingly unaware of the state of said characters. Mason ordered two brandies, hoping something warm and strong would rouse his tablemate from his trance.

Mason recorded Sadler's alias and address in his notebook before pressing onwards with Walt.

"Good work Walt. How did you find him?"

"That's not particularly important is it..." Walt's statement trailed off into a barely mumbled silence before it could fully form itself as a rhetorical question. He still seemed on edge, not quite ready to divulge everything. Perhaps, Mason thought, he would have to begin moving towards an interrogation regarding the other matters in question if he wished to learn any further facts.

"Well then why was it so important to drag me down here in the middle of the night?"

Walt did not respond to this question, but rather continued staring obliquely at an object that lay beyond the scope of everybody else in the room's vision. Mason decided to plunge straight in. There was no point wasting time here if Walt was simply going to shut himself off.

"Well did you manage to dig up anything interesting on Albright?"

The moment the name entered their chamber of seclusion Walt was suddenly snapped from his sleepy state. Animation came quickly to him, but in a disturbing fashion, as he seemed flung into the throes of a distraught frenzy. His body immediately unrelaxed itself as Walt became incapable of sitting still, and began twitching and turning constantly, his fingers locking and intertwining amongst themselves before subsequently attempting to unknot each other. The pupils of his eyes burst into agonising life, the filters, through which emotion and fear had been diminished to a vacant, distant, directionless stare, being unexpectedly lifted. Now the eyes darted around the room, observing everything and everyone on display, as though ensuring that particular persons were not present. When he began to ventilate his thoughts and finally spoke, Walt's voice was as frantic as his person. Gone were both the usual laid back arrogance and the casual mockery, along with the straight, emotionless delivery Mason had just witnessed. Instead there came flowing a stream-of-consciousness reel of information, almost indecipherable. For several seconds he would mumble at an indistinguishable pitch and volume, before his voice would become raised once more. Even then he would only enunciate and properly pronounce a small percentage of what he seemed to be attempting to say, leaving thoughts, sentences and even some words incomplete. Tides of coded language burst upon Mason and he struggled to determine what point, if any, Walt was getting at.

"It ... no it's impossib ... I have to get out of it Mason ... I ca ... You don't understand what I've been going through ... what I've se ... emplate the nightmares, the tragedies incurred ... you only kne ... don't be so idiotic, so simple, so juvenile ... clearly ... yes, I suppose so ... no, there's no point in even telling ... stubborn bastard, why did you have to pursue ... this can only end in ... how, bloody well how. I have to get out of here ... aso ... yes, that's it I'm leaving."

Walt pushed his chair backwards and stood up for some seconds in a quick uncalculated movement, before flopping back into the seat from exhaustion. His face had turned a pale white, only illuminated beyond the pallor of death by the lamps that lit the corrupted church, and it was saturated in a revolting layer of sweat. His eyes closed over as he held tightly onto the arms of the chair, breathing heavily and with obvious effort.

Mason witnessed all of this while remaining seated and dispassionate, yet curious and slightly nervous as to what had thrust Walt into such a state. He was lying when he tried to convince himself that he had not been fighting his own demons of fear these last few days, and that the world that encompassed him had not been growing steadily blacker as the days grew more intensely hot. However, the exaggerated fear and anxiety of Walt, along with the emotionally destitute state he was in, almost made Mason feel tougher by proxy. His fear, paranoia and desperate desire to end this job as soon as possible all lessened in the presence of a man clearly more majestically manic and painfully panic-stricken than himself.

The waiter returned to their table with their drinks, wearing the same unawareness of any potential goings on between the men. Mason pushed Walt's brandy across to him.

"You'll feel better after this."

Walt's eyelids slowly peeled themselves open and remained that way, though constantly threatening to fall once more, as though they were supported by a badly constructed scaffold. He mustered the strength to lift the glass and drink its contents, which in turn gave him the strength to produce a handkerchief from his pocket and wipe his dripping brow. The two men sat silent for several minutes, as Walt battled to compose himself, to bring some colour back into his ivory cheeks.

As he sat, impatiently waiting to hear what the next surprise from Walt's mouth would possibly be, Mason allowed his gaze to drift around the cavernous space, taking in the rich assortment of characters that surrounded their table, the disinterested audience to the theatrics of their secret saga. The pathetic cries for recognition of the remarkably wealthy presented themselves to him on all sides. An elderly man, exquisitely dressed, but with barely the teeth or sobriety to stop dribbling down his shirt-front, stumbled about the dance floor with a disgusting lack of self-respect or dignity. The woman in his arms, on the other hand, was young and astounding to look upon, the texture of her dark skin reflecting the flames of the burning candle-fire above in quite the opposite way to Walt's complexion. Her long limbs seductively wrapped themselves around her wealthy patron's flailing body, keeping him upright and undoubtedly keeping herself in the addictive grasp of high society. At a table to their right, Mason observed a man with an accent carried from afar throwing the contents of an unimpressive glass of wine upon a startled waiter and demanding he be brought something finer, much to the entertainment of his compatriots at the table. Countless other figures wandered through the spaces between such groups, each interesting in their own way, all dancing, drinking and debasing their way towards oblivion.

Mason turned his attention back to Walt who seemed to have regained himself somewhat, although he remained pale, sweaty and shaking, the left arm of his chair the final barrier between his semi-vertical posture and total collapse.

"Listen, Walt," Mason began, "the sooner you explain to me what's happened, the sooner we can both leave, and you can forget about this whole thing. You can go home knowing you've earned your money for once."

Mason's poor attempt at a joke failed to make much of an impact upon Walt's features but he nonetheless momentarily sat upright in his chair. Walt stared into Mason's eyes before leaning across the table towards him, propped upon his elbows, and with purpose in his gaze for the first time that night. He lit a cigarette and took several long drags, the murky smoke filling him with belief. Walt began to speak, but this time in a slow, deliberate manner. He still had the look of a man who had crept from a crypt, but nonetheless there was noticeable purpose present where there had, until now, been none.

"I'm going to take the money and leave. But I'm not just leaving this club. I'm getting out of the city for a while and I'd advise you to do the same thing. This whole business is beyond even you Mason. These people are not your ordinary, amateur scum my friend – they're powerful and they know what they're doing. Since you gave me this job, even though it's been just a short time, I've been on edge, just had a bad feeling. But things have been happening too. You'll tell me I'm crazy or paranoid, but I know otherwise. I know I'm not. I've been doing this work for a long time, as you know, and this case is different. There have been cars following me, parked outside my building at night, and pulling out from every corner I seem to park at. There are people... I'm recognising faces. Then there are the phone-calls, with no voice at the other end, calling over and over again, far too many times to all be wrong numbers."

Mason had sat listening intently for the duration of his time at the table, but at this exact moment his attention had been diverted by something elsewhere in the club. As Walt continued the panic gradually returned to his voice and he once more began to adopt his earlier frenzied rhythms

"And then there's ... the dreams ... if you can call them ... oh God! They're unbea ... no, but I can't even exp ... ieve me if I told you but it's true ... It won't stop ... they're going to keep coming ... I have to get out ... have to or I know I'll lose the last of my mind ... they're terrible, truly terrible."

As Walt had burst into this vigorously confusing collection of revelations, Mason had slowly risen to his feet, the distraction that had gripped his attention confirming itself before his eyes, to the point where he could no longer ignore it.

"Hey Walt, listen – stay right here. Don't move or talk to anybody. I'll be back in a few minutes."

He stood up and was about to step away from the table when he felt Walt grab his upper-arm and hold it with a strength unthinkable for a man in such a state, a strength that could only have been forged from fear. Walt peered into his eyes, with a begging, pleading, almost tearful look.

"You have to get yourself out of this Mason, it's not worth it. It's not worth the money, I can guarantee you that, no matter how much that is. You won't survive this, you can't. Promise me you'll walk away Mason, promise me!"

Mason forcefully shook his arm free of Walt's grip, barely paying attention to his pleas. His mind was too busy racing with other thoughts.

"Just wait here Walt, alright? I'll be back shortly. Just stay here"

Mason hurried off through the maze of tables before Walt had time to respond and instead fell exhaustedly back into the folds of his chair, cigarette still in hand.

As Mason had observed the cast of characters that circled them, one face in particular had seized his attention and held it with a forceful grip. Sitting several tables away had been a woman he was sure he recognised, but Mason had been unable to establish from where or when. The woman wore a long, tight-fitting dress of a dark and rich, sapphire blue. She had remarkably black hair that draped itself about shoulders which were bridged by a sparkling, bejewelled necklace. She was alone at her table, sipping a drink and smoking. As soon as she had drifted into Mason's vision, he had been struck by a strong sense of familiarity, despite being sure that he did not know her personally. Every now and then he had glanced inconspicuously towards the woman, without being able to recollect where he may have encountered her before.

Mason had temporarily set the matter of the woman's identity aside in his mind and resumed listening to Walt's speeches. However, when he looked back in her direction he was shocked, and immediately filled with a sense of inexplicable dread, to see her staring straight back at him, watching with a direct, piercing gaze. Along with the surprise came an instant reminder of where he had seen her before. Mason was almost positive that she was the same woman from the café days before, the woman who had been watching him when he had looked out from within the phone booth, who had stood up and left when he had returned her stare. He had only previously seen her through the bloody glass, decorated, as the world had been for those few brief seconds, in red. Now, blessed by her natural shades, she looked remarkably different, but something that lay in her stare, in the intensity of its essence, its brazen, burning scrutiny, had struck Mason as unique in the café, and now appeared to him again, almost certainly from the same deeply-set pair of dark eyes.

Only a matter of seconds passed between Mason meeting the woman's glare and her standing up from her table and beginning to walk away. This was the point where Mason had interrupted Walt's warnings and roused himself from the slump of his chair to follow her. It was the first time, as far as he was aware, that he had encountered one of the people who appeared to be following him when he was not in a disadvantaged position. The closer he came to her, the more he convinced himself that it was the same woman, and he was not going to let an opportunity to interrogate her, when she was seemingly alone and possibly vulnerable, slip away. Perhaps he could finally determine who had been stalking him – whether it was one of Albright's men trying to ensure that he finished the job on time, or whether there were other antagonists, with other motivations, involved. Her tall, slender frame wound its way between the dozens of diners around them as she directed herself towards the back of the club.

When the swarm of tables and chairs came to an end, Mason watched the woman turn before the altar and make her way, through the dance-floor, in the general direction of the bathrooms, the entrance to which lay on the border of the dim, candle-lit area on the right side of the vast room. He kept a distance between them, even though she neither turned around nor forfeited any sign to suggest that the suspicion of pursuit had entered her mind. Her hair and her waist swayed gently from left to right with each step, in a slow, elegant fashion, and if she harboured any worry or fear of being followed, her body language betrayed no indication of it. Regardless, as they passed first through the tables, and then the dance-floor, Mason made sure that there were always people between them to prevent a clear view of him, a view already impeded by the smoke-heavy air and the low lighting.

The calling of the singer continued to weigh upon Mason's mind, adding indistinguishable elements to this slow, subdued chase. He felt as though he were watching himself in a film, as he stalked this unknown woman through a bustling club, set to the score of the band's symphonies of heartbreak. The sound fitted perfectly to the atmosphere of extravagant delicacy and tragedy around him, and was complimented by the encounters his other senses experienced – a powerful smell of perfume, the glint of a golden bracelet under lamplight, the taste of cigar smoke lazily floating upon the air, the touch of the silk and velvet clothes of those who brushed against him as they danced, weaving their way past.

Mason followed the woman's exit from the dance floor and continued to tread upon the shadows of her soft footsteps as she turned into the tunnel leading towards the bathrooms. As he entered he quickly glanced to his right, into the gloom of the darkened area. It was impossible to decidedly determine what desires were being entertained within, as the embrace of light's absence melded one dark figure into another, and again the reactions of the senses were tested, this time in unidentifiable fashions – one foul laugh of defilement blended into another, surrounded by other, less recognisable, sounds, as the smell of expensive liqueurs blended with the scents of more powerful substances. However, at this moment Mason had more pressing matters to focus upon than the question of how the fantastically wealthy amused themselves in their constantly spare time.

The tunnel they entered was long and narrow, unravelling a pathway along a thick, ruby carpet, between walls only arm's length apart that were dressed by the drenching sweep of drapes of the deepest, most primal violet. The tunnel was lent light only by a shining candelabra at the far end, which held aloft four burning pillars of red wax, beyond which the tunnel split in two directions. On the wall behind the candles hung a large, gold-framed mirror, its polished surface sparkling in reaction to the flame, like water displaying the splendour of the sun's reflection. Also reflected in this mirror was the face of the woman who, having stopped in her movements, now stood with her back to Mason. However, in the glass she was meeting his eyes, once again with that penetrating glare that so unsettled him.

Mason quickly moved closer and stood immediately behind her, facing the image of her presented by the smooth, glass surface. She did not make even the slightest motion, but merely continued her stoic stare.

"Who are you?" Mason asked in a low, but angry, tone. "Why are you following me?"

The woman's face betrayed another expression for the first time. She appeared to be shocked and even, perhaps, a little amused. She spoke in a soft and seductive whisper, tinged by an upper-class accent not unbecoming of La Catedral's clientele.

"Me? Following you? Ha, I assure you I have no idea what you're talking about."

Mason clenched his teeth and growled in a more aggressive tone

"Listen, I saw you watching me and I know it was you in the café two days ago. Just tell me who you are and things won't have to get ugly, alright? Did Albright send you?"

Mason's outburst only seemed to increase the expression of surprise imprinted upon the woman's features as she continued to observe him, regarding him with seemingly equal measures of wonder, disdain and amusement.

"I may be completely mistaken," she whispered after some seconds, "but is it or is it not you who has just been following me? If I recall correctly, just minutes ago you spotted me at my table. You then ceaselessly stared at me. I got up to go to the bathroom. You have followed me through the dining area and through the dance floor, and perhaps would have followed me into the ladies if I had not stopped to accost you. Now please tell me how, exactly, from this series of events, you have deduced that *I* am following *you*?"

As she had said this she had leaned her slender body back against the thick, heavy frame of the mirror, and was almost reclining upon it as she took a cigarette and lighter from her bag. When her fingers began their delicate twirl about the cigarette, Mason noticed a tattoo inscribed into the palm of her left hand. Without thinking he instinctively grabbed it for examination. The thick, black lines laid out the scene of a large ship, floating upon a still sea. Behind it, and to either side, the horizon was engulfed in flames that rose high above even the ship's main masthead. The images of the fire, the water and the vessel flashed familiar memories through Mason's mind and he gripped the woman's hand tightly as he demanded, in a much louder voice this time,

"And what's this then?"

The woman snatched her hand back angrily.

"It's a tattoo for God's sake! What do you think it is?"

This response aggravated Mason's already unstable state further and in frustration he slammed his fist into the wall to the left of the mirror with a crash. This elicited a high-pitched shriek of fright from a young woman who had previously gone unnoticed, approaching the bathroom from behind them. She immediately turned and ran back towards the main area.

"Don't act like I'm stupid," Mason roared at the woman, feeling the rage within him resonating to a climax. "You can tell Albright, or whoever your boss is, that I'll finish the job, but it's not going to get him anywhere having people follow me around, setting me on edge, harassing me at every available opportunity, you got that!? Next person I see outside my office or my house is going to regret it! I'll finish the job, just back off!"

The woman kept coolly watching Mason, apparently not disturbed in the least by his violent outburst. She took a relaxed drag from her cigarette and blew the smoke out calmly, never taking her eyes from him.

"And what exactly are you going to do to these people you're speaking of, whoever they are?"

Mason met her eye contact with anger as she continued unanswered.

"Listen I don't know who you are or what on earth you're talking about, but you have some nerve setting yourself upon me like this."

She leaned slightly to the side and looked down the tunnel beyond Mason.

"Ah, my relief is here at last."

Two large doormen were walking briskly down the passageway, undoubtedly alerted to the presence of a troublesome man outside the bathrooms by the lady he had frightened moments beforehand. The woman looked into Mason's eyes one last time, with a knowing gaze that now indicated, at least to his fragile frame of mind, admittance.

"If I were you, I would finish your job, whatever it may be, on time, whenever that may be. All this work doesn't seem to be doing you any good, you're very worked up. If it's putting you in this kind of a state then I assume it must mean there'll be severe punishments if you can't see it through."

She watched Mason with a wry smile before turning for the corridor leading towards the ladies. As he went to follow her, he felt a strong hand grip his shoulder.

"Is there a problem here sir?" asked the taller of the two burly men who had positioned themselves behind him, a look upon their faces that indicated they relished the thought of a conflict arising.

Mason hesitated before replying. He realised now that he had acted foolishly. His strongest evidence for this woman having followed him had been a vague similarity about her eyes. Even if she was the same woman from the café there was nothing to suggest that their twice meeting, strange though it undoubtedly was, could be attributed to anything other than coincidence. In fact, even if this woman was following him, he had gone about investigating it the wrong way. Her ultimate statement had seemed to him loaded with meaning and, along with the art upon her palm, irritated the contemplative elements of his mind. However, perhaps this was just further sign of the case getting to his jaded thought process, of his brain becoming overly suspicious, of his paranoia at the mysterious cars and unexpected phone calls manifesting themselves in outright deception of the mind. Of course she was going to deny everything when he had no proof other than his own instincts. He should have attempted to follow her in a discreet manner, when she was leaving the club. Now that she was aware that he had noticed her, surely she would be more subtle in future, or else stop her surveillance altogether without him being any wiser for having detected it.

"No, it's alright, I'm sorry," Mason told the men. "I'm just a little upset, I've received some bad news. I'm going now in a few minutes anyway."

His mind flew back to Walt and the extremely peculiar thoughts that the terrified man had been divulging to him shortly before. He walked quickly to their table, only to find it deserted. The case of money and Walt were both gone. A single cigarette lay sitting in the ashtray, still alight, with a little over an inch of ash burned into a silver tube atop it. He looked around frantically but there was no sign of Walt. He cursed himself for having allowed this to have happened. He ran out through the front doors, but the streets, roaring with heat and flooded with the denizens of the lively, depraved nightlife, offered no indications of Walt's presence, and Mason, though surrounded by thousands, was left alone once more, to the darkness of the city and its stories and the horrors that prowled their way through his mind.

CHAPTER 14

Mason decided to return to his office rather than go directly home. Despite his exhaustion, resulting from the occurrences throughout the day and night, his mind had become far too restless and agitated to relax. He decided to determine whether or not there was any more progress to be made in examining the material that he had gathered from Sadler's house. Mason poured himself a glass of water from the hallway before settling his aching body into his office chair. He recalled the diary that had been the object of his contemplation before Walt had interrupted him, remembering that the man who wrote it had been mentioned by Sadler in his work journal. Perhaps this book contained some insight into the world, the mind, of Raymond Sadler and, if not, it might suffice in relaxing his own mind somewhat until a hint of the approach of sleep appeared. A tattered bookmark had been left in the middle of a lengthy entry. Mason skipped backwards through the pages to the beginning of this section and began to read.

April 16th 1843

These truly are terrifying times in which we live, burdened by the yoke of fears beyond our scope of comprehension. As events continue to grow stranger, more unnatural, the world which we occupy constantly shatters any presuppositions I may have once had that I have seen all there is to see, that there is nothing left to surprise me. There is a disturbing reality, or at least a shadow of, surrounding us, with little to act as its disguise other than our own refusal to recognise it. Once we remove the blinkered masks of our perception, than the passageways to realities of immense wonder, spectacle and despair lie gaping ahead, before we enter the jaws of death, and then, God knows...

At the day's end, as night comes to this lonely corner of the world, such strange things are happening all around us, such terrors and tragedies, which we are unaware of. Lights that flicker across the lakes when all earthly fires have been extinguished awaken unrest in my spirit, while the wild howling from the surrounding hills at night, such noises as I have never heard before, makes me pray for morning and anxiously wait, and then, alas, there is only the dark.

However, it is the events of the previous days that have risen above such possibly foolish fears, the creations of irrational minds tired and far from their loving homes, that will remain in my memory, that have shocked me and continue to haunt me with visions of the evils lurking within our world, if indeed it can truly be termed 'ours'.

The peculiarities I speak of were originally presented to us in the form of a story we heard from an unknown man, while we were resting after a particularly arduous journey. We had been crossing the ice plains for a little more than a week, as far as I could reasonably estimate, even with the help of my most trusted men, as we were in one of those eerie, far reaches of the planet where the sun may not set for days on end. Devoid of town or outpost to mark our time or way, we lived and dated merely in the chambers of our minds. For those days we travelled through biting winds and piercing sleet, driven with such force as to cut through the skin where it was unprotected. The sun blindingly bounced off the icy terrain that lay around us on all sides, bare and barren and beckoning death to our sides with bony, skeletal claws. Nothing of either life or nature greeted us, save for the most cruel of elemental furies, constantly mocking our cold and weakness and pain, a land in which the futility of man's pathetic attempts at controlling the world is shattered, as our place, prostrate at the feet of the natural world, begging for mercy, for forgiveness, is displayed high and wide, engraved across the stretches of frozen sky, scrawled upon the icy crags and glacial peaks of mountains that stretch for thousands of leagues below ground to mysterious underworlds of inhumanity.

No matter what course I had plotted, it had always ended with us being led through this land. We had rationalised every known route, but each one inevitably resolved itself here. If we were to reach our destination on time then it was essential that we take this gamble. Otherwise we may have missed out on a tremendously handsome payment, one that not a man amongst us could afford to lose, and we were all firmly unified in the decision that it was worth risking our lives for. As it turned out, the odds were stacked against several of our men, who lost this game with chance, and will forever be entombed in those icy lakes, their bodies floating and freezing for eternity, while their spirits wander through some demented afterlife. When the remains of our party staggered half-dead from this desolate desert of ice, we thanked every power in heaven, and stumbled through the door of the nearest rest-house, isolated upon the fringes of those

barren boundaries. Icicles that had once constituted our matted hair melted and
dripped to the floor, as we came back to life in front of a raging fire and warmed
ourselves with the drinks the locals use to keep their spirits aloft in such a dreary
world. Little did we realise at that stage that we were merely switching from one
landscape of savagery to another.

We sat circled around the hearth that pulsated its warmth through the
veins of the building. Some of the men contentedly sank into chairs, soaking
them all the way to their centres with the liquid melting from their frames, and
faded into delirium beneath heavy rugs of fur, their bodies finally succumbing
to exhaustion and slumber, something that seemed safe once more. Others felt
immediately rejuvenated by their new surroundings, and seized this opportunity
to snatch any strands of news from those who worked in the house or from other
travellers that had been led to this very spot, at this exact time, by the stock
the universe had designated to their wanderings. They ate and drank heartily,
spending the money they risked their very lives to earn, with little regard for
anything beyond the gaping holes in their bellies and souls. They lapped up the
conversation from passing fishermen and needed no encouragement to instantly
introduce themselves to the local girls. The rest of the men, those who had been
more, or perhaps merely differently, affected by the landscape that had been
their dominant, harsh, unforgiving mistress for what seemed an eternity, stared
at the flames of the fire before them. Perhaps they prayed for the souls of the
men that we had lost, perhaps they begged that they would never return to that
hell, or perhaps they were simply in rapture to gaze upon sights other than that
endless barrage of sheets of murderous ice.

The building was constructed of stone and wood, reinforced several times
through, to ward off the advances of the threatening cold outside. It lay upon
the edge of the ice-plains, acting almost as hospital for those foolish enough
to cross that merciless terrain, and marked the point where the vestiges of life,
and some degree of humanity, began to gradually reappear. Seven miles in the
opposite direction lay the town of Prawleton, upon the edge of an enormous
lake which one arrived at by winding for several hours through a large forest,
the last thing one expected to see after the ruthlessness of the barren ice. The
guest-house contained an impressively grand number of rooms, with local
fishermen and hunters seeking respite there at the beginning and end of their
voyages, while foreigners like ourselves landed upon it by chance in the midst of

our own calamitous adventures. A wide, wooden bar occupied the centre of the
room, with doors behind it that swung to and fro with the coming and going
of kitchen staff, accompanied at each movement by outbursts of steam and
profanity from the workers within. Set on either side of this protrusion were two
long-running benches, flanked by an assortment of barrels, logs and stools that
served as chairs for the makeshift tables. Around these tables sat dozens of men
and women, eating and drinking to different measures and extents of misery
and pleasure. The heads of innumerous animals, mammals and fish, both
common and unknown to me, hung from the four walls of this large room, most
likely paying the way for several of the men who resided there, men for whom
the blood of the most exotic animals was paving their paths through life. The
great fireplace, which could comfortably fit twenty or so men about its frame,
was situated in one corner, with a rug spread out upon the floor affront it and
chairs scattered around, welcoming the cold, the tired and the distraught to the
warming embrace of its dancing flames.

Now as the day grew older I sat beside the fire, for the most part solely in
my own company, the majority of my men having sufficiently resurrected their
fortitude and now seeking respite, either in their beds or in the arms of a young
woman. The only others who currently took up position near the hearth were
strangers to me, who lay upon the rug, asleep or drunk or both. I was lost in my
own bewildered thoughts, pondering the best paths to plan for the following day,
along with attempting to imagine ways to ensure the morale of the men held, as
even the lure of gold's delightful shine is not always enough to prevent a mutiny
when lives have been lost or, some would say, sacrificed. I lived solitarily in my
thoughts, circling the globe along plotted lines that existed only in fragments of
my own bothered mind, when I felt something akin to unease. My eyes darted
away from the flickering fire to meet those of a man sitting directly opposite
me, before the fire, who I had not previously noticed. He must have arrived and
sat down quietly, for I had not heard a sound (although admittedly I had been
deeply absorbed in my own ruminations). However, he now sat there with his
eyes fixed firmly upon mine.

His clothes were almost falling from him, so torn and frayed were they,
but somehow, due to the sheer number of layers he wore as wards against the
cold, a piece of fabric managed to hang just sufficiently to cover each part of
his large, muscular body. Worn about this dismal, filthy clothing, stained with

what appeared to be oil and blood, hung several belts and holsters, holding a wide assortment of hooks, hammers and knives, along with other tools, the purposes and functions of which my mind could only hazard a colourful attempt at guessing. A spear, only slightly shorter than the man himself, was strapped to his back. He wore thick, heavy, leather boots and gloves, the fingers of which were locked together in the frozen hold of ice. From his equipment, if nothing else, I figured that he was in the business of whaling or, if this were not so, settled in another profession involving just as much danger and terror, with as seemingly slight and disproportionate rewards.

His hair was long and as dirty, if not more so, than his attire and of a dark colour, though recently streaked with grey, almost indistinguishable from the filth that was tangled in it. It billowed out beneath the peaks of a cap, the colour, even the material, of which was weathered far beyond the scope of reasonable deduction. His face bore the markings of a hard fought life, nights spent on the lonely seas without sleep, struggling against the might of the world's oceans. They were the signs of a man who had once dreamed of a wife, a family, a fireside like this to call his own, but who's life fate had thrust elsewhere, condemned to battle the remorseless tyrants of the elements forever. His eyes glared at me with intent, though they were glazed over by a dull cloud that suggested he really searched for something that it was far beyond my powers to provide. It was the stare of a madman, a man with his life staked in the tomb, with nothing further to live for, but still too strong for the grave to finally take. Our eyes remained motionless, examining each other, for a long time before a sharp snap startled me. He was shattering the ice that bound the fingers of his gloves together, slightly melted by the fire's reviving licks. When he had finally ripped the gauntlets from his sizeable fists, he reached for a tankard that lay on the ground beside his chair and drained it in one go, choking and spluttering much of its frothy contents down the side of his chin. He wiped his mouth, stared back at me and opened his lips to speak.

"What would you say if I told you I slept with demons last night?" Under normal circumstances I would have struggled to suppress laughter at this unexpected question, but the look of abandoned hope that was so fixed in the man's eyes implied that there was no suggestion of humour to be found there. His voice was deep, rough and rugged, but seemed to have been thinned by the cold, as though, due to the swelling in his frozen throat, it was a struggle to forcibly squeeze every word from out of him. I failed to answer him, shocked by the abruptness of the statement and unaware as to his expectations. Was it a question that needed, or even asked for, a response?

"I have battled Leviathan and wrestled with monstrous beasts beyond the realms of all your imaginations and nightmares. I have spent the majority of my wasted, unhappy life journeying back and forth across landscapes of woe that are deigned to break the strongest of men, waging war on all the titans and fallen gods of this cursed planet but even I, yes I, though I doubted it not long ago, even I, it appears, still maintain the capacity to be shocked, horrified by the madness, chaos and witchery that lurks around us." His eyes diverted themselves momentarily from mine to acquire the attention of the barman and he signalled for another drink by the raising of the emptied tankard in his dripping left hand.

Despite my concerns regarding my own mission and the livelihood of my men, something about this unusual new company gripped me instantly and I found myself quickly falling under the spell of the tale he proceeded to relate to me. I told myself that it was best to remain silent, that I would obtain more from this hunter if I did not speak at all, that his confession would fall more naturally from his frostbitten lips. I sat still as stone, half fixated by the roaring fire, and otherwise by this soldier of ice before me. The barman approached with a fresh tankard, which the man devoured just as greedily, nonetheless managing to leave a few drops at the bottom this time. With his throat having been somewhat cleared by the liquid and somewhat warmed by the flames, his husky voice began to gain its natural power, and, bit by bit, became more forceful as he spoke.

"Yes, a strange night it certainly was. As strange as I have spent in a long and eventful life. I was returning from the seas after months of work with my shipmates, on an ill-fated voyage, and longed for nothing more than my hometown of Prawleton. The water beyond Prawleton, on which we sailed, is vicious, more forgiving than the ice-plains, but nevertheless a ruthless foe. If thrown overboard you are a lost man for sure, your shipmates incapable of doing much beyond watching your body instantly freeze and become another block of ice, floating through that white limbo. We had sailed through storms and violent quakes of infernal machination, battling our way to a livelihood, losing both good men and something of our minds. Just yesterday were on our way to dock in the nearest harbour outside Prawleton's, when our doomed voyage came to an end just a mile from the coast. We were brought face to face with the true perils of the waters, as a sudden wave, undoubtedly from nowhere other than the depths of hell, turned our vessel, stern over bow. Unlike the rest of the crew, who were lost, along with the entire cargo gained on the mission, to the ravenous cold of the sea, the gods smiled upon me and I landed by chance in one of the smaller hunting boats that had likewise been flung from the deck. I was alone in this fortune and quickly plucked a plank of the shattered ship from the sea. I used it as an oar to steer myself towards land. I soon made it to the nearest bank, on the far side of a thick, frozen wood that lies between the water and this very building in which we dry ourselves. I gathered my strength there for almost an hour, paying my respects to my fallen friends, before setting out for home." Here the man paused and took his eyes off mine briefly to gaze into the fire and drink another mouthful, a shine of sadness lighting his pupils as he reminisced over his lost comrades, before he continued his tale.

"I was weak and tired, but I knew that without heat or shelter the cold would be too intense for me once night fell, and Prawleton was too far away to reach by sundown. I needed to throw myself into the heart of the forest where I might find respite of some sort, perhaps even a cave, where I could build a fire and survive the dark. I took a last look at the twisted wreck of the ship, the prow of which broke through the thin ice, pointing towards the darkening sky. Shortly before, the place had become a mass grave for many men. Now it was as starkly still as a painting, the condemned prow the only sign that anyone had ever been there. I set off, away from the water's edge and through the dark of the trees."

"I knew the journey would take more than a day and, though preferring to last through the night without sleeping and arrive home in better time, my body soon began to feel the strain of hunger, cold and tiredness. My progress was slow. The floor of the forest was uneven, with many unexpected, hidden holes and ravines disguised beneath thick layers of snow, which resulted in my tripping and stumbling often. Every time I landed in the snow my clothes became soaked through, bringing the chill closer to my bones. I had walked for what I gathered was six or seven hours, but I knew there was a distance of twice that ahead, and my mood began to dwindle towards the point of despairing. I would have to find a suitable resting place or I would not live through the night."

"I staggered onwards, growing ever more tired, frozen and hungry with every step. I guessed that it was several hours after midnight and without the assistance of light I could barely make out my own hands extended before me, which sought to seek a safe passage through the trees that obstructed my way. I could feel myself losing control of my senses, growing ever weaker, and I felt sure that I had reached the end of my journey through life. It was just as I was about to collapse upon a mound of snow-covered ferns, to abandon myself to whatever destiny nature intended, that I saw a gentle glowing through the trees in the distance. Although my mind had by this time stopped functioning to the best of its abilities, and I realised that I may have been succumbing to hallucinations, I decided to approach. I could not help but wonder, with fear, what sort of procedure was being conducted in these woods, this remote, in these bitter conditions, plunged this deeply into the darkness of night. I am not a superstitious man by nature and have generally always believed that there are terrors situated in reality far more horrifying than those that our mind may conjure in the otherworldly. However, it is impossible to be born and raised in Prawleton without having spent your childhood assailed on all sides by the tales of these woods, what devilry takes place there late at night, how many have entered and failed to reappear, how often unearthly noises have echoed from deep within its belly during the late hours. Regardless, I reckoned that whatever ghastly beings may have lain in waiting for me, they could scarcely condemn me to a fate worse than perishing of cold and hunger, frozen on a forest floor. I summoned a final effort from the depths of my innermost fortitude and began inching my way forward."

As I listened, I noticed that the longer the stranger spoke, the more interest he attracted from those around us. At first I had comprised his entire audience, but further listeners had gathered near the fireside to hear his tale. By now there were close to ten other men sitting silently in the half circle around the hearth, looking into the flames, but listening attentively to the stranger's words. When he arrived at this point in his narration, I noticed several of those around me begin to shift uneasily and whisper amongst themselves at the mention of the local town's legends and the light burning dimly in the depths of the black forest. Outside night was coming on, and a fierce wind had begun to pick up from the ice-plains and hurtle towards us, bellowing though the chimneys of the building with a ghostly, whistling wail. All the while the stranger kept his eyes fixed on mine alone and, only breaking now and then for a drink, continued his story.

"I approached the dull glowing slowly and warily, trying through my blurred, failing vision to determine what it was that I looked upon. However, with the trees in my way and the contrast between the brightness of the light and the darkness of the woods, I could not immediately ascertain its origins. I moved closer and closer until a strange sight greeted my tired eyes. The glowing came from a fire in the centre of a clearing that stretched out some fifteen feet in each direction. The fire's fuel appeared to consist of little more than logs and branches, but emitted an unusual, white glow, quite unlike the roaring, amber tint of the flames with which we presently warm ourselves. The strangest sight in the clearing, however, was the four young ladies who surrounded this ivory blaze."

"They were all remarkably thin, blessed with beautiful, bone-white skin, and each of them wore long, dark hair that fell to their waists. Their faces were dominated by their unusually large and round black eyes, like small, mounds of shimmering coal, which all seemed to be focused on some deep understanding that lay burning in the depths of the log-pile. What shocked me immediately was that the four of them were dressed in the lightest of robes. These robes were white in colour and covered their full bodies' length, but seemed to consist of little more than a thin layer of silk. Despite the cold and their lack of suitable clothing, they seemed oblivious to the infernal elements that raged around us. They circled the fire in a slow, trance-like dance, their hands rotating in small complex patterns at waist-height. I watched this bizarre ritual, unobserved, for what seemed a long time without witnessing any change in their behaviour. However, the chill and hunger that had been displaced from my thoughts by this unique sight had not been forgotten by my exhausted body and, all of a sudden, I happened to keel over, falling forward into the clearing."

"All four sets of eyes were slowly turned upon me. I feared for a moment until I recognised sympathy and pity in those beautiful, black pupils. I immediately felt a sense of trust, as though I were in the caresses of ones who would help, who would never harm me. Although in my haggard state I could barely make out their features, asides from their eyes which loomed above me examining my weakened body, I could hear them talking amongst themselves, in high-pitched but gentle voices, discussing what was to be done with me, where they would take me. One of them eventually leaned over my face and asked whether I wished to come with them to their home, to rest and recover. With my remaining minutiae of strength I managed to nod in response. The moment I did so I felt a new energy come over my body. The cold and hunger and pain all instantly vanished and, without consciously doing so, I had risen to my feet and seemed to be walking, through no doing of my own, amongst the four of them, along a path that now stretched clear before us, even in the darkness. I found myself slipping in and out of the waking world. Asides from my view of this path, my vision remained blurred and my head groggy, but I felt my body transporting me through the forest in safety until we reached what appeared to my eyes to be an old, wooden cottage, standing alone in the midst of those abandoned woods. Before I had time to wonder where I had been brought, we were inside. All this I can only recall in brief snatches of memory, momentary flashes followed by seconds of unrealised blackness. I seemed incapable of controlling my body, or of refusing the hospitality of these strange women, but a comfort had come over me and I believed wholeheartedly that they were to be trusted. I felt safe in their care. I remember sitting in a comfortable chair beside a roaring fireplace, in new clothes, warm, dry and comfortable, beneath several layers of thick blanket. The room I was in had a reassuring sense of homeliness. Finely-crafted furniture sat beneath exquisite water-colours that graced the walls. I was brought warm and nourishing food from a table laden with extravagant dishes, and felt an exceptional wine being poured into my mouth. I scarcely have memory of anything more. Shortly afterwards I must have given way entirely to the heavy weight of exhaustion that had hung about my shoulders for so long. I fell into the deepest of sleeps."

As the hunter's story had progressed, more tenants of the establishment had gathered around, until all the seated places at the fireside were occupied and intrigued characters began to stand, drinks in hand, around the edge of the group, listening with consternated and curious expressions. Outside the windows, the sun had long ago abandoned us to the night, sinking below the horizon for respite from another tireless day of labour. The wind maintained its howling swirl throughout the building and, as we watched the snowfall outside settling into a deep, solid, white sea, we all became thankful for the presence of the fire, to ward off the chills of that cold world and the icy freeze of the imagination that lies inside each and every one of us, no matter how we try to conceal or deny it.

The looks of dismay present in the audience had not gone unnoticed by the stranger, even though he still spoke solely to me.

"Yes, perhaps I was foolish to place myself at the mercy of such unearthly creatures. However, I implore you not to forget that I was at death's door. I had little choice other than to allow myself be embraced by the seeming generosity of these women. I was too delirious to make rational decisions, to recall everything I had heard about this place and, as I have said before, I had little to worry about that could be much worse than death at the hands of the elements."

This slight interruption in his recital aroused several mumbles from the crowd around, many of whom still seemed to consider his actions foolish, to wonder what could drive a man into accepting invitations from such abnormal hosts.

"Now, as I told you, I fell into an intense sleep, dark and devoid of dreams, or so it seemed to me at the time. I still find it difficult to organise the events as they came to be, or at least that I believe came to be, in my head. Everything seems so ... unlikely, so unreal, that, indeed, if I had not touched and felt with my own fingers, I would doubt my very sanity. I was woken from this sleep by a sharp tugging pain at my neck. My eyes still melted shut with drowsiness, I shook my head from side to side to escape this sudden pain, but found, to my surprise, that I was only granted slight manoeuvre on either side before encountering this tugging pain once more. A restraint of some sort was also preventing me from moving my arms, which seemed to be securely manacled behind my back. I heard a deep, male voice, so different to the sensually gravitated pitches of the mysterious women. I could not hear the exact words coming from the man until I managed to shake myself into a waking state sufficient for the gathering of some indication as to what was taking place, and the moment I opened my eyes I was granted the most shocking and unexpected sight."

"I was standing upon a platform, looking, bewildered, out at a crowd of people, who stared at me with faces of distrust, fear and, most of all, hatred. They stood in silence, all eyes directed at my face, and I tried, once again in vain, to loosen the bonds that restrained me so uncomfortably. My hands were held fast by a thick length of rope. Then I heard the voice again, strengthened by the power of authority, amplified by its own sense of righteousness, shouting out above the silence that lay between the crowd and I.

"... and finally for the robbery, torture and brutal murder of four young, innocent women. Whatever chance of mercy you may have aspired to before these ungodly crimes is now of little relevance – you will be punished accordingly."

Desperately, I looked about the faces that made up the crowd, still struggling to understand how I had come to be here. They remained staring back at me, offering not the slightest of clues. I realised that the tugging at my neck was due to a noose that hung dauntingly about it.

"I have no choice but to sentence the accused, who now stands before us, to hang by the neck until death."

I tried to cry out, to beg for a moment to present my case, to ask what had happened, to implore for just a little time to gather my thoughts, but it seemed nobody could hear my voice, or else they chose to ignore it.

"May God have mercy on your soul."

I made one last attempt to shout, but the air was taken from my lungs as the ground beneath me gave way, and I fell until I felt the pain and wrenching snap of the rope. At that precise moment I sat up, soaked in sweat, lying upon a piercingly cold, stone floor in a dark, unfurnished room. I was still dazed and, despite being thankful that the execution had been but a dream, I began to worry, as once more I failed to recognise my surroundings."

The entirety of the house that was not stretched upon their beds upstairs had by this stage gathered about the edges of this makeshift half-circle. Now there were neither comments nor mutters regarding the contents of the tale. Rather they all gazed upon the man, who still looked into my eyes alone, listening intently to every word that flew from his twisting tongue, heightening the foreboding sense of mystery and discomfort that we now all felt, living and breathing through the very brickwork of the building itself.

"However, something about the inside of this room struck a familiar note in my mind and it resonated inside my head for several seconds as I looked around me. The only light came from a dirt-smeared window on one wall, which barely managed to penetrate the darkness at all, and it took some time for my eyes to adjust themselves. Eventually I began to make out the silhouettes of shapes that I vaguely recognised. As my distorted memory of the events of the night before came slowly back to me, fed to my confused brain in minimal doses, I saw that I was in the same room in which I had gone to sleep. I remained beside the fireplace but now I lay upon bare stone, rather than the chair I had fallen asleep in, and the previously roaring fire was now an empty hearth, devoid of anything but cobwebs and birds-nests, looking as though it had not been disturbed in decades. The surrounding room shared a similar appearance of having been long forgotten. Where I recalled there having been comfortable furniture, attractive paintings and a table ordained with flavourful delicacies, there now lay sparse patches of weed, filthy, smoke-blackened walls and piles of rotting wood. Freezing-cold air blew through the room, and a foul smell drifted along with it. Cold sweat trickled down my body and I tried to stand up, to remove myself from the icy, stone floor on which I had slept. A weight lay across my legs, preventing me from rising with ease. In the darkness I could not make out the exacts of its dimensions. At first I kicked it aside a little and then reached down to attempt moving it with my hands. I felt something that I instantly recognised, something that terrified me – cold skin."

"Immediately I was on my feet and running about the room, frantically feeling along the dark walls with my shaking fingertips to find an exit. I discovered a doorway and, after pulling on the stiff, wooden handle for what seemed an age, I flung it open, spreading the daylight from the serene, woodland morning outside across the scene of horror that lay within."

"The dark stains upon the walls, that had appeared to be black, now reflected red in the light and it appeared blood had been smeared across them. I stood, completely stunned, looking upon a scene of absolutely diabolical levels of violence. Body parts lay strewn across the floor, some rendered unidentifiable through acts of brutality. What I recognised as a hand lay close to my feet and I took a step backwards as I looked upon its fingers, frozen in motion, curling upwards towards the ceiling. The weight that had so startled me to begin with lay facing the door. I remembered aspects of the mutilated features as having belonged to the body of one of the ethereal nymphs that had taken pity on me the night before. The remains that were remorselessly scattered about the desecrated room indicated the presence of more than one massacred corpse. I managed to fight the feeling of nausea in my stomach until I saw, lying upon the floor beneath the small window, the decapitated head of another of the four. A putrid, burning-hot liquid slithered its way up the insides of my throat before releasing itself over the brim of my lips and onto the ground before me. As my vision was directed downwards, I noticed for the first time that I too was covered in blood – my hands and clothes glowed red in the morning light. I looked once more upon the torture chamber that presented itself to me, still and quiet amongst the birdsong outside as though it were the most wholesome sight imaginable as opposed to a vicious mass of unreality that defied the reasoning of my senses. I turned and ran."

"I ran for a long time, hours most likely, without stopping. I fell several dozen times, but the shock and terror flowed through my body like a tonic of invulnerability and urged me on, forcing me to ignore the usual bodily needs. I ran, in no particular direction, until I reached an edge of the forest where a tributary of the sea ran. I collapsed at the side of the pool and buried my head in the cold water. I quickly washed the blood from my hands and clothes. The cold water felt refreshing and I drank to try and somewhat revive myself. I wasted little time in moving onwards and followed the stream for the rest of the day, walking what must have been half the circumference of the forest to avoid re-entering its folds, not daring to set foot in the land between those haunted trees again. I eventually found myself upon this edge of the forest and, by all the gods, never have I been so happy to see the company of fellow men of the earth as when I walked through this door."

The glow from the roaring fire now served as the only light in the room, the lateness of the hour having lent it a macabre tint, the workers having been too engrossed in the man's account to have bothered lighting the lamps that hung from the walls. As he finished speaking, an unsettling hush floated hauntingly about the group, all remaining seated or standing in the same position. Nobody dared break the silence, or to even slightly shift their stance. The whole gathering continued to stare at the ever-present tongues of fire that raged up the chimney, waging war against the freezing wind that threatened to blow down upon them, as though these fiery forks fought the last battle for the defence of humanity from such evil as the stranger had described, as though the seeds of such witchcraft would be blown into the building, borne on the wind itself. The man finished his drink and looked me in the eyes for the last time.

"I cannot explain what happened. I am deeply, irrevocably disturbed and reckon that I may never sleep another peaceful night for the rest of my years. All I can say is that there are things that exist beyond our supposed reality. When I thought that I had seen everything, the most shocking of all had been waiting for me the entire time. I did not kill those ... 'women', yet I dreamed of my being punished for it. I felt their blood smeared across me and tasted it dripping from my lips as I washed myself at the river. This region of ours has always been known for its strange happenings, but this is a matter of another devilry altogether. This was violence of such merciless force, such..."

The man trailed off before finishing his sentence. I heard his voice waver painfully and it took him some time to gather himself once more.

"Something is happening out there. Trouble is coming to Prawleton and all who call it their home, I assure you. I will be spending a sleepless night tonight, waiting behind a locked door."

The man did not speak another word aloud, but simply stood up from his chair and walked through the circle, which opened silently for him as he approached. He muttered something in the ear of the house-owner and took himself up the stairs, not to be seen again. The rest of us maintained our muted guard of the furnace. We stayed for some time, each contemplating in his own mind the story he had just listened to. Then, all at once, through a silent and mutual recognition that the night was not one designed for the benefits of mortal men, each and every person present gathered themselves and walked upstairs to their bedroom without saying another word.

I slept poorly that night, haunted by unwelcome visions of unnatural cruelty, which seeped their way into my subconscious no matter how hard I fought, winding through the weak defences I had tried to enforce by contemplating the more joyous aspects of life as I had drifted towards sleep. I woke often, finding myself in a sweat that reminded me of the hunter's story, and in my waking state I would rush to light the candle at my bedside, in order to ensure that it was not another substance that soaked me so.

At sunrise we settled our debts with the proprietor and began upon the road for Prawleton. A clear, brisk morning awaited us outside, though a strange air of unease and nervousness hung upon our entourage. The men rode in silence, each thoroughly absorbed in his own thoughts, the subject of which I ventured I could guess with moderate accuracy. We only conversed when necessity required us to do so, only regarding the bare essentials of our trip such as which route to take. Even the men I had noticed going to bed at an early hour the night before, whom had thus not been present for the stranger's tale, seemed to have an unearthly shade cast upon their characters, and they too proceeded without words, both sensing the unhinged condition of their comrades and being absorbed themselves in the aura of impending disaster that descended upon us. Without anyone voicing a desire to do so, we unanimously plotted a course that circled the edges of the dark forest, rather than making passage through, which lengthened our trip by a number of hours. It was as though the unspoken fear and angst amongst the troupe surrounded us in the flitting of the breeze and had soaked into the very air we breathed, encompassing every aspect of our travel that day.

The sun laboriously crossed the sky as the hours passed by. We travelled quickly until at last, after surmounting a mound that sat on the far side of the forest, in the late hours of the evening when shadows were being stretched across the length of the land, the flickering lights of the town came into view. A weight seemed to fall from us with the recognition of signs of everyday life and we slowed our pace to approach Prawleton. From a distance it did not seem much more than a typical example of the villages that occupy these parts. They had sprung up for little purpose beyond the provision of nearby homes and food for the hunters and fishermen who gambled their fates, along with those of their families, on the plains, as they travelled too far into the depths of frozen abysses to constantly trek back and forth to further, more illustrious, centres of human activity. Close to a hundred buildings of log and stone were scattered across the landscape that crawled its way down towards the waterfront. Boats swayed in the small harbour that jutted out into the lake, their reflections shimmering brightly in the purifying waters. The lights from flames lit up the windows of homes where families ate and inns where travellers rejoiced or relaxed or revelled or drank. However, it was a large concentration of torch glow that seemed to emanate from the centre of the town which most attracted our attention as we entered Prawleton.

Firstly we found ourselves a rest-house. We came upon a dour, squalid, little hut, but one that was empty, devoid of further strange characters to insinuate prophecies regarding atrocities that may yet have befallen our journey. The innkeeper had plenty of food available and was kind enough to feed us all. As we ate he rambled on with local tales, despite none of our group affording him much interest or attention, making slight reference to strange goings on in the region, to crimes and black magic. As I settled the bill, I questioned him as to the nature of the collected lights that we had perceived on approaching town. He was unable to offer an answer but satisfied me that it was most likely a gathering of some sort in the town square, just a short walk away. While the vast majority of my men departed for bed immediately after dinner, and the remainder were content to let their minds gently simmer in alcohol fuelled contemplation, I felt that a visit outdoors, surrounded by other people, not so saturated with thoughts of despair and foreboding, might fortify my constitution and that the air might assist in clearing my angst-ridden brain before sleep.

I strolled briskly along many of the town's principal streets, breathing in the reviving, icy breeze that floated inland from across the lake, only to find their cobbled paths deserted. I decided to allow myself to wander in the general direction of the town square. As I drew near, the sounds of numerous raised voices came to my ears and the glow of the torchlight began to rise higher above the roofs of the buildings. I quickened my pace and soon turned a corner around an abandoned blacksmith's quarters, to be surprised by a remarkable sight.

I found myself at a corner of the town square, an unexpectedly large space considering the town's miniscule size. The square was flanked by the most important buildings of the town – the magistrate's office, the cathedral, the library and other striking structures that I could not identify. All these constructions were of a far more impressive architectural nature than the rest of the town and framed the large square in an elaborate fashion, along with numerous statues extolling the deeds and virtues of the town's patrons and heroes. Indeed if one had suddenly woken from a sleep on that particular spot, without recalling the route by which one had arrived there, it could easily have been mistaken for the centre of a thriving, prosperous capital. However, it was the events taking place upon the clear, open sprawl of the square itself that held my interest.

The moment I turned onto the square, the sound of raised voices was amplified into a tumultuous, simultaneous roar of what must have been thousands of people. The residents of the town were packed tightly into every available space in the opening and many were gathered along side streets that led from it, unable to get closer due to the sheer enormity of the crowd. Most of them carried burning torches, which accounted for the bright blaze seen from afar. They shouted and wailed, waving these burning staffs, and though I failed to make out any individual cries, as their screaming seemed to mesh together like the wail of some wounded monster, I soon saw what it was that every set of eyes there were focused upon.

At the opposite end of the square, in front of the cruel-looking spires of the cathedral that rose, twisting toward the blackening heavens, a crude gallows had been erected. It appeared to me to have been hastily and inattentively constructed, as though it were not a regular feature of life in Prawleton. Five figures and four nooses occupied the raised, wooden platform and I pushed my way through the crowd to get a better view. Upon coming closer, I experienced a shock that I am not sure I am capable of summarising, let alone expressing, in mere words upon paper. I felt my breath taken from me and I swayed upon my feet, being both pushed and supported by the crowd that packed me in tightly on every side, ensuring that there was no opportunity granted to my body to collapse to the ground.

Four of the current inhabitants of the deathly scaffold were young women dressed in thin, white dresses. They were all remarkably similar in appearance, with beautiful pale skin and luscious, black hair that brushed against the smalls of their backs. Each was blessed with a pair of uncannily large and absorbing, black eyes that gazed out innocently above the heads of the furious mob. I felt a powerful tremble of fear as I recognised the four women that had appeared to my mind the moment the hunter had described them on the previous night. Surely there was no room for coincidence here. The images that had painted themselves in my mind, with such an unnerving and burning intensity, as I had listened to his story, had been despotic premonitions of the very creatures that now stood before me. Though they appeared harmless, the very personification of harmony and grace, they were all bound to the gallows by the four nooses that were wrapped tightly around their slender necks.

The fifth person upon the platform moved about unrestrained, prowling the space affront the women, draped in attire that suggested a position within the clergy, a position situated firmly in the upper echelons of that establishment judging by the quality of these embellished robes. He was a tall man, no more than sixty years of age, but certainly not much younger, with a mane of shockingly bright, white hair that danced about his shoulders. His eyes were ablaze amidst a fierce countenance that seemed locked in an undecided, frenzied battle between fear and self-righteousness. As with most of the occupants of the square, he carried a blazing torch and he scanned the crowd with animated eyes as he shouted in a powerful, booming voice, strengthened by the power of authority, amplified by its own sense of piety.

"Our town must, once and for all, be purged of the unclean, poisonous influences of such venomous creatures! These demons have plagued our well-being for years, filling our woods with evil spirits! Now they go so far as to descend upon the homes of our own friends and families, of our own children, with their unspeakable aims and tainted desires. They shall be punished and Prawleton will be purged to become a place of peace once more."

At this the crowd rejoined in their screeches with renewed force, all their rage mingling into an uncontrollable surge that seemed to shake the very buildings that echoed their cries from one side of the square to the other. They raised their torches higher and bayed for the blood of the women. Their spokesman continued.

"For bringing evil to Prawleton! For placing curses upon our forests, our once fertile fields and prosperous waters! For filling our hearts and minds with fear, angst and worry over immeasurable lengths of time! For poisoning our dreams! And finally, for the robbery, torture and brutal murder of one of our own hunters on the night before last, you are hereby brought to pay for your misdeeds. Whatever chance of mercy you may have aspired to before these ungodly crimes is now of little relevance – you will be punished accordingly."

I continued to grow fainter as I heard this list of accusations spread forth, with the charge relating to a hunter particularly shocking me to my core. I began to fear, or perhaps hope, that it was I who had been dreaming all along, that indeed these strange illogical coincidences and impossibilities concerning who it was that lived and breathed with beating heart, and who did not, amounted to nothing more than the winding, twitching patterns of my brain as I slept. I scarcely had time to develop my thoughts further before the man's monologue drove itself on once more.

"I have no choice but to sentence the accused, who now stand before us, to hang by their necks until death. May God have mercy on your souls."

As he spoke these words, the crowd once more intensified their furious cries and, at a sign from the feral clergyman to an accomplice at the rear of the gallows, the floor beneath the feet of the criminals gave way. They fell momentarily, before there was a loud, hideous snapping, clear even above the noise of the mob, and their bodies twitched briefly before succumbing to stillness.

The crowd cheered itself into silence and a sense of relief gathered about them, allowing their minds release from the morbid matters at hand. Myself, I felt deeply troubled and unnerved. I was concerned by the eerie instances that surrounded my knowledge of the whole affair – the question of who the murdered hunter had been? And then who indeed had been the man that had appeared before us in the guest-house the very next night? Who were these four women and who had the four bodies in the man's story belonged to? Moreover, and most of all, I began to worry about my own sanity and the influences such unnatural, remote latitudes of the globe, with their archaic beliefs and methods, were exerting on my psyche, and I decided to return to the rest-house and ensure that my men and I left Prawleton at first light, before any word of these happenings were afforded opportunity to reach their ears and taint their confidences as they had mine.

However, as I pushed my way back through the throngs of townsfolk towards the street by which I had entered, I heard frightened screams arise behind me. I turned to see what was happening and to my disbelief was rewarded with a grotesque picture of abject horror that I fear will live inside of me until I pass beyond this world. The corpses of the punished, that had hung so lifeless mere minutes prior, had begun to stir. We all stared, incredulous, as the pale arms initiated movements. They grasped the edges of the rim where the floor of the gallows had opened beneath them and slowly pulled the remainder of the animated bodies they were attached to back atop the platform on which the startled clergyman still stood. As their heads reappeared above this horizon, it became clear that the eyes of the women had now assumed a devilish quality, relishing with malice the petrified looks upon the faces of all who stood there captivated, too stricken by shock to react. As they rose to their full height, the preacher once more began to scream out to the townspeople, this time in a tone lacking any of the control that had hitherto been present, his voice having been altered and provoked by the suddenness of his being stripped of power by these monsters, his eyes now driven by madness alone.

"May the Lord save us all! People, thrust forth your torches that we may burn these demons back to hell!"

As he shouted, he plunged his torch far into the depths of the scaffold, from where the women had risen. The townsfolk nearest to the construction followed suit. As the women struggled to free themselves from the ropes, expressions of evil glee upon their faces, the crowd threw scores of flaming torches upon and beneath the wood, and it was instantly alight. The clergyman leapt from his podium and all drew back some distance. Flames greedily ravaged the logs and rose high towards the spires of the holy church, as the gallows soon became a funeral pyre.

However, the preacher had not yet finished his wild declarations.

"Hurry people, we must not rest. The Lord has delivered these demons into our hands, and we must destroy them in his name. Deep down we all know what we must do, we all know our town's histories! We must destroy their temple!"

The crowds let out another rousing roar, this time of fear mingled with *anger, and in agreement with the wisdom of the preacher. Many had fled from the square, but those that still surrounded their leader began to join him in his cries.*

"Yes, we have all awaited this moment for years!"

"It is their sanctuary, that vile, cottage in the woods! It has to be destroyed to truly rid ourselves of this witchcraft! Otherwise they will not rest until they have consumed our entire town with their evil."

"That is where they bring their victims! That is where they have sacrificed our children, our wives, to grant themselves this wretched afterlife!"

"You know the stories, the legends! Let us put an end to them once and for all!"

The crowds that remained let out an almighty cheer and, only stopping to gather more torches and some hunting weapons from nearby homes, began a quick procession from the square in the direction of the forest upon the edge of the town.

The ring of a telephone in one of the nearby offices, deserted at this hour of repose, shook Mason's attention from the text that he had become so absorbed in. He glanced at his watch. It was almost 4 a.m. – far too late to be occupying himself with the reading of centuries old diaries. At first he contemplated attempting to sleep then and there. Then he thought about returning home but instead decided to go to a nearby late bar that he sometimes frequented on sleepless nights, believing that a quiet drink would do his nerves more good than immediately turning towards bed. Mason locked up his office and returned it to darkness with the flick of a switch.

CHAPTER 15

Upon awakening the next morning, Mason had, for some reason, felt an almost overwhelming urge to visit Rachel again, an urge he could not dispel. He could not precisely establish what had planted this seed of unease – perhaps something he had read when trawling through the writings on his desk, perhaps something that she had said when they had previously spoken or perhaps just a natural intuition that belonged to those accustomed to this line of business. He listlessly paced his office for a large part of the day, trying to determine exactly what it was that irritated him so, what it was that his subconscious was urging him to discover. Regardless of the cause, he felt, with a strange, sudden, and to Mason surprising, nausea, that something was terribly wrong and that it was his responsibility alone to ensure that the woman was not in danger.

Despite the oncoming evening, and the hour being at hand when most people would be leaving work, the roads en route were completely deserted. The intense, scathing heat remained hovering above the city like a thick, stifling blanket, smothering the incandescent warmth inside, depriving it of breathable air, and perhaps as a result people were hiding indoors, seeking shelter from the chastising fire. As he pulled up outside the building, Mason contemplated what he was going to say, or why indeed he had really come. Surely he was in possession of a whole host of more important concerns at this moment, not least of all a case in which, if unsuccessful, he could become far more of a victim than this woman, who was little more than a bystander in the affair. Regardless, his feet continued to carry him across the street towards the apartment block and Mason decided to accept the fact that he was here now, and ready himself for whatever lay waiting inside. For a sensation deep inside the pit of his stomach told him with a firm certainty that surprises of an unpleasant nature were lurking around these corners.

He clasped his hand upon the handle of the front door of the building. It was covered in a disgusting, greasy substance, perhaps due to so many sweaty hands wrapping themselves around it during a day of such harrowing humidity. As he stepped through the door he saw an attendant sitting at a desk that he had not previously noticed. The attendant was asleep and the sight of this immediately heightened Mason's sense of undeniable dread. He turned for the crumbling stairs and bounded the steps three at a time to the third floor, to reach her before it was too late.

The door to Rachel's jaded apartment now came into view at the end of the corridor. As Mason approached he observed that the lock had been smashed almost entirely off the door. His mind raced to recall his last visit. Had he broken the lock? He felt sure that he had left the door securely closed

He pensively entered the room, making sure to close the door behind him, his right hand clutching the blade buried in his pocket, eager to carve. The material of the handle felt rough and recently used, as though there was a foreign substance sitting atop its ingrained fabric. Mason took in his surroundings quickly and was surprised to see that the old room had been restored to what he could only assume was the glory of past times. The carpet was now thick and comfortable beneath one's soles. The crafted details upon the wooden furnishings had been cleaned and restored with exquisite care. The curtains were drawn, dragged together to form a meeting of material that appeared more comfortable and enticing than many of the beds Mason had slept in. There were no magazines, newspapers, cigarette butts or empty bottles lying upon the soft, new carpet. Bookcases covered the wall behind him and a small, oaken table beside them supported a bottle, two crystal glasses and a fine, silver vase filled with immaculately delicate orchids.

Everything else was in its original place, only more exquisitely announcing its presence. The mirror hung upon the same wall space, but had been recently cleaned and shined, and beneath it an enormous fire blazed in the marble fireplace. Mason wandered to the curtains and flung them open. Outside the sun had finally set and the night sky fought in its place, lightless, listless and lifeless, adding a further sense of comfort to the light beaming from the hearty blaze.

Mason then remembered why he had come here, if indeed he had had a reason in the first place. He turned around to see Rachel lying stretched out, asleep, upon the settee as he had seen her for the first time, with her head resting upon the familiar, pink pillow, decorated by the red candle. On this occasion she was adorned with an alluring, purple, full-length dress of exquisite silk. Her hair was now clean and free falling along the length of her back. Her face was free of bruises or blotches, her pale skin now glowing beautifully beneath the flames of the furnace.

Mason was relieved to observe that the woman's situation had somehow remarkably improved. Regardless, he felt an inexplicable need to talk to her, to make sure no trouble had come or been brought her way.

He approached her gently and whispered "Rachel" in her ear.

She remained motionless. Again he uttered her name, this time louder, and elicited no response. He tapped her lightly on the cheek, hoping to rouse her without causing alarm.

To his horror he merely roused a vile, thick, black liquid from inside her mouth and watched it slowly roll down the side of her face like boiling tar. Mason jumped back in shock as the liquid continued to emerge from the crevasse of her mouth, rolling down her body, now meeting the dress and staining it irretrievably with its dense, ebony evil. As it passed her neck he noticed for the first time several marks that had engraved themselves upon it, dirty, black imprints, in the shape of a large man's fingers. He leant forward to examine her and discovered that she had deliberately been placed upon the pillow to lend the appearance of normality, but when he lifted her closer Rachel's head rolled to and fro like that of a broken daffodil.

He became violently weak, beginning to tremble uncontrollably, and embraced her neck, feeling almost nothing there at all. It was as though the bones inside had been completely removed and there now remained little beyond a thin layer of skin, flesh and the black liquid, which continued to pour forth, stronger now, more powerfully. As he held her corpse he realised that the plan of his hands fit the spread of the prints upon her white neck. He looked at the palms of his hands and let go of the body, realising that they too had become absorbed by the black. Then the substance began to descend from the angles between the walls and ceiling, and treacle down the decadent wallpaper, devouring it, along with any memory of it having ever been beautiful. Mason turned to run but saw that it had dripped down so far as to cover the door. He saw the mirror's face, and his own inside it, succumb to the oil, until it dripped down to extinguish the fire and the room was plunged into black by the pitch.

He waited a moment for his eyes to adjust.

Mason sensed something behind him and turned his head slightly. His eyes could just about distinguish a pale, white hand resting upon his shoulder from behind.

He closed his eyes in fear as he felt it clutch him tightly.

He heard a frozen, dead voice whisper a single word.

"Alan."

Mason woke up screaming in his office chair.

Mason was fully aware that he no longer wished to finish this job. He now knew where Sadler was to be found. He could collect him as soon as he wanted. On previous assignments the target would have been returned by now and Mason would be at home enjoying his money at his leisure. In this case however, he felt that every step towards bringing Sadler to Albright was pulling him deeper down, deeper into an inferno of his own creation, deeper into his own fears and closer to unspeakable acts that even his previous unscrupulous clients may have frowned upon. The more he learned about Albright and the more he contemplated Walt's advice, along with what he was beginning to look upon as the gradual fading of his own steady sanity, the more he feared the completion of the job. Albright's words wormed their way through his mind:

"Remember, Mr. Mason, that you are being extraordinarily compensated for the completion of this job. Likewise, you will be the victim of severe punishment should you fail me."

He thought of last night's dream. It had disturbed him as much as any experience that he could recollect from his waking life. Mason feared very few things that he could understand, that he could feel and fight, but the dream had penetrated him, with a vicious fervour, to the deepest, minute, insecure dwelling within his mind. He could not explain to himself why this was. He simply sensed that his current feelings were similar to the sensations in the previous night's dream. The events of the vision seemed to him to have been inexplicably vivid and true. Not a mere dream, nothing as dramatic as a premonition, but a concoction of the two, as though the nightmares contained something of himself, of what he had done, what he had involved himself in, what role he had assumed by becoming involved and what chain of events his actions were gradually setting in motion.

Mason glanced at the photograph of Rachel that Albright had given him. She did not look like this anymore, as he had seen first-hand. She had only looked similar to this in his nightmares, even with all the black and her shattered neck bone. He pondered whether he had assisted in causing this change in her, from beautiful to strung-out wreck, and perhaps he was also assisting, or inadvertently contributing to, a future change from a wreck to a corpse.

Mason tried to collect himself. What was happening was not his fault. Sadler had been missing and Rachel's life had clearly been in chaos long before he had become a part of their realities. It took more than a few days for a person to become so resolutely broken. This was not his fault. He had to admit to himself that he felt more sympathy towards Rachel than other bystanders in his previous cases, but nonetheless it was neither him nor his actions that had caused her to be involved. If anything it was Sadler's fault for entangling himself with a man like Albright – the minute he had done so he had endangered her. Mason was just trying to find Sadler. Whatever he experienced in pursuing this task, this course of actions, whatever consequences, were the responsibility of other sinners. He was simply trying to finish his job.

Mason could not entirely dislodge the feelings of doubt that seeped into his convoluted thoughts, but nonetheless managed to convince himself that picking Sadler up was the most sensible thing to do, for all concerned. If Sadler had to pay for his crimes, than he would do so. Sadler had created this catastrophe and involved those he knew, causing them to suffer for the simple and unfortunate act of knowing him. Mason reckoned that once he had finished the job, then Albright's hounds, the mysterious faces and his nightmares would disappear, that all of the innocent bystanders in the case would be allowed to progress with their lives, leaving Sadler and Albright alone to conclude their unfinished business between themselves.

As another morning dawned outside, Mason picked up his keys and reminded himself of the address of Sadler's hotel. He was going to finish this today. Whether he was doing it for the love of money, professionalism, or simply out of concern for Rachel's life, he could not entirely decide. However, no matter what answer he used to deceive himself, he always knew that it was far from the truth.

CHAPTER 16

Mason entered the hotel, edgy with tension but also feeling drained of all of his energies. He had already almost reached the point of exhaustion and he knew that the coming hours were going to be difficult. However, one final effort, he told himself, and this entire enterprise would soon be forgotten. He entered the lobby behind a group of four men, waiting until they approached the desk and occupied the receptionist, before stealing quietly through the waiting area towards the lifts.

Mason stepped into the first lift that arrived, pressed number four and stood waiting for the doors to slide silently shut. As the lift, with a gentle jolt, began its motion, Mason was given the impression that it was going down rather than upwards. For a moment he was startled, before he remembered how the building had appeared to be small, for a hotel, from the exterior. It would seem that the lobby had been built on the ground floor, and the rooms for the guests lurked deep beneath, in an underground maze of electric light.

The four walls of the elevator, including the closed doors, along with the ceiling and the floor, were all mirrored. This created a dazzling effect, with hundreds of thousands of reflections dizzyingly bouncing off one another in a blinding fashion, spiralling away in every direction, eternally becoming more and more miniscule. Mason glanced around at the infinite projections of his image, plunged further into darkness as the gloomy light of the lift became more obscured with each subsequent reflection. Every one of his movements, no matter how slight, was replicated by this never-ending train of doppelgangers, each one mimicking the action of that preceding it with lightning fast reflexes. This vision, along with the downward motion of the elevator, produced an uneasy effect upon his already unbalanced mind-state, as though each and every individual aspect of himself, whatever lay within his soul, be it of virtue or evil, were being simultaneously dragged through this fantastical descent. No matter which direction he looked in, he saw himself stretched out forever, to inevitably continue beyond the scope of his vision. Even under his feet he continued to mark the view with his omnipresent person, gazing at a landscape beneath him that was nothing but alternate and equal versions of his self floating in darkness, with the bulb overhead emblazoned eternally in each reflected chamber, never sufficient to fully reveal his images, but enough to make the furthest shadows seem menacing. If he closed his eyes he merely felt the motion of the steel casket rumbling its way through the heart of this unusual world. The lift shook unsteadily before stopping and Mason felt relieved to look upon a different scene when the doors opened upon a brightly-lit corridor.

All was quiet. It was early in the morning, too early for the cleaners to be doing their rounds. Mason approached the door of room 417. Like most of the interior it was rotting and devoured by termites, or other creatures with equally voracious appetites, and it easily gave way to a little pressure. Mason entered the room quietly and looked around. There were very few possessions visible. Sadler had left in a hurry, if his house had been any indication, and it showed. The room bore very little trace of anyone having lived in it, save for a dishevelled, leather bag on the dreary, stain-filled floor and a man lying unconscious on the bed.

Mason looked at the man. He appeared slight and slender. He was in a deep sleep and Mason suddenly felt like an intruder. Sadler's face was young, no more than thirty years of age. In the days prior to this moment, Mason had forgotten the image displayed in the photographs that he had received from Albright and, instead, had constructed notions of a monstrous opponent in his mind. He had allowed Sadler to assume the face of a powerful enemy, a ruthless journalist exploiting anybody he could for easy profit at their expense. He had subconsciously taken it as a given that this moment of their meeting would be a monumental occasion, a physical altercation in which he was determined to triumph, with Sadler fighting tooth and claw for his freedom. Instead he looked down at a young man, sleeping comfortably in his bed, assumedly no match for his strength, one who was possibly a good person, possibly innocent and possibly a victim. Mason realised just how much of the picture of Sadler, that he had carried in his mind, he had unwittingly created in the act and art of deluding himself. For a moment he hesitated and contemplated getting as far away as possible, leaving the city and forgetting the whole affair. Then he remembered Rachel and the likelihood of her being brought to further harm. He thought of his own safety...

The figure in the bed suddenly awoke with a start.

"Who are you? What do you want with me?"

Mason panicked and stood silent and still for several seconds, face to face with his prey. The next moment the attack in Sadler's house flitted across his memory and instinct overcame him. Mason clenched his fist and struck Sadler heavily. The boy sunk back into the sheets.

Raymond came to, sitting on the damp floor of a room that was unknown to him. His head was pounding with pain and the taste of salt, sweat and blood swirled around behind the line of his lips, mixing in his mouth. His eyes ached with the effort of allowing themselves to be opened. He barely managed to make out a lantern swinging slightly from the low ceiling, just faintly offering visibility to the dimensions of a filthy, stone basement. The room stank with a sharp, stinging smell and the air was heavy with something that left a bitter taste upon the tongue. Raymond attempted to move but found his arms bound behind him to a thick metal pipe that refused to budge.

He had no recollection of how he had arrived here. The last few weeks of his life had been a daze of terror, subsisting solely on the fuel of survival, constantly fearing the worst and making a tiring, distraught attempt to prevent it from happening. He had managed to sleep only an hour or two at night for as long as he cared to remember but, nonetheless, the last memory he could recall before being in this room was of his drifting into a listless, unrewarding sleep. Now he was overcome with a strange feeling of despair, of the loss of all hope. Despite his not recognising the room, he was sure that there was only one place that he could realistically be. They had won and now he was going to meet his end. There was no further hope to be bestowed upon any of the people whom he loved or the few whom he secretly hoped still loved him.

A noise from nearby drew his attention back to the confines of the room. A shrieking, metallic noise, as though someone were cutting through sheets of steel with a chainsaw, came from somewhere close by and heavy footsteps echoed through what sounded like a narrow walkway, coming closer and closer to the room. Raymond could still only barely, and briefly, open his eyes and the light from the lamp stung them whenever he did so. He managed to peel his left eyelid upwards to make himself aware of a blurred view of a door hanging open and a tall, heavy-set figure coming through it. Raymond closed his eye again and hung his head. His vision was too weak to make out any exact features of this person, but what did it matter now? All was lost.

Raymond heard the figure's footsteps and deep breathing grow louder, until he could tell that it was standing merely a few inches from the end of his outstretched feet, probably staring down at its defeated prisoner.

"It's been quite a job with you Sadler," a man's deep and aggressive voice poured out. "I think we'd both feel better if we just finished it now."

Raymond did not respond, but just sat shivering and shaking from the cold, the fear and the explosion of pain in his head. Then something buried within a memory associated with the pain triggered a flash in his swollen brain and he recalled a figure, possibly and probably this man, staring at him silently as he had awoken in his hotel bed.

"How did you find me?" he stammered in a hoarse, broken croak.

"Forget that for now," responded the man, "let's just get the final details over and done with."

Something about this comment registered itself as unusual to Raymond. What details were left to be resolved? Surely this was already the end of the matter? He allowed a slight flicker of hope to enter his mind and he tried to hold back the panic bursting inside him. He decided not to divulge any information to this figure for the time being. He would see what his jailor knew first.

"Where's the brooch Sadler? I searched your hotel room, top to bottom, and I searched you, but I can't find it. Tell me where it is."

This statement surprised Raymond even more than the previous one. It was the last thing he had expected to hear. Panic continued to escalate inside him as the possibility of capture by another person simultaneously gave him courage. Clearly the figure was not here to merely kill him – to hurt maybe, but at least not to immediately kill. Raymond speculated that perhaps there was the faintest hope of this man being turned to his side. The prospect excited him and again he had to fight to remain calm, reluctantly focusing instead on the stabbing pain in his skull.

"Where is the brooch?" the man asked once more, this time in a slower, intimidating tone.

"I've no idea what you're talking about," Raymond rasped in response. "Why did you bring me here?"

"Tell me where the brooch is. Now. I'm not going to ask again."

"I swear, I don't have any brooch, I don't'..."

Raymond's speech was interrupted by a sudden swift and strong kick to the side of his aching head. Agony shot through his body and he became dizzy. As more blood ran down his face, he decided that the temptations of unconsciousness might in fact be the best end to this nightmare. The figure dragged him to his feet, slapping him frequently to keep him awake.

"Please don't hit me again! I don't know what it is you want, I can barely think with the pain!" Raymond desperately begged.

The figure leaned in closer to Raymond's face and leered –

"I'm just returning the favour."

Raymond opened his eye just enough to distinguish a large red scar running down one side of his captor's forehead. Their eyes met and, as the swinging lamplight briefly brightened the stranger's features, Raymond recognised the man from his house. The man he had caught off guard and struck to ensure his escape. Now, more than ever, he was convinced that he was not imprisoned where he had originally believed himself to be. This man did not know everything. Raymond was sure of it. The fact that Raymond was still alive, the way the man spoke and this brooch that he was demanding – none of it indicated that the stranger was intrinsically linked to the heart of the matter. The panic quickly swelled up in Raymond until he could bear it no longer. His pulverised brain was overcome with excitement and he embraced it. This man could be turned. He just had to know the truth.

Words began streaming from his mouth almost without control. "So you haven't brought me to them yet ... you don't even know what's going on ... haha ... you don't know anything! ... please you have to help me ..."

The figure had clearly had enough of this and took a step back now that Raymond was standing of his own accord. He seemed to have given up hope of learning whatever it was that he wanted to know and, as the words continued to spit rapid fire from Raymond's lips, the prisoner watched as the fingers of figure's right hand curled into a large, gloved fist.

"Please ... you can still help me ... I ... I'll find a way to repay you ... don't be a fool ... you're selling your soul ..."

The hand had finished drawing back and was now moving forward towards the battered side of Raymond's head.

"You can stop them now ... you're the only one ... there's nothing to be done if they take me ... you have to listen ..."

The fist was now only inches from his face, the pain and subsequent blackout inevitable.

"Please ... once they have me it's over ... for both of us ..."

Mason's fist crashed into the side of Raymond's head and the young man fell back to the ground unconscious.

Mason was driving quickly towards the waterfront, to end his involvement in this case for good. He bent his way around the curves of the city's decayed shell, travelling its maze of damaged highways, searching for the seafront escape, for escape from what his life had become. Tonight it would all be over.

The young man was bound and unconscious in the car boot. Perhaps he had handled the situation too roughly in the basement. The young man was small and weak, and Mason had been heavy handed.

However, this feeling dissipated quickly. Earlier in the day, but what now seemed weeks ago, Mason had decided that he was delivering Sadler no matter what.

Every now and then his mind flickered back to the issue of the brooch and the question of what it was that Albright really wanted. Was it the photographs, or was it something completely removed, that he had still managed to remain unaware of? Would Albright be angry if he turned up without the brooch? It was doubtful. Mason had previously toyed with the idea that there had never been a brooch at all and he was now more sure of it than ever. Albright had merely used it as an excuse to send him after Sadler. Albright would probably not mention the brooch and would perhaps even go as far as possible to avoid the subject. Mason had recognised the glimmer in Sadler's eyes as one of hope when he had repeated his question about the brooch and guessed that Sadler really did know nothing about it. Had that been the reason for the sudden, overwhelming need he had felt to knock Sadler out, to silence him before he was faced with the truth? Was he secretly afraid of discovering what was happening, now that he had finally decided that turning the man in was the best course of action? Was he incapable of handling the possibility that he would hear something from the boy that would complicate his own troubled thoughts further, which would result in his having these nightmares trapped inside his mind forever? He wanted it to end now. He had resolved to end it and did not want his brain blighted by undesirable truths about what he lingered upon the brink of doing... No. Sadler had refused to cooperate and Mason was being paid to follow through on this job.

Mason continued to ponder as he drove through the dry, dusty, desolate valleys formed by the looming buildings that furiously streaked up towards the scorched sky on all sides. What had Sadler meant by saying "it's over ... for both of us"? Who did both of us refer to? Mason had already decided that turning Sadler in was the best thing to do for everybody involved. Surely it would both ease the horrors in Rachel's life and finally get himself out of this business for good. He could not understand the boy's protests and therefore failed to sympathise with them. If the matter was simply a question of Sadler's blackmailing

Albright, or indeed any other personal matter between the two men, then Sadler had had all of this coming to him for a long time.

Try as he might though, Mason could not shake off the feeling that he was heading towards the committance of some grievous deed. He stopped the car at the side of the deserted road that spiralled down to the docklands and stepped out into the night air. He was only a matter of minutes away from the bar now. Soon it would be over. Tonight there would come an end to the nightmares, to unwanted characters following him, to the responsibility he felt for those who had been dragged likewise into the case. These feelings of injustice could be ignored, could be replaced by admiration of the good he was doing for other people, for Rachel, for Walt, for himself, they could be suffocated deep down within his soul, buried forever, to be forgotten. He could leave this city, detach himself from this world and finally live something akin to a normal life.

Mason looked upwards, anticipating a view of the stars to be displayed, to lend him courage and strength in their beauty. However, the heavy weather had left a thick fog creeping over the city at night time. This drifted across the sky and mixed with the smoke and pollution of the docklands to produce the effect of an oil spill hanging in mid-air, black as the natural sky but tinted and tainted by an unnatural sheen. It produced a queasy, stomach-churning effect on Mason as he stood solitary in the silence. He wiped his forehead with the back of his hand and felt a bruise, still raw and throbbing with pain, from Sadler's blow. Rage returned to the forefront of his mind. He took a final breath and got back into the car.

As he placed his hand upon the keys to start the engine, Mason heard a dull thumping noise coming from behind him. A sickening sense of déjà vu came over him, as though he had heard the sound somewhere before, sometime recently, someone banging, pounding, begging for mercy or escape... Then he realised it was coming from the boot of the car. Sadler had come to and was banging upon the roof, rallying for a final plea, a desperate last attempt at freedom. Mason remembered a dream he had had several nights ago. The pounding was now more frantic, stronger and more rapid.

"Please," he was sure he made out, "you have to help me."

The sound of the engine would silence it. Mason sat there for a few seconds more, one hand fingering the keys, the other etching its way along the path paved by the bulging bruise upon his temple. He heard one last pound before he turned the keys, the roar of the engine drowning out all other noise, and resumed his journey towards Albright.

CHAPTER 17

Mason's footsteps echoed around the shoddy walkway that directed his approach towards the familiar building, which loomed before him from out of the night. The silence surrounding the steps heightened the ominous tone of their volume, fuelling his feeling that he was now walking a path along which he would never return, at least not the same man as before. Each meeting of boot and board brought him closer to both escape and damnation.

Mason had parked his car beside the painted sign that had signalled the location on his first visit here. As he had stepped from the car and began the walk to the building, he had realised that the banging in the boot had stopped.

The oily blackness was still smeared across the night sky and, as before, no light was coming from the strange building. Sound and sight were not necessary senses in this darkened underworld, merely a sense of direction was required, something calling one towards their destination or destiny, leading them there whether or not they wished to arrive. Mason surveyed the building quickly and took a deep breath, before descending the stone steps to re-enter Albright's parlour of inequity.

His fist pounded heavily upon the iron-studded door. There was no noise for several seconds until the same gruff, grimy doorman as before pulled the blockade back. This time the man did not utter a word. He stood aside, an emotionless expression painted upon his rugged face. Mason likewise failed to offer any greeting and stepped through the doorway into the corridor. He began walking without waiting to see whether the man was escorting him.

He immediately breathed in the same sweet, pungent smell as before, and for one brief moment he was sure that he finally recognised what it was, before it escaped him once more. He turned the corner, at the end of the corridor, into the bar area which still wore its appearance of depravity, only now it was empty. No tattooed arms passed between pillars and no shadowed bodies plotted in darkened alcoves. This sense of desertion unsettled Mason. Whereas previously the place had seemed dangerous and threatening, teeming with turmoil, it was a threat that he knew how to meet, inebriated sailors and petty thieves, adversaries he could deal with if necessary. Now he felt as though some unspeakable horror was imminent, that he was trapped in a mausoleum deep beneath the black waters that waited and wailed outside its thin walls. He thought again of the face that had greeted him in Sadler's study and pondered whether it waited for him somewhere within the passages of this evil maze. He remembered Rachel's freezing, limp hand resting upon his shoulder, hearing his name whispered from somewhere, or had this even happened... Mason tried to pull himself together and walked with renewed purpose towards the door to Albright's room.

He did not bother to knock, preferring to barge uninvited into the room without betraying any of his anxieties, now that he had recovered a brief amount of his usual iron will. He knew that he could not settle this business with Albright if he had any doubt or fear in his mind. Inside it was empty and he began across the room, making straight for the opposite door, the one that Albright had exited through after their meeting, before something caught his eye. Mason stood in the centre of the high-ceilinged room, his heavy steps softened by the thick carpet, the extravagant splendour of the chamber further nursing the budding discomfort one felt within. He looked up at the paintings on the walls that he had previously examined, each depicting its own individual sea-faring scene. The paintings maintained the same colours, the same textures and each hung in the same position, as though they had waited there untouched for centuries. However, Mason was sure that something was not right about them, that even though the general appearances of the paintings were unchanged, there were nonetheless subtle differences in the scenes they depicted. Mason felt a slight chill shiver its way down his back. He rubbed his eyes and looked closer in disbelief. Undoubtedly it was just his memory playing tricks on him, his tortured mind suffering delusions, but it seemed to him that this time the whale was closer to the ship and the harpoon did not appear as reassuring as before. He swore that the mysterious vessel in the second picture had been anonymous on his last visit, but now it flew a banner depicting swords and flames, and its crew outnumbered that of the closer vessel by a significant margin. In the next picture the boat was at a more severe angle, upon a larger, more ferocious wave, about to capsize at any moment, while in the last painting there was no longer a bird of prey in the scene at all, but the ship's crew lay scattered across the deck, reduced almost to skeletons with hunger, and hauling disease-ridden bodies overboard. Mason stood, stricken starkly still by his incredulity, feeling almost nauseous in the realisation of his own dawning madness, until his scattered thoughts were shattered by a familiar elegant, powerful and threatening voice.

"Good evening Mr. Mason."

Albright was now sitting behind his desk, with a glowering stare fixed upon his visitor. He was wearing the same dark, velvet suit and assumed the same position he had taken up the previous time Mason had met him, but now he looked remarkably different. He retained the force of his visage, his domineering presence remained, and he still dwarfed the rest of the room, causing it to disappear, drawing one's attention immediately towards himself. However he looked as though he had aged immeasurably. The lines on his face were more prominent, lending him a much older countenance than before, and his formerly grey hair was thinner and now almost completely white. His posture was crooked as though his body had been bent by years of neglect. His hands, placed upon the desk, were wrapped in wrinkles. Mason noticed that Albright's voice, though doubtless reeking the same evil power, though still thunderingly quiet, now cracked and broke with each utterance, as though there was an object that could not be cleared constantly lodged in his throat. The only features that seemed unchanged were his piercing eyes, still ever watching and waiting.

"Please sit down Mr. Mason," Albright began.

"I don't think I'll bother Albright. I'm here on time; let's just get this over with."

"Yes Mr. Mason, I must say I am pleased, and a little surprised, to see you here tonight. I trust you have Sadler somewhere nearby?"

"I brought Sadler, but I want to see my money before I hand him over. This case hasn't exactly painted the best picture of you and I hope that after tonight we won't have to have anything to do with each other ever again."

Albright's old, rupture-ravaged lips broke into a smile revealing his gleaming, still-white set of teeth. His eyes remained fixed on Mason's all the time, challenging him to break eye contact and lower his pupils. Mason, despite putting on his best outward demeanour of impeccable professionalism, was struggling to maintain composure, to fight this duel of words, wits and stares, and wanted nothing more than to look, or even run, away.

"Naturally, as is the case in our line of business," Albright replied.

Albright picked up the telephone that sat on his desk and after waiting a few moments ordered whoever was on the other end to bring in Mr. Mason's money.

"After all," he continued after returning the receiver to its pedestal, "is not our line of business essentially the same? Neither of us let our emotions, or what some lesser people would call morals, stand in the way of our goals. That is why I hired you, because I knew that you would deliver regardless of what you discovered, not that there is necessarily anything to discover," he said smiling again, "and that I can trust you to remain silent after this affair ends tonight. Of course, you will tell me if I am acting unwisely by placing my faith in this assumption?"

Mason was tormented by how Albright pronounced the words "ends tonight". He had run the phrase through his own mind several hundred times that evening, but somehow felt that Albright's definition of ending the affair was drastically different to his own.

"And what about the brooch Albright?" he said, ignoring the question.

Albright stared at him for a time, as if plundering Mason's soul for any information or telling emotions that might lurk there, as if to determine whether his ability to stand firm was to be trusted, as if to see whether the strains of the days prior had snuck underneath his skin. Mason could not establish what the conclusions of this optical examination were and Albright broke into a dry, rasping laugh. The noise was like a rotten branch being wrenched from a dead tree, and as his head shook so did his long, unkempt strands of white hair. After seconds of laughing Albright spluttered into a fit of phlegmy coughing. It seemed to Mason, despite the still eminent emittance of authority and power, that Albright was about to keel over at any given moment and plummet down to the embrace of the infernal world to which he surely belonged, this word no longer capable of maintaining his demoniacal being.

"Ah yes, the brooch. I trust that you have also brought that to me?'

"No, I didn't find this phantasmal brooch. Or see it. Or hear anything about it. I don't think Sadler has any idea of what it is either and I pushed him pretty hard for information. So tell me what this brooch is and why you brought it up at all?"

"So you treated our dear Raymond a little roughly did you?" the smile lit up Albright's dilapidated face once more. "I knew you were a man who could be trusted to go all the way. Regardless, if you do not have the brooch let us not mention it anymore."

Albright leaned forward on his desk, his face now adjusting itself into a more menacing expression, the eyes burning with a fire even more rapacious than usual.

"I do not think it is necessary to warn you not to pry into this matter any further, especially now that your work is complete, and to forget all about it after we part tonight. If you brought Sadler to me then that is sufficient."

Mason felt as though he was being physically assaulted by Albright's predatory gaze and found that he could scarcely continue to support his own frame without considerable effort. He desperately attempted to stay on his feet, to meet Albright's pummelling stare. He knew that he should forget the matter, that he had already decided that this was the route he was going to take. There was no need to unnecessarily involve himself any further. However, if it was going to end tonight and he had already descended to this level of the deep, then he wanted to know more. The thought struck Mason for the first time that if Albright knew of the suspicions he was harbouring, of the evidence that he could possibly produce against Albright's name, than this issue of the brooch could turn out to be the least of Mason's problems.

"I thought the brooch was what the whole matter hung upon?"

A supreme quiet cocooned the cavernous chamber. Albright remained fixed, leaning forward on his desk, penetrating with eyes that burned like evil, midnight lamps. Mason somehow managed to remain staring back, shuddering inside his flesh, wondering what the next move would be. The tension that saturated the room was almost breathable, touchable, something that could be grasped and beaten to a bloody pulp. In those moments Mason thought about everything that had happened those last few days – the cars following him, the figure outside and inside Sadler's house and its expression of hate, his nightmares gradually becoming more disturbing, powerful and real, the torture he had performed on Sadler, the photo reel, the mosquito's blood splattered across the phone booth window, the madness that was seizing a dangerous grip on his brain as he watched paintings taking on new faces before his eyes and men impossibly ageing decades in a matter of days. He felt that at any moment things were going to come to an unexpected and possibly brutal conclusion. He himself had engaged in terrible acts of late and now the hour had come to atone for them. He renewed his attention on the vigorous vision of Albright for what he suspected might be the final time and, as he awaited his ultimate moments, he suddenly heard a loud bang behind him.

Mason quickly turned and, at the same time as he realised that he had not been hurt, he acknowledged that the sound had been the gruff sentry entering the room and closing the door roughly behind him. In his right hand he carried a briefcase.

"Your money is here Mr. Mason," said Albright slowly and deliberately, without any of the softly mocking tones he had assumed before. "We have taken Sadler from your car and now it is time for you to leave. There is enough money there to live lavishly for the remainder of your natural life. Leave now and forget everything that has happened. I hope, for your sake, that my faith in your steadfastness has not been misplaced."

Albright continued staring until Mason finally caved beneath the pressure and broke eye contact, feeling relieved to finally have another person in their presence. He walked briskly to the door, took the briefcase from the man's hand and left the room without even examining its contents.

Mason walked back through the bar, along the foul passageway and up the narrow steps once more. He emerged out onto the blackened walkways just as Sadler was being brought into the building. The screaming and protests had stopped. His body was being dragged limply by the underarms, by two large men. As Sadler was being brought closer, he managed to slightly raise his head as if to make one final appeal to Mason, one last, striving plea. Mason lowered his gaze and quickened his pace, not raising his sight from the planks beneath his feet until the tyres of his car appeared on the horizon of his vision. He flung the briefcase on the passenger seat and sped from the waterfront, before he had time to gather his thoughts or make any rash decisions that he might later regret.

After reaching his deserted office Mason checked the case. Everything was there. He tried not to think about what had happened. When he could no longer ignore it he thought about Rachel and convinced himself that he had done the right thing. If not, he had at least made the right decision, both for himself and for others. He then proceeded to drink until he reached a self-created oblivion in which he could forget. Something inside of Mason begged him not to go home that night, warned him that unimaginable events were waiting, salivating with eagerness, to take place. However, something else, something dead within him, told him that it made no difference anymore.

CHAPTER 18

Mason had returned to Sadler's laboratory. He was sure that the answer to this nightmarish puzzle was buried deep within its recesses, the antidote to the repugnant poison seeping through him, the cure to allow him to sleep peacefully once more. Perhaps if he had just had some more time, if the deadline had not been thrust so restrictively upon him, things could have been different. However, it was still possible that by finding the lost photographs, or anything else detailing Albright's deleterious activities, he could somehow change things and alter the fates of potentially innocent people.

Loud, passionate screams bounced around the room behind the door opposite Sadler's, where the Inca had dwelled. The door to Sadler's laboratory seemed to be new, a temporary one, most likely installed by the owners of the building to prevent unwanted visitors entering the room. Mason threw his full force against it several times without the door giving way. A creeping sense of exasperation crawled over him, realisation that the door was, in fact, not stronger than before. Rather he had grown older, weaker, tired and broken in the last days. As this thought dwelt within his mind, the door flew open with a loud crack and Mason thanked the neighbours for the vicious, violent noises they were emitting, providing apt aural disguise for his illegal search.

The red lighting lit the venomous snake of passages that endlessly slinked up and down. The passages now seemed to extend further into the darkness and there appeared to be a greater number of them than had originally occurred to Mason's troubled memory. He recalled his previous search and, despite the fact that he had been sure there was nothing more to be found on that visit, he now felt that either here or Sadler's home were the only places in which he could resolve this riddle. For the moment the thought of returning to Sadler's house splashed a hostile and feverish fear across his brain.

As he placed a foot forward he looked down and saw hundreds of photographs scattered along the floor of the waiting passageway. Despite the unkempt nature of their layout, strewn wildly about the passages, a trail was discernible of particular pictures that formed an individual pathway in the midst of the others and appeared to twist around the end of one walkway and continue along the next. They left Mason with the impression that somebody had walked the path briskly while holding a bulging pile of photographs in their hands, from which these pictures had continuously fallen. Mason stooped down and picked up the first photograph.

It was a frame of Albright's face, close up and staring at the camera. It was an old photograph and Albright was younger looking, as Mason had first seen him. His eyes threatened to set the picture alight, as though cigarette burns would appear in the centre of his sockets at any moment and devour the portrait in flames. Mason threw the print back to the floor, not wanting to engage in another war of wills with those marauding pupils. The next picture was nearly identical, taken almost immediately after the first, with Albright's figure shifted slightly to the left but still staring down the cameraman. The next photograph was similar, only again a split second after the previous one. Mason began to quickly follow the trail along the ground, around the first corner, watching Albright as he, interminably slowly, turned until his back was to the camera. Growing impatient, he now only bent down to examine every third or fourth picture, as Albright began to complete a three-hundred and sixty degree turn and almost faced the camera again. Mason gasped in horror as he saw the face that greeted him. It was the older Albright, the one he had seen the day before, with that vicious grin cascading across his countenance. What were these pictures and who had managed to create this masterfully, deceptive optical illusion? Despite the feeling of dread that harried Mason, he realised, due to the nature of Albright's condition, that these must have been taken in the last few days, since he had begun work on the case. These were new photographs. There was someone else out there, a potential ally, taking pictures of Albright. Perhaps there were pictures that could answer his questions...

Mason continued to follow his course along the map of photographs, like a bloodhound stooped to the ground, unsure as to what was bothering him but not daring to stray from the scent. After what seemed an eternity of prowling the passageways looking at Albright's constantly ageing face, Mason was eventually in the final stretch leading up to the desk where he had found the roll of undeveloped film. The trail here was thicker, with countless prints littering the walkway before the desk. When he looked back the distance between the door and the point where he now stood appeared much greater than it had from the other side. In fact, in the dim, red light of the room it was barely visible – the room seemed to snake back and forth into the dark forever. Albright's face now looked as though it was rapping upon death's door, but that smile still leered at Mason through pestilential, broken lips.

As the tyrant's profile continued its descent to the grave, the images displayed in the pictures upon the floor suddenly changed dramatically. Now they were taken from a very low angle, as though they were the work of a small child, and displayed the walk along the pier leading to Albright's lair. The photographer came closer and closer to the colourful sign that announced one's arrival and, as they turned in the direction of the building, Mason watched unnerved as his own figure appeared in the frame, standing as he had the night before, staring at the boards beneath him. Who had taken this? Surely there had been no-one else there that night? He remembered turning his eyes to the ground and walking, staring only at the boardwalk, until he had reached his car. Had he been so absorbed amidst his own consternation that he had failed to notice an anonymous figure creeping across the waterfront?

The photographer continued past Mason towards the building, down the steps, along the corridor and into the bar where no light existed save for that which emanated from an iron, black candelabra standing in the centre of the room. Mason flicked through the pictures with a greater rapidity, desperate to see what had taken place after his departure. The photographer moved towards the centre of the room and appeared to lie down on a table that stood behind the candelabra. The lens faced the darkness in the direction of the door that granted entry to the inner rooms, from which a man was emerging. Mason knew that it was Albright before the man had even stepped into the light, his dominating essence seeping from the pictures as though he were in the laboratory right at that moment, standing behind Mason, leaning over his shoulder to gather a glimpse of the picture, breathing his rank, deadened breath. As Albright stepped into the light, a long, silver-handled knife in his right hand brightly reflecting the glow of the candles, the photographer seemed to react by sitting upright. Mason approached the last handful of pictures as the camera focused on a mirror that hung upon the wall at the foot of the table. Mason scooped the next shot up from the phantasmal, red floor and, almost simultaneously, let it fall again. The reflection in the mirror showed Sadler, bloody and bruised, being held by the same two men.

Mason scrambled across the cutting room floor to the final photograph in the series and was dismayed to see that it again depicted a different scene altogether. It was a picture of himself, lying face down, fully clothed, in an unknown alleyway, his face beaten almost beyond the point of recognition. Rubbish from nearby bins vied with telling signs of a struggle for space atop the canvas of his coat.

Suddenly a phone on the desk began to ring, breaking the monotonous, constant hum of the overbearing overhead lights. Mason's heart began going through strange spasms, beating with violent vitriol at irregular intervals. He stumbled to the desk and grabbed the receiver, too traumatised to even speculate who could be on the other end. The only sound that came down the line was a high-pitched cackling, not unlike the laughter of a delirious child, but closer to that of someone who was unhinged to the point of suffering. Mason shouted angrily, demanding to know who was there, but the cackle was his only answer. He noticed that, for some reason, the phone was still ringing. Now the laughing stopped and a familiar voice, but nonetheless one Mason could not identify, said

"It's me."

"Who are you?" Mason shouted.

"What do you mean? It's me."

"Who for God's Sake, who?"

"It's me, it's Alan."

For some reason the phone was still ringing.

Mason woke in a stupor, lying dazed upon his bed, his sheets soaked through with the sweating produced by his turbulent visions. He struggled to raise his exhausted body from the mattress, the exertion of the nightmare having drained his energy as much as the actions of his time spent awake. He emptied the glass beside his bed of the water inside it, now dusty and warm, and collapsed back onto the mattress, before he realised abruptly that the phone on his desk was ringing

He had spent the dawn in a state of semi-consciousness, being too hung-over, shaken and tired to muster the strength to do very much of anything, but too paranoid and frightened to return to sleep. Every few minutes his eyelids had knowingly started to buckle beneath the weight of exhaustion, but as soon as slumber forcefully attacked, Mason had snapped awake once more, dreading any more fearful assaults on his mind. All night indecision had undermined his thoughts, as he had attempted to make sense of the events in the days that had led to the present. He was tormented by constant contemplation of Sadler's possible fate and could not free himself of an eerie anxiousness, one that whispered that this affair was still far from over. The sense of completion that he had so hungrily thirsted for, so fantastically anticipated, had not yet arrived. The closure he had so desperately striven for still eluded him. Had his dream informed him that Sadler was finished, that there was nothing more to be done? If so, then why had the horrific nightmares continued? Were they connected to Sadler and the case through nothing other than the unsettled designs of his own tumultuous subconscious? Yesterday Mason had hoped that, even if the waking hours of the rest of his life were now doomed to be spent in a guilt-gilded cage, he would at least be able to sleep peacefully, to escape the reality that had been set in motion on the day that he had taken this job. The dream he was rising from, after having finally fallen asleep for more than a minute, suggested otherwise. As morning spread itself across the city's melting, concrete blocks, his attention turned to the ringing telephone.

Mason approached it warily, dreading the consequences of answering, struggling to identify the distinctions between reality and the chasms of his dreamscapes, struggling to decide whether this was the same phone upon the same desk as the one from his nightmare, whether, indeed, he had woken up at all.

Mason's troubled voice croaked "What do you want?" down the line.

There was silence for what seemed to him an unbearable stretch of time, as Mason stood waiting, suffering, not so much fear anymore as fatigue, fighting a feeble battle against feelings of resignation to whatever fate awaited him. Eventually the voice, sounding less aged and broken than the night before, gracefully glided from the receiver.

"Mr. Mason. How are you feeling today?"

"What did you do with him?"

"That is not your business to know. It does unfortunately seem, however, that you may be too concerned to be trusted"

"Where's Sadler? What was this all about? The photographs? If so, I know all about it Albright! Killing Sadler won't make a difference!"

"Killing Sadler... Mason, I hired you, as I said before, because I thought you were a similar man too me. I heard that you took a job without hesitation, besides those arising from monetary issues. I heard that you left your few scruples at home and completed your task before erasing all traces of it from your memory. I now gather that I must assume my sources were uncharacteristically incorrect. Fortunately I prepared myself for all the possible outcomes arising from any such behaviour on your part. I even somewhat anticipated this course of events. I was hoping this phone call would not be necessary, would not yield such disastrous results. Nonetheless I expected that it would and now it is too late for you."

"What are you talking about Albright?" Mason spat. "We're nothing alike! We're not similar! You'll murder anything that gets in your way! I don't kill people!"

"You can delude yourself however much you desire Mr. Mason. Regardless, a chain of events that we had hoped to avoid has been set in motion and it is now time to part ways for good."

"Don't hang up on me Albright! Don't you dare threaten me! I'll come after you and expose you, for what you really are!"

There was a pause in which Mason could hear only a low, hissing sound that he could not label – laughter or something else altogether? Albright's voice uttered a final farewell.

"Mr. Mason, you have sealed your own fate and now you are doomed. Goodbye."

Mason shouted down the line for several seconds after Albright had gone. Animosity now consumed his whole person. His concern for Sadler's fate and his part in the potential crime had transformed his fear, paranoia and guilt into unbridled rage. He shuddered with anger, contemplating the consequences, both to date and those yet to come, of his actions, of his own greedy decisions. However, after he had lain sprawled upon the floor at the foot of his bed for some time, his mind dwindling only faintly in the realm of consciousness, he began to calm down a little, as though the realisation of what he had done was setting in, the realisation that he had reached a point from which there was no turning back and finally the realisation that he had done wrong, but that he nonetheless still had the power to set things even somewhat right once more.

Despite this sudden, compelling craving that overcame him to right his reproachable deeds, Mason, unlike in the last few days, now managed to separate the emotional, impressionable aspect of his brain from his logical thoughts. His mind was now, to some degree, focused, perhaps because he knew, for the first time in a long time, what the right thing to do was. He would no longer be fighting an inner moral argument during every passing second of the day. He was no longer going to be fighting on the side of wrong. Mason gathered from Albright's vague threats that the man was clearly not going to leave him be. There was obviously something in store for Mason and, based on what he thought he knew about Albright, he felt it safe to assume that the latter's vengeance would be final, bloody and brutal.

"You have sealed your own fate," he had calmly stated and Mason knew then that this was going to be a battle to the end.

However, if it was possible to find the missing pictures, to gather enough evidence and submit it to the police, to help build a case against Albright, then perhaps Mason could finally bring about justice and for once in his life do it within the confines of the law, punishing the actual

UNDONE

criminals of the world rather than aiding them. His clarity returning, the single-mindedness of his thoughts harnessing his wild, irrational instincts, Mason began to think clearly for the first time in days.

The first thing to do was to remove himself from his home as quickly as possible. Considering all the figures that had been shadowing him and the cars that had been following his daily undertakings, Mason knew that he had to disappear before he even began to think of striking back. If a punishment was coming, it was coming fast and soon, and it knew exactly where to find him. He packed up a few things, took the briefcase full of money and left his apartment, possibly, he thought, for the last time. The sun outside continued to reign victoriously, the night before having failed to alleviate the aching heat that embalmed the sweltering bricks of the buildings, and Mason almost burned his hand in his efforts to open the car door. He stopped on the pavement for a moment, watching the slumped figures slouching by, more stooped, more broken than ever. The distant tops of the taller buildings leaned over the road, threatening collapse, while the trees that lined the avenue seemed ready to explode into flames at any moment.

Mason drove hurriedly to his office, constantly looking each way to ensure that he was not being followed. The sole reason for his taking the seemingly senseless risk of visiting his office was to pick up Sadler's roll of damaged, undeveloped film, which he had secreted in his office desk. Mason knew that Albright's underlings could be waiting there to pounce, but he believed that if the developed photographs could not be found, then this film could turn out to be very important before the end of this matter, even if only a handful of the pictures on it could be salvaged. He had to ensure that he recovered it before anybody else was made aware of its whereabouts.

He hesitantly climbed the stairs and walked along the corridor towards his office. There was complete silence running through the building, due to the early hour, and not even the slow creaking of the lift, ascending and descending in its daily routine, was present to shatter the unsettling lack of sound. Mason knocked loudly upon his office door and waited outside for several seconds. When he received no response he placed his right hand on the knife in his pocket and

[150]

with his left rapped upon the door again, this time loudly calling out:

"Mr. Mason, are you in there?"

Still no sound came from inside and there was nothing out of the ordinary visible through the keyhole. Mason opened the door and, after ensuring that both the waiting and consulting rooms were deserted, went straight to the task of searching his desk.

He had left his office in quite a disorderly state, having had more pressing issues on his mind than the organised layout of his workplace, and the piles of material he had taken from Sadler's home mercilessly littered the room. He went straight for the drawer in which he was sure he remembered storing the film, but inside it was empty. Alarmed, Mason spent several minutes sifting through papers and photographs, before he became aware of the sound of footsteps pattering along the hall nearby. He searched with an invigorated sense of urgency, the steps coming closer to his door all the time, the prospect of the office being their intended destination seeming more likely with every moment. Attempts to make as little noise as possible, while trying to search through the mounds of paper and assorted pictures, were not particularly successful and Mason resigned himself to the fact that he would not find the film in time. He silently slid across to the front door, locked it from the inside and hid himself behind the closed door of a small, closet-sized space attached to his consulting room, containing nothing more than a filing cabinet, packed with papers, and a few old suits, long destroyed by moths, that hung from a rail. Mason drew a deep breath and waited in silence.

The footsteps came to a halt outside his office. Mason could only see a small area surrounding one corner of his desk through the crack where the door hinges met the frame of the closet's walls. The sound of the door handle being tried was the first thing he heard, followed by the jangling of keys. He heard them turning in the lock and freely granting entrance to their holder. Whoever it was had managed to procure a set of the keys for his office, despite Mason being very insistent on the issue of himself and the owners of the building possessing the only copies. He heard the footsteps, now clearly audible, of two people, one heavy set and the other lighter, along with the noise of papers being carelessly knocked to the floor.

"There's nobody around. I told ya he wasn't dumb enough to come here," spluttered a man's deep voice, interspersed with struggles for breath and an interruption for the purpose of clearing phlegm, that one could safely assume was the utterance of the duo's larger member.

Mason clutched his knife with a firm grip. He did not want more violence and he could not be completely sure that these were Albright's men. It was better to utilise this position of unknown observation, to see what it was they were interested in, and stick to his plan of finishing this in the proper fashion, finding the lost pictures and bringing Albright to account for his crimes before the courts. Nonetheless, he clung tightly to the rubber grip that embraced the sharp and ravenous steel, in case of his having to tackle anybody who came into that small, dark closet with the wrong intentions.

"Relax. Let's just look around a bit, see if there's anything useful here," said a different voice, that of another man, calmer, more precise with each word and using a disdainful tone towards his companion.

Mason could now see a slender man, dressed in a dark-blue suit, through the crack, rustling quickly through the piles lying atop the desk. He was only afforded a view of the back of this unwanted guest, but Mason guessed that he was reasonably strong, despite his slightness, and that he was used to being listened to. He could hear the larger man's heavy breathing all the while, refusing to leave his post by the door.

"Look, I told you, some of these books are Sadler's, signed and written in by him," said the man in blue. "This stuff could turn out to be useful."

The other man was seemingly not very interested by the discovery of these documents, but briefly joined his companion by the desk anyway. Mason could see the back of an obese man wearing a filthy, tan-coloured coat that almost hung as far as the floor. The dirty, thin, black hair at the back of his head was stuck to his balding scalp with a mixture of grease and sweat.

"Fine, grab them and let's get outta here. You waste your time readin' that crap if you like but it's not gonna get us any closer to findin' this guy. He's gone into hidin' and we gotta go out lookin'."

As Mason wondered exactly which man it was they were trying to find, the intruder in blue, ignoring the fat man, gathered a large pile of books and papers from the desk and the two men left the room locking the door behind them.

Mason waited a full ten minutes before he emerged from hiding. The place was in such a state of chaos that he could not definitively establish what information the men had taken with them. Had they been looking for him? Or were they perhaps other bounty hunters still looking for Sadler? Mason found it odd that, regardless of who they were and what they wanted, they had not bothered to thoroughly search the office, as though they had already been sure of his not being there. Perhaps they had been looking for something or someone else altogether and had deliberately come at a time when they assumed Mason would be absent. As he randomly browsed the piles of papers, trying to stumble upon any indication of what they had been searching for, he accidentally knocked a stack of folders onto the floor. As he did so Mason momentarily experienced a powerful sense of déjà vu, the semi-remembrance of something similar having happened before. He stooped down and looked under his desk, the base of which was raised about two inches from the floor by its stumpy, wooden legs. The roll of film was settled against one of these legs, its shiny sides enlivening the murky light. Satisfied by this discovery, the achievement of his original intention in coming here, Mason decided that it was best to leave the premises before even less desirable visitors called upon him.

Mason pocketed the film and promptly left the office, locking the door behind him. He slowly walked downstairs to his car and ensured that the men were nowhere to be seen, before reversing out into the afternoon heat once more. He drove distractedly for several minutes, devoid of destination, simply ensuring that nobody was repeating his chosen route. Mason then made up his mind to get off the streets as quickly as possible and into a safe hiding place where Albright's men could not find him, at least not without significant effort. A dreary hotel seemed as safe a place as any. He decided he would settle in the first suitably unexceptional one that he came across. He sped the car up and roared across the city in search of safety.

CHAPTER 19

Mason checked into a dirty and discreet hotel on the outskirts of the city. He had driven around the crumbling, downtrodden area for quite some time to reassure his safety and, when he had satisfied himself with the fact that his whereabouts were unknown, pulled into a tacky, cockroach-ridden hole, designed for adulterous couples and wretches who wished to disappear from the eyes of society. Mason walked to the end of a corridor that the receptionist had instructed him towards, occupied only by several, sleeping dogs and what seemed to be the janitor, who barely managed to stay sitting upright in a chair that leant against the dilapidated, water-stained wall.

The room was small, smelt of mould and had only one miniscule window, the latter fact only serving to magnify the powers of the odour and the omnipresent heat. Mason did not care. All he needed was a place to vanish while he gathered the scattered shards of his mind together, orchestrated them once more and formulated a plan. Music was coming from an ancient television set which teetered precariously over the edge of a set of splintering drawers. Advertisements were playing. Mason felt somewhat less solitary with the television on and quickly discouraged any intention of tampering with it. He walked to the fridge and opened the door against the express wishes of its rusted hinges. Inside it was empty, save for a sickly black, bile-like scum that covered its walls. Mason winced from the stink and pulled away. It was impossible to remain in that closed space for any considerable period of time without refreshment. He returned to the desk downstairs and bought some bottles of an unknown brand of beer that seemed to exist only in the congested confines of this hotel. Mason opened a bottle and collapsed on the bed to collect his thoughts. The news was coming on the television.

What was his next move going to be? He reckoned that the best course of action was to collect as much evidence as possible against Albright, about what had happened, and turn it all in to the police. He would continue trying to find the developed pictures and, if he was not successful, attempt to develop the damaged roll anyway. Hopefully the condition of the film was not completely unsalvageable and some precious information, no matter how little, could be garnered from it, information that might publicly expose Albright and make him pay for his crimes. Sadler would be likely, and entitled, to press charges against Mason for kidnapping and assault, but perhaps Mason's acceptance of this was what would be necessary to bring this nightmare to a close.

His immediate goal would be to try and find a location where he could develop the photographs himself, as he did not want them falling into the wrong hands. At some point he would have to make contact with Rachel, even to just call her and perhaps tell her to get out of the city for a while. Then he would...

"Alan Mason".

The sound of his name hammered itself into his head and he leapt to his feet, spilling his drink across the bed.

The sound had not come from the hall outside, as experience was quick to suggest. Rather it had come from within the room itself. It had come from the television. The screen displayed a woman standing at the entrance to a dirty, rubbish-strewn alleyway, one which was flooded with police and surrounded by barricades. Mason stood transfixed in horror as, one by one, photographs of him began to appear on the screen. A picture of him entering Sadler's house, another of him departing with his head drenched in blood, a picture of him leaving Rachel's and a last one outside the building that contained the laboratory. Mason felt himself instinctively reach for another drink. This was the last thing he expected. What could the public possibly know about, or have to contribute to, this drama? However, he managed to surprise himself with a subconscious suggestion that he had a suspicion of what the woman was going to report.

"Yes, that's right, one Alan Mason," the reporter continued, "a private bounty hunter, is wanted by the police for questioning in connection with the murder of a Raymond Sadler."

Mason felt his body weaken, as he began to tremble and an intense urge to vomit surged through his insides.

"Sadler, a young photographer, was found this morning in the alley behind me by a local woman."

Mason wanted to collapse, to hide from the world, to suppress all feeling in the depths of the alcohol, to seek nothing less than utter escape.

"Sadler appears to have died of gunshot wounds. He had also suffered several stab wounds and extreme blood loss. Officials on the scene have already indicated that he was extensively and brutally tortured for some time beforehand. The pictures you see on your screens are photographs of Mason, a tall, dark-haired, well-built man, who has frequently been spotted in the vicinity of Sadler's home in the last few days. Early reports are scarce but suggest that Mason had recently been questioning those close to the victim in regards to his whereabouts. If you see or hear of Alan Mason please inform your local authorities immediately. Do not try and apprehend him yourself – he is armed and extremely dangerous."

Sadler was dead. Sadler was dead and Mason was the police's prime suspect. He shivered painfully as he lay sprawled across the bed. Each breath felt heavy, as though his lungs were sandbags, while his spine shirked and shredded against his insides like a frozen dagger. He had delivered this defenceless boy to a sinister, dangerous man and his cohorts, and they had murdered him – tortured and murdered him. Mason wondered to what extent the signs of torture upon the body had been the result of his own extreme interventions...

He had been idiotic, blind, naive. Cars had not been following him, people had not been calling him, lurking behind him about the city, merely to intimidate him. Albright had hired a fall guy, a scapegoat, and all the while they had been monitoring his progress and collecting evidence that would suggest his guilt. He had planned to kill Sadler all along. Albright had never doubted Mason's ability to catch Sadler – he was a scared photographer up against a professional bounty-hunter. He had merely wanted to keep watch of his employee and create a documented record of his actions while Mason went about completing his task. Albright had known Mason would eventually turn the boy in and, in the event that Mason ended up turning against his client in the process, Albright had needed to be able to frame him for Sadler's murder. Photographs existed of Mason entering the murdered man's home and leaving bleeding, at his girlfriend's, at his workplace. Surely there would be further implicating documentation of his manhunt and they would possibly present the testimonies of all the people he had questioned in his efforts to find Sadler – Rachel, Sadler's Inca neighbour, perhaps even Walt. There were mountains of notes, photographs, journals and books, about and belonging to Sadler, in Mason's home and office. Albright had directed it all perfectly. He had hired a man too blinded by money and his passionate ego to examine the case passively, to not fail to plunge headfirst into the accomplishment of his goal; one that he knew would inevitably deliver while perfectly assuming the role of Sadler's murderer in the eyes of the public, the press and the police. Albright had threatened and intimidated him, seemingly to solely speed up the process and ensure the timely completion of the job, but also, and more importantly, as a means of surveillance. Albright had disposed of the problem that Mason had delivered at his doorstep, all the while collecting the necessities required to dispose of Mason afterwards, and he had sent this mirage of evidence to the people who desired to see it the most. Mason had been completely manipulated, used and, most of all, fooled.

Now, as a result, Sadler was dead. Mason wondered exactly what Albright and his men had done to the young man before they had finally sent him from this world. What had possibly made torture necessary; why not just kill the boy? Mason knew that there was blood on his hands. He was fully cognisant of his having played a leading role in this monstrosity. Memories of the dream from the previous night muscled their way into Mason's mind, as seen through Sadler's eyes, of his own body lying in a similar alleyway. However, this was no time to dwell on coincidental superstitions. He managed to persevere in keeping a hold on the steel that he had lent his reserve earlier that day, accepting his guilt in the matter, trying his best not to relinquish the tight grip that he had assumed upon the full proclivities of his wits. The police would be on his trail now but it did not mean that he had to forfeit himself, to lie down and let Albright triumph in the devilish saga he had orchestrated. It was still possible to present his own photographic portrayal, evidence to counter the wave that would inevitably be brought to crash against him. It was still possible to administer blows of legality against Albright in return and perhaps bring some sense of comfort to Sadler's soul, maybe even to his own. Anger began to return. He was not going to be used in this way only to passively surrender, to allow Albright undisputed, unanimous victory, without encountering resistance of any kind.

The television, to which Mason had become oblivious, continued announcing its news.

"... And after weeks of this unbearable heat, I'm happy to tell you folks that there could be rain over the next few days. Don't rejoice just yet though, as it's the result of severe pressure changes that are quite likely to set heavy storms upon us. There's even a slight possibility, believe it or not, of snow coming along with them. This is Barbara Madsen reporting."

The first, and most crucial, thing Mason had to do was to get out of the hotel. If the drunken clerk downstairs had been watching the news, he may have just remained lucid enough to recognise the man whom he had checked in a short while before. Mason decided he would hide himself in the house where he had held Sadler before bringing him to Albright. It was an ordinary building in a quiet neighbourhood and he had rented it over the telephone using an alias. At that moment it was the only place he could think of going where he would not have to interact with any strangers, to risk exposing his identity, and that the police would not already know about. Mason left the grotty room, quickly turned down the corridor towards the back of the building and bolted out through the fire escape.

The world seemed a trap to Mason as he slid through the stale and musty city streets. He was a wanted man – by the police, by Albright and by God knows who else. He had spent the majority of his morose life accustomed to being involved in pursuits, to living in the shadows, to looking out for enemies on every corner. However this time he was not doing so as a hunter, but in order to hide. It was now he whom the net was being drawn tighter around, woven with streams and strands of nothing other than the unavoidable pain of inevitable, and possibly deserved, fate. Mason pondered how this would all play out. It was quite plausible that he was condemned beyond all hope, that his final exertions would be little other than minor deeds that might someday be mentioned in the footnote that would be his life story, that they were only the brittle branches of bare trees lining the austere avenue that approached his grave.

He slouched in his seat while his car waited at a red light, facing the long stretch of road that ran downhill to the bay of the city. The broken, withered necks of the docklands' cranes pricked up along the evening skyline, while the decayed, metal bodies of shipwrecks that no-one had bothered to clean up were haphazardly deposited throughout. The setting sun was glinting off these enormous frames and it lit up the murky, brown bay-water that surrounded them. It resembled a puddle of rust more than anything that had the right to allow itself assume accurate description as a body of water. There had been fish and plant life down there an age ago but now it was little more than a collector's museum of obliterated iron corpses and perhaps bodies of another kind.

Mason was still slumped in the car seat, surveying this bleary landscape of dirt, when he was violently flung forward, headfirst into his windshield, with a powerful crash. The familiar feeling of blood trickling down his face announced its arrival. The windshield had been transformed into a spider's cobweb of white, dizzying lines. Before he could regain his senses or compose himself, another terrifying thump slammed into the back of his car, folding it like melted plastic, soft enough to be shaped and moulded with ease.

Mason managed to bury his foot in the accelerator, not knowing which direction he was taking or from whom he was fleeing. The crushed rear of the car was being dragged along by the sheer determined will of the front. Mason could feel its misshapen body trailing upon the ground, as though there were another vehicle entirely in tow. The back wheels had clearly been destroyed and it was unlikely that he could out-run any foe. He glanced in the rear-view mirror and, between the cracks that had splintered their way across its pane and the cascade of sparks being fired out from the back of the vehicle's body as it scraped the concrete, he could just make out a roaring, brown Jaguar, once more bearing down upon his shattered and twisted excuse for a car. Amidst the chaos he could not clearly see the face of the driver and refocused his sight on the road ahead, as his attacker readied another assault.

They were coming close to the water's edge. Mason struggled to keep control of the car as it swung wildly like a faulty corkscrew, sliding and swerving its way across the street. In the confusion caused between the blinding of the sparks and the other cars with which they narrowly avoided collision, along with the high speed at which they careened along, it was impossible to attempt any evasive manoeuvres and Mason was unable to even make a turn off the main road. The car shook from the force of a third blow, throwing it several feet forward and transforming it into little more than two front seats and an engine. Mason's head pounded from the impact of its having struck the windshield and this time he felt his body slammed against the door beside him. A loud cracking noise, whether in his head or without, told Mason that something, somewhere, had snapped.

The car hurtled along, somehow managing to build up a dizzying, if out of control, rapidity. The road continued to steeply decline towards land's end, beyond which lay the drop, down into the poisonous bay. Mason readied himself to attempt swerving the car around the corner at the bottom, to turn sharply and hopefully position himself behind his opponent. He knew it was a risky strategy. At the moment it was difficult to simply maintain a straight line and the back of the car was now so close to becoming one with the front that another heavy blow could crush him. However he had no choice, as outrunning the other car in this condition was an impossibility. He glanced in the mirror again. The Jaguar was snarling angrily behind him, like its exotic namesake, with an intense and insatiable bloodlust, ensuring its prey suffered just the right amount before it dealt the final blow. Despite the screeching of tearing metal in his ears mixed with a slight deafness that had come upon him from the force of the first attack, Mason could hear its engine growling aggressively, hungrily howling and screaming for the sounds of suffering.

They reached the bottom of the hill and Mason stamped upon the brakes while twisting the wheel with all his strength. The car was too badly beaten. The front began taking tentative steps in the desired motion of swinging around, until the immobile back impeded its progress by stubbornly refusing to move. This clash of intentions instead sent the car spinning into a dangerous circle, threatening to flip over at any moment. As he desperately struggled to regain control, Mason saw the Jaguar pounce. It smashed into the passenger side sending jagged metal spikes of what had once been the door flashing inwards towards him, knives forged from the very fabric of his car. Shards of glass showered his face as he closed his eyes, doing his best to shield his head with his arms. The daggers stopped short only a few inches from him. The momentum caused the car to slide towards the water's edge and hesitantly hover upon the precipice, halfway between the solid stone of the land and the grip of the bay beneath. As Mason struggled to remain conscious he saw the Jaguar reverse and speed off, and he felt the wreck of the rear of the car slowly pull the remainder of the vehicle backwards, dragging it down into the vile marsh that waited below. Mason blacked out...

He awoke in a world of total blackness – a blackness that could not have associated itself with any features of the natural world. He was sinking. Nothing in the line of his vision stirred, other than himself and the ruptured carriage he was riding down through this evil paradise. Outside, amongst the black, lay what seemed to be the residue of crumbling buildings, or perhaps the signature of some other design. A growth of polluted weed smeared this universe, mixed with what appeared to be the sunken artifices of man. What hellish vision had he now fallen into?

His head ached and his sight was blurred. He attempted to take a breath, to relieve the horrible throbbing in his chest. All he drew in was mouthfuls of the foul, dark liquid. Drowning with this intake of water, Mason suddenly regained a sufficient portion of his senses, remembering the attack and the crash. He had sunk deep into the depths beneath the murky surface, down to where the true nightmares began. Frantically, he thrashed about, attempting to open the car doors. It was futile. The crashes had mangled the vehicle into a misshapen death-trap. As he desperately tried to open the door to his right he realised it had been crushed too severely, so that a door barely existed, while to the left the internal knives and daggers stabbed to discourage any attempt he made, sending trickles of blood bubbling up through the mire, mixing with the stolen life forces of its other victims.

Mason's lungs grew tighter; the car was completely filled with the black water. He did not know how long he had been submerged. He was also ill-informed as to how long a human could hold their breath before slipping off to the other world. The nightmare vision, that faced him from outside the car, added to the growing belief that he was already residing there. His body began to give in, the tough skin and powerful muscles buckling beneath the pulverising pressure of the swamp, a physical human power submitting to the unharnessed fury of the dank pit. He began to grow dizzy and faint as the need for air overcame him. Mason's eyelids were like leaden sheets, the dim world grew even darker, and he began to feel his soul slinking off to the damned realm for which it was bound.

A sharp cracking pain snapped him back to life a moment later. Mason had slumped over and hit the open wound on his forehead against the edges of the hole that the crash had opened in the windshield. The time it took Mason to realise this enticing opening existed seemed to him like several minutes when in reality it took less than a second. As he floated through this bizarre lake, between life and death, if indeed there was or ever had been a difference, Mason saw this escape and, although sure that he was already well upon his way to hell below, saw one last chance at redemption.

Despite being submerged so deeply within the well of water, he summoned an uncanny, seething strength, a raging reserve of fuel, that ultimate determination not to perish, not like this, not before it was over, not to let the others win. Mason brought his feet crashing into the windshield three times, before the glass gave way and the hole was sufficiently large. He slipped through the gap and within a short time was at the surface.

The air did not initially feel good. Every breath felt like newly sharpened razor blades slicing through his insides, as though the air were a consumable liquid into which someone had slipped tiny, spiked slivers of metal. Despite the agonising effort, Mason breathed and, after a few moments, sucked in the air as though he were drinking in heaven itself, as though each gasp brought him closer to a joyous world, one which he had moments ago come narrowly close to forfeiting any hope of entering forever

As his body regained some small degree of composure, Mason paddled to a ladder that led up the wall of the defunct harbour. He emerged to the pier on top gasping and struggling for life. A crowd of onlookers, who had seen the crash, had gathered around, concerned for the fortunes of the driver below. However, when Mason stood upon dry land again, no one dared forward any attempt at comfort or indeed contact of any kind. He stood, a hulking, muscular mass, exhaling little other than pure rancour, with every inch of his body and clothes coloured a blistering black. The only parts of his body still clearly visible were his open eyes and these stared past the crowd to something beyond, burning fires of fear and fury within their sockets.

From a distance the creature looked on, as Mason resurfaced from the sea of pitch. The creature experienced the wrap of tendrils of distant anger, of primordial rage, upon seeing that its prey had escaped its death. Urges to annihilate began to surge through its body once more. It licked its torn lips with relish as it thought about the next meeting with this man. Its master had forced it to bide its time for long enough. It had watched the man squirm beneath the force of intimidation for days, as it imprinted paranoid thoughts upon his mind. Now the stage to act was set. Now it was the time for torture and mayhem, for the rending of flesh from bone, the snapping of sinews, the laceration of ligaments, for the warm taste of the prey's life slipping away. As the blur of shadows that made up the crowd of outsiders parted to allow the injured man passage from the waterfront, the creature licked its dripping lips once more and disappeared.

CHAPTER 20

Mason sat, watching the house he had rented from the opposite side of the street, scrutinising all who looked in its direction, or even slightly hesitated while walking past. A place that would have made a pleasant home, with a front of white, wooden slats, surrounded by a cheerful, little garden, in turn surrounded by a cheerful, quiet neighbourhood. Out here the buildings did not slope from the weight of the heat like those in the city centre and neither did the people. The presence of greenery and wide streets, in which the height of the structures still afforded a view of the sky, gave off an air of the area being significantly cooler than elsewhere. A breeze floated along the main road, flitting wistfully from person to person, brushing their faces, already blessed with smiles, simply from being in such serene surroundings. Nobody would suspect the history that lay behind those white slats

Mason sat beneath the spread of a large oak tree which cast a dark shadow about his person, one that ensured nobody would easily recognise him as the man from the news, the man wanted for murder, armed and dangerous. He had skulked through the back alleys and rooftops to get to this neighbourhood, now fearing that either the police or another assailant, or both, could be anywhere. A cloud of bright, red blossoms from a nearby tree drifted by, some settling upon his lap. Mason brushed them off his new suit. He had lost almost everything in the car crash. All of his clothes had been ruined by the foul, black water. He had replaced them using a crumpled wad of notes that had been folded in his jacket's inside pocket and had miraculously survived the near-drowning. He now wore a simple, grey suit. His face was partially masked by a mustard coloured, wide-brimmed hat. He had dipped into a bar and ordered a drink, much to the puzzlement and dismay of the bemused barman who had offered an expression of disgust at the sight of his filthy figure, only so as to use the bathroom, where he cleaned himself as best he could in the sink. The smell of the foul mire still clung to him, caked beneath his fingernails, matting his hair, and it rose to his nostrils from beneath his clothes every time he moved, reeking of rusted iron and rot.

The money was also gone. The briefcase he had taken from Albright had lain in the backseat of the car, now at the bottom of the black pit. Enough money for a lifetime of leisure, slowly being putrefied, devastated by a polluted, pernicious chasm of water. However, Mason did not have the time to worry about the ill-gotten money for now. He was simply trying to survive, to rest somewhere safe for a few hours and pull his thoughts together again. Besides, this had ceased to be about the money a long time ago, perhaps even before Sadler's death. He had wanted simply to remove himself from the situation, to detach himself from this menagerie of sordid characters. He had not then realised how difficult this feat would prove to be. Another whorl of blossoms shook Mason from his brooding. After almost an hour of sitting in observation, nothing and nobody of note had been in or around the building. He brushed more red petals from his lap and crossed the street.

The quiet façade of the front of the house concealed a similar demeanour inside, and all was tranquil as Mason carefully drew the front door open. Silence mixed with the smell of old rose petals in the hall, the only entities occupying the stark space. Mason climbed the stairs and stumbled exhaustedly into the shower. After he had scrubbed his body free of the dirt and dried off, he collapsed onto the bed and unintentionally subjected himself to the power of sleep. As he had crossed the landing between the bathroom and bedroom, his eyes had glanced in the direction of the stairs descending towards the basement. Sadler's blood and skin possibly still clung to the chains down there, along with the damp and the darkness.

Mason awoke with a start some hours later. He had been having another startling dream, one that, on this occasion, he could not remember. Whatever element of now massacred optimism he had ever nurtured inside of himself told him that he should be grateful, that escaping these nightmares was one of the goals he was striving for. However, he initially found this forgetfulness strange and a little frightening, considering the vividness of his dreams of late, their strangling power, the pounding images hammering their imprints into his mind. The only aspect of the dream that still lingered upon his memory was Rachel.

In the madness of the previous twenty-four hours or so he had mostly forgotten her. What would happen if the assailant who had come for him went after Rachel? Perhaps she had been bought off. Perhaps at this very moment she was in a police station somewhere, helping to compile an even stronger case against Mason. It was even possible that she truly believed he was the one responsible. Either way, whether he cared to admit it or not, her safety had leant significant weight to his decision making process throughout the affair and he was concerned with, indeed he felt he needed to know, what had become of her.

As Mason picked up the telephone and dialled for the operator, hoping in turn to procure Rachel's number, he stood looking out of the window into the night that had taken hold of the peaceful neighbourhood. The moon caressed its background of blackened sky, its brilliant face distorted by both the clouds and the pollution of the city that floated past, lending it the appearance of a misshapen egg. He waited in the dark, allowing the phone to ring for several minutes without answer until he gave up. He decided that he would get dressed and call over to her place himself. As he was turning from the window, Mason saw two bright spots crawling slowly up the middle of the street. They further slowed their momentum as they neared the building he was currently in until, with a sudden movement, they turned in an arc and slid into the driveway, the two lights slicing open the darkness of the front garden. Mason could hear the sound of broken gravel crunching beneath the heavy, rimmed tires of a large, black car.

A large figure stepped out from the driver's side after turning off the engine of the metal chariot. It was too dark to accurately determine any of the stranger's features. Mason felt a mixture of excitement and unease. A vision of the face he had seen in Sadler's house just nights before flitted across his mind, seizing it with an almost crippling fear, before releasing its grip a moment later. He decided to hide in the bedroom wardrobe, picking up an empty wine bottle that stood upon a nearby desk, the only object in sight that could easily be used as a weapon, his knife having been lost with the money amidst the bottom of the bay. Who could this person be and what had brought them here so late at night? Indeed how did they even know that this place existed? He had a strong instinctive inclination towards the notion of encountering the police, but the more he thought about it the more he doubted that a solitary person arriving in an unmarked car so late at night was to be counted amongst their numbers. If it was his assailant from earlier that day did he really want to take his chances, still ignorant as to what breed of adversary it might be? Mason decided it was best to remain in hiding for the time being. He heard the hall door downstairs open with a loud bang.

Mason held his breath, straining to hear every movement of his night time visitor. Heavy footsteps wandered their way through several downstairs rooms. Every now and then the steps would stop, settling themselves in a particular spot. Then the sound of rustling amongst the contents of a drawer or the opening of a cabinet could be heard. As Mason had spent very little time in this house, and had only rented it for instances when extraneous circumstances deemed its use necessary, there were very few of his actual belongings about, certainly nothing of importance or interest that he could recall. As he waited silently, barely even breathing, clutching his crude weapon, Mason heard a voice come to his ears from below. He could not hear the words clearly enough to determine what was taking place but was almost sure that there was only one person speaking. Despite this, the voice became louder, sounding aggravated, enraged, as though it were in an argument with itself. After a few seconds of silence between each consecutive outburst, Mason realised that the trespasser was using the downstairs telephone. Mason slipped from his hiding place. He crept quietly to the opposite side of the room and put the black receiver of the bedroom telephone to his ear. As he suspected, the two telephones operated on the same line. The voice downstairs was immediately amplified.

"Is he here?" the voice roared angrily. "I don't know where he is! What do I care? He could be asleep upstairs in bed for all I know! Listen, you paid me to do one job and one job only. I just called in here to try findin' a few things to leave in his apartment with the gun, make the rest of the boys believe it a little more. Maybe some more convenient pictures or bloody clothes, anythin' I can find. I'm still not convinced that the evidence is watertight. I'm ensurin' this job gets done right, but whatever else you're into is none of my business, okay?"

As Mason heard this last statement he suddenly recognised the voice as that of the fat man from his office, who had been so unwilling to approve of or involve himself in the thinner man's investigations. He remembered the unhealthy breathing and the disgusting, ever present sound of phlegm at the tip of the throat. Whoever was listening at the other end of the line was silent.

"Listen," the man continued, slightly more subdued, "you really don't want him to bump into us, or vice versa. It just complicates things. If he actually finds himself in custody, it's possible, not likely but possible, that he'll have some evidence or a different angle, to convince the guys that somethin' else might've really happened. I don't wanna run into him and have to make the arrest that's gonna ruin everythin'. You just keep working on silencin' him for good and then, when he can't say nothin', the evidence they have now will be the only thing left to tell them what happened, alright?"

Mason had come so far, was so deeply submerged in this subterranean empire of subterfuge, that it came as no surprise to him that his enemies had police on their payroll too. After other recent revelations and instalments of breaking news, it was going to take something monumental to shock Mason. Either way, until he could produce something that leant weight to his own version of events, the police were essentially his enemies, even the good ones. The voice on the other end remained silent. Mason was sure he could hear Albright's toxic respiration vibrating down the line, seeping out of the receiver to poison the very air he was breathing.

"So I'm goin' to his house now to plant the pistol, okay? Then my part is essentially done. Kill the son-of-a-bitch and I'll see to it that afterwards everyone finds the right bits of evidence and nobody finds anythin' that might inspire alternative theories. Then I'll be back in touch."

The man paused for a few seconds, as if drawing in a final chestful of air to enforce the impact of his parting statement.

"Make him bleed".

The line went dead and Mason crawled back into his hiding place. He listened to the contemptible policeman stumble around the rooms some more before the steps dragged their heavy owner back out through the front door. Mason waited until he had heard the car roar into life and reverse onto the street, before he hesitantly emerged from the wardrobe. Yet again he was placed on the back foot. He would have to take care of this 'pistol', and whatever it might serve to insinuate, before the more admirable members of the police force discovered it.

Although Mason had been followed, attacked, almost killed and knew that half the city was probably after him, it was the first time that he had ever heard someone specifically, remorselessly, state the intention of bringing about his death. The detective's last words resounded in his skull. He had to end this soon.

CHAPTER 21

It was almost five o' clock in the morning before Mason managed to pull himself back into the car. He had scraped enough money together from his temporary home, the last money he had access to in the world, and hired the car from an all-night rental company. The bare, uncomfortable seats felt like beds of silk beneath his suffering body as he had fallen inside. Now Mason was sitting upright and scanning the darkened streets around him. No lights had been lit and neither cars nor people, it would seem, were on his tail. As far as he could perceive, he had come and gone without notice. He switched the engine on and drove away.

Mason had returned to his apartment earlier that night. After overhearing the policeman's conversation he had reckoned it was best to go straight to his home, before day broke, before the detective had the entire police force re-examining his house and discovering what he could only assume was the gun that killed Sadler. He had parked the car two streets away and snuck up to the building carefully. As he suspected, a police car was parked outside the front door. However, Mason easily managed to gain entry undetected, simply climbing up a drainpipe at the back of the building and breaking in through one of the bathroom windows. There was no sign of any prior break-in that night and he could not prevent the thought from perturbing him that the obese, abhorrent detective had probably entered his apartment legally, with police supervision, while he himself had to slink and crawl in like an undesirable insect.

After entering the apartment, Mason had spent hours, undisturbed by the watchmen outside, feeling his way through the all-consuming darkness, hoping to find the weapon that could be the final nail in his coffin, the initiation of the soil being tossed upon his rotted carcass, placing cries of strife upon the lips of anybody left who may still have doubted the extent of his guilt. Even after his eyes had adjusted to the gloom, it was still a strange task exploring his apartment without the assistance of light. His hands crept beneath sheets, through drawers, behind clothes in wardrobes, searching desperately for whatever weapon lay hidden, hoping silently, deeply, to secure some sort of victory, some strike against his tormentors in this limitless nightmare, this constant downhill tumbling on the road towards his obliteration. For hours he checked and re-checked, behind sofas, through the cupboards of the kitchen, on the tops of bookcases. Mason found nothing. As the clock crept towards four in the morning, Mason began to wonder whether the detective had actually come to deliver his parcel, and cursed himself for not having left in time to follow him. It was possible that the detective would not make his drop-off for days. Mason sensed defeat and anguish scaling towards the rafters of his mind. He sat down on the floor, leaning the back of his neck against the soft comfort of a couch, trying to decide what his next actions were to be.

As he sat pondering, he suddenly remembered the package that he had received from Albright, with the photographs of the man who was now dead. Surely, if they were framing him, the contents of this envelope could act as evidence of Mason's innocence, or at least of Albright's involvement, and would have to be disposed of. Mason had buried it below a loose floorboard underneath his table. He dragged himself across the floor until he reached the board in question, only two feet in width, and violently jerked it out of its rightful place. Underneath, glowing despite the darkness, shining with its own gleam of gleeful intent, was an old fashioned pistol. Beside it lay a heavy, two-foot long, metal pipe stained with a dried-up, red liquid. Mason shuddered as he grabbed the instruments of death. They felt dangerous in his hands, as though the evil they had been implemented to ensure could no longer be prevented, that they had already served their purpose, done their due damage, and were now merely mocking him and the ignorant and the innocent, urging them on to further perfidious deeds. As he suspected, the other items were no longer beneath the loosened board.

Mason had snuck back out of his building via the same route and secretly returned to his car. Now, as he drove away, he tried to determine what his next move would be and what to do with these weapons. He could not leave them at his current hideout. If the crooked officer had found the rented home it would surely not be long before he tipped off the more righteous members of the police force as to its existence. Although he reckoned that the tools of death could possibly be used as evidence of the set-up, of the police corruption, he had to admit that he did not actually know what indecency they were indicative of. He did not know for sure whose blood or fingerprints were painted upon them and, even though the answer seemed obvious, it was not wise to assume exactly which crime scene they could be traced back to. There was possibly more than one. If he tried to present them as evidence of his innocence in regards to Sadler's death, he may have just ended up as a suspect in another case. In the current circumstances, with so many already convinced of his guilt, he decided it was better for the weapons to vanish, for their part in this game to be done away with entirely.

Mason could not think of anywhere suitable to hide them. Every location that entered his mind had a flaw, a possibility, no matter how slight, that one day somebody would find them there. The swamp of the harbour initially seemed perfect, but if a bystander reported the car crash, which could be traced back to him, perhaps they would trawl the sludge below. Generally a trawler went through the water there at least once a year anyway, searching for corpses and other bodies of evidence, as the crime rate continued to escalate in that beleaguered pocket of civilisation. No, the only solution was to destroy them completely, to wipe them from existence, to ensure that whatever wicked information they threatened to reveal would remain unknown, unsuggested to the impressionable world.

The sun was beginning to rise, as the night's attempt at offering relief from the blazing orb came to another end. The tall buildings along the horizon glowed with a deep, beetroot tint, a warning of the callous ferocity of the day to come. Mason did a sharp U-turn and sped in the direction that led towards the distant, industrial district on the edge of the city. An ideal solution to his problem was situated there, an abandoned but still semi-functional steel mill, where anything could be mangled, twisted and warped beyond recognition. He had used it before.

The creature watched Mason slip back into his car. Saliva gathered around the corners of its wicked mouth, as it licked the lips that surrounded its yellowed teeth. The time had now come. The death of Sadler had transformed the monster, it felt its bloodlust renewed. The desire for carnage it had felt rising during the days it had stalked Mason had now reached celestial levels, as though the release of blood would be the opening of the gates to the sanctity of an ungodly afterlife. As the years had crawled back from its aged body, the creature felt its old strength reborn, felt its muscles flexing with fresh force, felt the power surging through its revitalised body. This, however, was accompanied by the overriding urge to use said strength, the return of the irresistible need for destruction that had been merely simmering beneath the shallow surface of a body now bursting with overwhelming, and barely restrained, force. Mason would die today, of that the creature was sure. It knew that Mason had taken the weapons but it did not care. It was an impenetrable stalwart against the pull of rational thoughts, against the intricacies required in elaborate schemes of framing or police interaction. Its desires guided its mind and its needs were all it could dwell upon, more and more with each passing minute. It had accomplished all of its other tasks, destroyed all those that had stood in its master's way. Even though the taste of blood was still fresh, almost wet on its tongue, as long as Mason breathed it would not be able to quench this thirst. The monster managed to sustain a sufficient level of focus to operate the Jaguar it sat in and peeled away from the pavement after its prey. Mason would die today.

The industrial district sprawled out beyond the glass of the car windshield like the bones of an enormous, monolithic beast, dead and rotting, its pieces devoured by time, surrounded by dry sand, without a living thing in sight. The rising sun reflected a dull, dusty shine off the ruinous, desert landscape, scarred by abandoned factories and incomplete, forgotten constructions. Scraps and shards of beleaguered building had somehow found their way from the confines of their enclosures and crawled towards the road that Mason's car now navigated, turning sharply every few minutes to avoid another piece of wreckage. Fellow humans had been illusive back in the city, due to the early hour, but out here, in this destitute, dried-up excuse for a land, it was inconceivable to come across anybody who was not also concerned with the completion of some deleterious activity. In the distance one could make out the silhouettes of colossal, cumbersome drills, assumedly once designed to suck the earth dry for oil, now standing still as statues, unused in years, and beyond these the empty horizon hovered atop the sprawling, lifeless desert.

The car came to a stop outside a large, grey, antiquated and forsaken warehouse. Above the black, iron gates that hung open, an inscription read:

"Parksen and Sons Metalworks. Providing the finest for over 50 devoted years."

Mason wondered when the business had last been open. In this barren land it felt as though nothing had ever truly functioned, an apocalypse of failed, half-hearted schemes. Mason got out of his car, passed through the gates and walked along the cracked, litter-strewn path. The wooden door hung almost open, holding onto a single hinge, its paint completely peeled leaving its former colour a mystery. It somehow managed to keep its laboured grip upon the wall as Mason nudged it aside to walk past and enter a room of incalculable magnitude.

Machines of warped metal blanketed an area that seemed too overwhelmingly large to fit into the dimensions of the building as it appeared from the outside. Ancient machinations of branding, welding and twisting steel lay before him, their cogs and wheels reaching to the ceiling, obscuring the maze that continued to stretch forth behind them, only seeming to grow grander as Mason passed each one. Around the perimeters of the room several metal walkways rose high above ground level, granting the workers of old ample opportunity to access the different, lofty levels of the tall machines. Tools that may once have doubled as the mechanics of medieval tortures hung upon the wall. A thick layer of dust and cobwebs coated every inch of the warehouse and it rose in an explosion that made the air momentarily unbreathable, as Mason pressed a familiar button and several of the grinding engines creaked and achingly stretched their limbs into life, with loud, pained groans, the results of decades of almost complete inactivity.

The high-pitched squeals of these long-dormant devices, struggling to fight back the unwanted symptoms of years of disuse and rust, were loud enough to silence the sound of another car coming to a slow, decisive halt outside the forgotten factory.

Mason approached a machine used for the flattening of twisted metal into thin, creaseless sheets, before sharp, spinning blades sliced them into smaller strips, to be used for the reinforcement of unstable structures. A powerful, round, iron stamp viciously crushed everything that drifted its way upon the narrow, now-torn belt that nervously passed beneath it. Mason placed the iron pipe on the ruined strip and it was dragged, against its will, beneath the pounding force of this remorseless disc. The sound of it being flattened and diced was inaudible under the growling groan of the other machines. As he watched it disappearing, to emerge unrecognisable elsewhere in the factory as a simple block of utility steel, Mason unwittingly allowed an unwanted question to drift across his mind – what had been the outcome of the people who had been involved in the previous cases that had required him to pay this place a visit? Had he been sending people to a fate similar to Sadler's for years? Was this merely the first time that he was being forced to realise, to come face-to-face with, the existence of a crime that had been commonplace throughout his life?

He removed the gun from his jacket pocket. After studying it for a few seconds, he placed it upon the belt and watched it being ground down, witnessed an artefact of some interesting history, possibly fabricated, being erased, vanishing to be left unknown and undiscovered. Mason stood contemplating the weapons he had destroyed along with the events of the preceding week, the creeping, sneaking and hiding, the wretchedness his life had been reduced to. The sheer necessity of survival had taken control in the previous two days, slightly taking his mind off the overriding fear, confusion and questioning of his own sanity, the déjà vu, the dreams, when he remembered them, that had become even more powerfully, and tangibly, horrifying, often being eerie pre-echoes of what he could now only barely discern as his waking life. Were these echoes things that had come to pass or were they horrible premonitions of some nature, dark canvasses upon which the future was being painted. Mason felt uncomfortable thinking about it, remembering the shadowing cars, the fiery Jaguar and the face in Sadler's home that had haunted his subconscious at every moment since. As the gun disappeared from view, he pushed the button again and the machines died slowly and loudly, desperately struggling to remain in motion, stubbornly refusing to be doomed to another eternity of inactivity. The powerful devices came to a halt and Mason turned to leave as silence once more gained a hold on the sprawling, deserted warehouse.

A sudden, unnatural sound shot across the room, a disgusting gurgle, the sound of a bleeding throat, infected, filled with pools of stagnant spittle. Mason spun around in horror as this bizarre sound reached his ears. Standing upon one of the walkways, three levels up from the ground, leaning against the railing and leering down at Mason with that hideous smile, stood the man from the car outside Sadler's house and from inside the study on that vividly disturbing night.

The man still had that face devoid of any hair, but the skin that had previously appeared pale and pasty now consisted of a much darker tone, a lurid, ashen pallor. His tongue licked its way across a wide mouth, with lips the same colour as the rest of the deformed face, which formed that horrible smile that Mason had already encountered, that threatening and menacing grimace which revealed a row of long, sharp and pointed teeth. The eyes of the thing stared at Mason with the same passionate hatred, but now contained a new malicious excitement. They were two deeply black pupils, set upon eyeballs that were an unpleasant mix of yellow and white. Saliva dripped from both corners of its scarred mouth, savouring this moment of surprise.

Up until this moment, Mason had seen nothing of this fearsome figure aside from its face. Now it was dressed in a cheap, cream overcoat but it was clear that it was enormous by the proportions of an average man. It rose to a tall six foot six or so, and appeared even larger to Mason as it towered on the platform above him, glowering at him with glee. Even beneath the folds of the coat it was easy to identify muscle bulging to an unnatural extent, stretching every seam of the material, threatening to rip the fabric surrounding the monster's shoulders at any moment. It seemed as though the walkway itself was struggling with all its might to support the weight of this behemoth, this force of nature. It stood there for what seemed several minutes to Mason, skewering the image of his weaker flesh with its glare, moving nothing other than its thirsty tongue, which swept the saliva from its lips into its mouth, only for the poisonous liquid to flood back over the brim seconds later.

Mason dared not turn away, to allow this thing to proceed in initiating its duty, which he could only assume was the fulfilment of his murder. The figure stretched out a powerful arm to point a swollen forefinger at Mason. A foul utterance erupted from its throat, sounding as though the figure was coughing up blood and bile that had been caught in its internal passages for an agonising age. The figure pulled a lever to its right and the deafening roar returned of machines coming to life, echoing around the kaleidoscopic room, that suddenly seemed to Mason significantly magnified, an impenetrable puzzle from which one might never escape. As the growl of the engines swept all other sound from Mason's mind and sent his senses into a dizzying whirl, the figure ran along the walkway, through a blast of steam and out of sight behind the maze of machines, readying itself somewhere to tear its prey apart.

Mason turned upon the spot as the engines whizzed and whirred about him, more of their number switched on bit by bit, drowning him further in confusion. He looked around for something, anything, to use against this titanic force. Clearly it had waited until he had destroyed the weapons before revealing itself, leaving Mason weak and defenceless, just a battle of bodies, of pure physical force. He slowly advanced in the general direction of the entrance, which lay several rows of machinery away, out of sight, a sacred holy-ground offering salvation from this playground of punishment. As he passed wall after wall of metal in this world of twirling steel and grinding iron, he quickened his pace, getting ever closer to the door. His excitement rose to a panic as he further extricated himself from the heart of the factory. He became careless, running faster and faster, ignoring what might be waiting behind any of the machines, the thought racing through his mind that he could reach his car before the monster reached the ground floor.

An immense clenched fist, veins threatening to burst through the dark skin with a combination of force and tension, swung from around a corner behind the glowing blaze of a welding station and smashed its way directly into Mason's face. The power of the blow threw Mason back several feet until he crashed against a great, grinding blade, growling angrily after an age of despondency. His body ached from the roughness of the landing while his head swam from the force of the assassin's strike. The impact alone left him feeling as though he had been charged by a rhinoceros. He struggled to his feet and, with his eyesight blurred from the severity of the blow, attempted to stumble away, in what direction he did not know, any passage away from the shadow of the gargantuan figure that lay in the periphery of his brutalised vision.

Mason, battling to remain upright, leaned against the jungle of iron, pulling himself forward, possibly no longer even towards the door, his body threatening to fall with every movement. A haze of machinery spun around him as he tried to refocus his sight.

He heard the loud crunch before he felt the full impact of another superhuman strike. The creature emerged from somewhere behind him and all Mason had noticed was the gleam of the sharp teeth that seemed to be savouring the taste of his corpse, adding to the excitement of the kill. Next he lay slumped against one of the walls, beneath where the apparent torture instruments hung, his consciousness threatening to surrender before long. His head hung to one side, affording him a view of the dark, heavy boots approaching, almost cracking the floor beneath them as they slowly advanced, the gurgling of the beast contending with the roar of the machines and the ringing and throbbing in Mason's bruised, swollen skull. His entire body felt shaken by the crashes to his temples. His stomach was winded and his bones trembled beneath thin layers of wounded flesh and pale skin. He had no idea how many teeth were missing, loose or cracked in his mutilated mouth as he spat out a mixture of bone and blood, leaving remains rattling around the inside of his mouth.

Mason made an effort to battle the oncoming eternal sleep, to elevate himself to his knees. His limp body almost refused to obey but he felt himself going beyond the realms of mere physical exertion as he rose to his feet and threw out a fist, infused with all the remaining muscle he could manage to muster. Despite Mason's doubtless strength, it was nothing compared to that of this thing that stood before him. He felt his right hand being stopped midway through its punch by the force of an open palm in the opposite direction. The creature's hand wrapped itself around his fist, crushing and cracking several fingers with loud snaps. Mason screamed as he felt his hand being rendered useless, felt the ripping beneath his skin. Blood had by now begun to run into his eyes, drenching his already blurred vision with a demented, red curtain. The evil smile now appeared even more deliriously eager to murder.

Mason felt one of the creature's giant sets of fingers wrap around his throat, lift his body and slam it into the wall he had laid against seconds before, squeezing the air from him as easily as it departed from a punctured tyre. His body jerked and twisted involuntarily, struggling to combat this colossal strength that dominated it so forcefully. He could feel his soul slowly starting to slip away as the grip around his neck tightened, as his eyes became foggier and the throbbing in his head sunk to a numb semi-consciousness. He feebly stretched out his left arm to attempt one last strike and felt his hand brush against something sharp and jagged hanging from the wall alongside him, something that seemed to tear at his fingers as they touched it. It was assumedly one of the medieval tools he had spotted before. Mason could just about determine that the creature's eyes were still directed at him. It was sucking in through its grimacing, colourless lips, waiting to gorge on the flesh of its prey with those protruding pointed, predator's fangs. Mason came close to passing out with the effort it took him to quickly, with one agonising movement, lift the heavy blade from the wall with his left arm and swing its murderous spike round towards the side of the creature's head, plunging it in deep beneath the monster's ear, before pulling the weapon out once more. The beast let out an unearthly, howling shriek, like the sound of thick glass being scraped upon by blunt nails, released its grip on Mason's throat and reeled backwards, now clutching its own neck with its monstrous mandibles.

The adrenaline rush, the survival instinct, now surging powerfully within Mason, overrode the pain and feebleness of his body, and he lunged forward striking again, this time in the stomach, knocking the creature to the floor. Mason leaned upon the spike and twisted it as his enemy howled. As he withdrew the weapon, scraps of organ and tissue came along with it, stuck to the barbed blades. Mason sat atop the beast and began stabbing furiously, again and again, without thinking or hesitating, driving the metal deep within the monster's body, enjoying the infliction of pain, now savouring their clash in his own bestial manner, greedily drinking in the monster's moans with a barbarous thirst. Blood splashed across his clothes and his face, mixing with his own, as Mason struggled to decide whether this was merely the continuation of another violent nightmare or was actually taking place.

The creature lay twitching spasmodically, breathing heavily, drowning in a fountain of its own blood. Mason saw the blunt blade of an axe hanging upon the same wall where he had found his first murderous instrument. The weapon was surprisingly light and, with only one able arm to wield it, Mason plunged it into the creature's enormous chest, before pulling it out in another spray of gore. The beast succumbed to the violence and lay still.

Mason collapsed, exhausted, upon the dusty, littered floor and slumped against the rear side of a rattling furnace, that shook to the point of near explosion due to a lack of fuel inside with which to run on. The force of his own violence had shocked Mason, the number of times he had stabbed the defeated body, mercilessly plunging the blade in, enjoying the sensation of ruthless power until life had been extinguished. He had been reduced to their level, to a mere animal, killing, perhaps for survival, in self-defence, but nonetheless with relish, with an uncontrollable, primeval passion.

Half of his shattered body was limp or even numb, the other half ached. After the painful ringing through his skull and the savage sounds of the struggle, the simple, mechanical clanging of the machines now sounded like a peaceful silence. Mason began to crawl on all fours towards what he thought was the exit. He heard a crack behind him.

Mason slowly turned his head in disbelief and the sight of the corpse moving met his incredulous eyes. Fingers first, then arms and knees, began to move slightly, sluggishly, before the torso slowly lifted itself from the ground. The creature's head gradually directed its glare towards Mason, fixing his delusional mind with its stare of contempt. Then the ravaged beast began to crawl, supporting itself with an inconceivable strength, towards Mason.

Panicking, not knowing where to turn, in which direction to hope for escape, Mason found himself trying to pull his own fractured frame up the steps of a staircase towards the walkways overhead. His left hand still clutched the axe, while with his right arm he leaned on the banister despite the broken fingers' cry of pain. He slowly scaled the flights of stairs, looking back every few seconds to see the monster a little closer, pulling itself towards him on all fours as it left a river of red in its wake. He reached the second floor and began to drag himself along the metal walkway, the sweat and blood that dripped from him falling through its considerable cracks, oiling the ancient cogs of the machines far below. Eventually the exertion overcame him and Mason fell upon his back.

He turned to see the monster's head appearing at the top of the stairway. Moments later the rest of the body followed. Mason watched in horror as, painfully, steadily and inexplicably, the monster lingered on the spot for an instant before rising to its knees and then standing, almost completely upright. It stumbled towards Mason, its stare now one of determination, the venomous smile absent from its bloodless lips, replaced instead with an animalistic urge to simply finish this abnormal, otherworldly feud. It slowly stepped forward, inches at a time, leaning on the side railing that shook beneath its huge body, leaking litres of its life with every movement. Mason watched in fear as it drew closer. This time there would be no toying with him, no punches or throws, just a simple crushing of his skull or snap of the neck.

Mason decided his course of action then and there, and followed it through without hesitation, before he had an opportunity to alarm himself and change his mind. As the old, rickety walkway shook beneath the lurching bulk of his opponent, Mason picked a particular spot, eaten away by rust and disrepair, where two sheets of the decaying metal had been connected and, somehow clutching the safety railing with his deformed right hand, struck the walkway with the axe, using all of his force. The landing shook beneath him and threw the two of them off balance, as a deep gash appeared in the metal, loosening the flimsy support beneath their feet. The monster continued its unstoppable forward momentum, nearing the end of its hunt. As Mason readied another strike it was only a step away from him, one arm outstretched, ready to eradicate.

The second blow cut to the heart of the walkway, leaving a gap so large that the two connected sheets of metal began to twist in opposite directions, turning almost onto their sides as they battled. The creature, midway through its final lunge at Mason, grabbed for his feet just as the tension between the two sheets peaked and, with a sharp, shrill screech, they snapped and fell away from each other. The combatants' side of the walkway bent downwards, swinging from side to side, just barely attached by its other end to the next stable sheet above. Mason had let the axe fall and now clung to the railing with both hands. He could feel his grip on the dangling railing weakening as the weight of the beast pulled at his right leg, the strength of the creature tearing through both his resistance and flesh.

As they swung in their struggle of suffering, Mason heard a loud rip. He readied himself for the descent of the walkway to the ground beneath, for the two of them to drop to their death together. Instead he felt a surprising lightness return to his leg and looked down to see the monster falling, a small piece of the material from his trousers clutched in its fists, towards the wicked machines below. The beast fell two floors into the heart of a machine, grinding and slicing beneath it. With its unnatural strength used up, the creature had no chance of resisting the pull of the mechanical cogs that sucked it into the man-made jaws. Mason watched as its giant body was rapidly thrust inwards by the unstoppable force of the wheels, being massacred to a revolting pulp, sinew and bone snapped and bent beyond the recovery of even this sadistic monster. After he pulled himself up to the remaining walkway once more, Mason looked over the edge to see destroyed body parts emerging to the surface of the wheels in different places, as the monster was rendered piece from piece, finally destroyed by the power of the iron's crushing and tearing. Mason dragged himself to the nearest stairs, where the surface beneath him was stable once more, and collapsed as though entering a coma, unable to maintain consciousness any longer, unsure as to whether he would wake or not, whether his body had been beaten too badly, too far beyond the brink of self-sustenance.

CHAPTER 22

Somehow, instead of falling into the folds of the abyss, Mason's body awoke, reviving itself in an abandoned warehouse, caked with dirt and dried blood. As he staggered to an upright position, his heavy, swimming head, spun by a seemingly constant force, would not afford his eyes an opportunity to focus. Mason slowly descended the staircase and stumbled towards the door in an attempt to finally leave this mausoleum of murder and madness. He winced as, through force of habit, he used his right hand for support, which each time reminded him, with stabs of pain, of its mutilated fingers. As his eyes regained some semblance of sight he looked around to see the body of the thing strewn about the room, some parts still stuck in machines, others lying isolated on the dusty, stone factory floor. There was nothing to be done with it. It would be beyond his abilities to ensure that the body parts were disposed of, so scattered was their current state. Regardless, nobody would be coming out to this place anytime soon. He had more important things to be concerned with. He realised that he had arrived at the point where the law abiding brand of justice he aspired to administer was becoming an unattainable dream. He had still not contacted Rachel and this homicidal attack had shot his nerves, sent his mind into feverish concern for her safety. She was the only, even moderately, innocent person connected to the case who was still alive. She had to be saved, perhaps for his own sake as much as hers.

Mason picked out a small blade from the armoury hanging upon the wall and dragged his forlorn feet through the front door. Outside the sun was beginning to settle, to be buried beneath the industrial graveyard. He had lain unconscious in the factory for most of the day. Virulent visions of massacre and mayhem had surged through and haunted his sleeping brain, but once more he could not remember the exacts of his dreams. It occurred to him that since his hearing of Sadler's death, his real world had become more dreamlike, more surreal, macabre and brutal, while his dreams had mostly returned to being visions that vanished with daylight.

Mason noticed the Jaguar that he had encountered the day before, parked behind his own car. He broke a window to open its door, before half-heartedly searching the interior for anything that might be of note. There was nothing. He decided to memorise the license plate number, telling himself that perhaps it would turn out to be useful, but he was fully aware that his mind would, in reality, discard the digits almost instantaneously. An inner voice told him that he already knew how all this was going to end.

Mason drove towards Rachel's home, determined to ensure her safety, terrified of what could happen if he did not reach her in time. He had been occupied one way or another for the entirety of the preceding two days but now nothing would stand in his way. With all that had taken place, with all the destruction he had contributed towards, he believed that she was his responsibility, that it was largely his fault that the stakes had been so terrifyingly raised in this torturous game.

His limp right hand barely managed to lie lifeless on the seat beside him while his left manoeuvred the vehicle through the roads of this listless town. Despite the oncoming evening, and the hour being at hand when most people would be leaving work, the roads en route were completely deserted. During Mason's sleep, the intense, scathing heat had finally broken and, after weeks of dryness and drought, heavy drops of irregular rain began to splash upon the scorched earth. They hissed themselves into the form of steam as they came into contact with the burning hot concrete and evaporated immediately, leaving no trace of their having ever existed. Perhaps people were hiding indoors, hibernating safely, seeking shelter from the storm that was prophesised by the sky, coming to replace the chastising fire that had ruthlessly governed the city for weeks. As he pulled up outside the building Mason contemplated what he was going to say, or why indeed he had really come. Regardless of the answer, Mason decided to accept the fact that he was here now and ready himself for whatever lay waiting inside. For a sensation deep inside the pit of his stomach told him with a firm certainty that surprises of an unpleasant nature were lurking around these corners.

Mason stepped out of the car into a crisp, biting wind. The sudden change in temperature seemed uncanny and he wrapped his loose-fitting suit jacket around him as tightly as it would stretch. He clasped his hand upon the handle of the front door of the building. It was covered in a disgusting, greasy substance. As Mason stepped through the door he noticed an attendant at a desk that had not previously been there. Perhaps the tenants of the building were somehow getting demands met, for better living conditions, for improved security. If the latter were true, then the solution offered had failed to have the desired effect, as the attendant was asleep. For some reason this immediately heightened Mason's sense of undeniable dread. He turned for the crumbling stairs and bounded the steps three at a time to the third floor, to reach her before it was too late.

The door to Rachel's jaded apartment now came into view at the end of the corridor. As Mason approached he observed that the lock had been smashed almost entirely off the door. His mind raced to recall his last visit. Had he broken the lock? He felt sure that he had left the door securely closed

Mason cautiously entered the room, making sure to close the door behind him, his right hand clutching the blade buried in his pocket, ready to carve. The material of the handle felt rough and recently used, as though there was a foreign substance sitting atop its ingrained fabric. It was dark inside and he flicked the switch on an old, dusty lamp, barely emitting sufficient light to battle the gloomy, sordid squalor of the room. Mason took in his surroundings quickly and saw that the room was in the same state as it had been on his previous visit. Magazines, newspapers, cigarette butts and empty bottles were flung about carelessly, the gaps between them on the floor revealing rare patches of carpet, the latter of which stretched itself to breaking point just to maintain any slight command over the rotting, wooden floor beneath.

Everything else was in its rightful place, announcing its presence just as unpleasantly as before. The mirror hung, filthy with a sticky, oil-like substance which seemed to slither down its ugly surface, above the abandoned marble fireplace, still blackened from the smoke of ancient, glorious fires. The thought of this long extinguished fire caused Mason to shiver. He walked quickly to the drawn curtains and threw them open. Outside the turbulent night sky fought back against the dim light of the room, pits of black surrounded by heavy clouds that had the hinting touch of ice whispering about their fringes.

Mason then remembered why he had come here. He turned around to see Rachel lying stretched out, asleep, upon the settee as he had seen her for the first time, with her head resting upon the familiar, pink pillow, decorated by the red candle. He succumbed to an immediate sense of relief, followed shortly afterwards by another sickly feeling of déjà vu. On this occasion she was adorned with an alluring, purple, full-length dress of exquisite silk. Her hair was now clean and free falling along the length of her back. Her face was free of bruises or blotches, her pale skin now glowing beautifully beneath the faint light of the lamp.

Mason was pleased that the woman's situation had somehow remarkably improved. Regardless, he felt an inexplicable need to talk to her, to determine which side she was on, to make sure no trouble had come or been brought her way. Was this finery the result of a deal she had struck with Albright to keep her under his control, to tell the police about Mason's questions? Or was it easier to simply kill a woman like her, someone nobody cared about from a part of town that nobody visited. Mason had to be sure, he had to discover her story. For all he knew there could be more assassins, more violent underlings of evil on the way there that minute, blades glinting beneath the forks of lightning that were sure to strike from the sky before long.

He approached her gently and whispered "Rachel" in her ear.

She remained motionless. Again he uttered her name, this time louder, and elicited no response. He tapped her lightly on the cheek, hoping to rouse her without causing alarm.

To his horror he merely roused a vile, thick black liquid from inside her mouth and watched it slowly roll down the side of her face like boiling tar. Mason jumped back in shock as the liquid continued to emerge from the crevasse of her mouth, rolling down her body, now meeting the dress and staining it irretrievably with its dense, ebony evil. As it passed her neck he noticed for the first time several marks that had engraved themselves upon it, dirty, black imprints, in the shape of a large man's fingers. A horrific sweat broke out over Mason, the liquid immediately freezing to a startling cold the instant it formed itself upon his skin. He felt the physical pains in his body, the numerous wounds and soon-to-be scars, but this blow was deeper. The one goal that had kept him walking, struggling upon his doomed path, had been intrinsically linked to the safety of this woman, the one innocent life remaining. The marks were buried deep into her flesh, almost penetrating her throat with their remarkable power. The creature had prepared its revenge for Mason. Clearly it had been here before turning its attention towards him, ruthlessly eliminating everyone who now posed a threat to Albright's abominable machinations. He leant forward to examine her and realised that she had deliberately been placed upon the pillow to lend the appearance of normality, but when he lifted her closer Rachel's head rolled to and fro like that of a broken daffodil.

He sensed bile brimming, boiling inside of him. He became violently weak, beginning to tremble uncontrollably, and embraced her neck, feeling almost nothing there at all. It was as though the bones inside had been completely removed and there now remained little beyond a thin layer of skin, flesh and the black liquid, which continued to pour forth, stronger now, more powerfully. Mason noticed the immobility of his numb right hand, before the rest of his body went limp and he crumpled into a heap upon the floor. He opened his mouth to howl in anguish but could only force a pained whimpering noise to emerge. Mason had not wept in a long time, since an instance which he could not recall, and was unaware if this was how it was supposed to feel. He sat staring out of the window as the skies grew whiter, not through the act of brightening but in the crescendo of preparation for the impending storm. Every one of his different emotions battled to burst forth from his soul at once, but nothing came. All he felt was bitter, bitter cold, the futility of his life and the guilt of the sufferings of so many people. Rage gradually began to assume control, rage and bloodlust. The law of the civilised world could not serve him anymore and counted for nothing. Justice would be done by any means necessary.

CHAPTER 23

Mason's frail figure ploughed through the storm, almost oblivious to its driving force, its insistent bursting against his body, as it screeched challenges to his constant, steady stride. The sky was an intoxicating blend of dark and bright. The familiar shade of the deepest black, polluted sky splattered with an unstoppable, seismic spray of white snow. It assaulted those below with such severity, such ravenous, venomous bite that it became unreasonable to belittle it with the title of snow, rather sheets of sharp, slicing ice, striking from the sky, as if tridents thrown by some god of the storms.

They crushed against Mason's suit, entrenching themselves in its material and ultimately settling there. The melted drops of liquid meticulously brought out the different hues of blood smeared across his clothes, presenting him as though he were a character in a stained glass pane of sparkling red and white, placed against a blackened backdrop. The storm was too deep, too dense, and the night too dark, to see further than a few feet ahead. To any observer deranged enough to be outside on this detestable night, Mason must have appeared a strange, pitiful being, stumbling through this vicious, pitiless world, his clothes thin and torn, one limp arm dragged along by the remainder of his body, a pathetic figure slowly using every portion of whatever strength he still possessed to make it through this blizzard, persisting towards whatever cruel destiny awaited him.

Within himself, however, Mason roared like a furnace. He scarcely noticed the weakness of his body, the fragility of his state, and paid no attention to the raging torments about him. The powerful blasts from the sky were pummelling his unprotected face, relentlessly assaulting his exposed mouth and eyes, but he strode forward barely even blinking. His careening mind ignored his body, ignored the world, ignored everything but the thought of punishment. Or revenge. Whether there was a difference anymore.

He was fully aware of the reality that when all of the facts were summarised, he still knew virtually no details of the case, of what had really happened to these people and to himself, or why. He was unable to understand how a lot of the things that he had seen were even possible, but such matters were no longer important to him. His mind blazed with quiet fury, focusing itself with murderous method. He felt guilt, remorse, anger and most of all an overriding urge, desire and need to bring about retribution. Not the just retribution that he had convinced himself was still achievable, that could still be grasped, mere hours ago. This was justice of another kind. This affair had sprawled and spewed itself beyond the realms and rules of those uninvolved. There was, and always had been, only one way it was going to end. He now acknowledged this beyond doubt, resigning himself to realising the futility of his attempts to salvage his situation, and his life, by normal means. He had been foolish in convincing himself of this possibility when all along the actuality of the finale had dangled to and fro beneath the ignorant layers of his conscious mind, knowing that sooner or later it would surface so vehemently. Now death was all that remained. This was the only path left to tread. In the city, that stood twisting and bending, contracting under the force of the storm, its heat pounded beams and columns struggling to adjust to the new conditions and demands of their habitat, nothing was left for him. The police hounded him, both the corrupt and the just, and had claim to an avalanche of evidence, while he had nothing. The life of just one person besides his own had encouraged him to keep going, to pursue and finish the job in the hope of that life's protection. Now that person had perished. He had little reason to live, but plenty of reasons to take the life of another.

Perhaps his entire life of evil had been bringing him to this point, walking without hesitation along the waterfront, to the lair of his nemesis. Perhaps the spirits of all those people that he had kidnapped, because really there was no other word for it, that he had never cared for nor known the fate of, had orchestrated this operatic tragedy that led him along the rotting planks, his right arm dangling lifelessly, his left clutching a pistol, the steel almost becoming one with the skin of his frozen hand in the consummation of ice. He had found the old weapon amongst the belongings of the dead woman, clearly buried too deeply to have been of any use to her. He deserved this. He had deserved this for a long time. His existence had been awaiting its due for an age, dealt out now by the reading of the weights that hung upon the scales of right and wrong. Perhaps he would have suffered an ulterior horrific fate years ago if it had not been for the necessity of this moment. He had needed to realise his guilt, to know that so much of this massacre was on his head, to recognise that to an extent he had killed Raymond Sadler. He had needed to know that if he died tonight nothing lay for him beyond the grave other than pain. He could only hope that perhaps somewhere, some force of the universe would recognise that for one brief, passing point in his cursed, despicable life he was attempting to do the right thing and, if not the right thing, the only just action that he could distinguish; that it would recognise that he had tried, and most likely given his life, to remove an evil greater than himself from the world, to wrestle Albright down towards the inferno in a violent, eternal grapple.

"Mr. Mason, you have sealed your own fate and now you are doomed."

These were the last words Albright had spoken to him and they had rung true. However, Mason had sealed his fate far before that conversation and had possibly always been doomed to this surreal and sinister conclusion.

His body, devoid of physical feeling, existing and sustaining itself solely on pulsating, seething, hate-filled force of will, continued to travel across this wasteland of biting snow, brittle wood and broken steel, until something displayed itself in the darkness before his battered eyes. Between the blizzard and the bluntly, overpowering black of the night, a sign was visible. It hung, suspended by two brass chains, from a wooden post. Despite hanging loosely, exposed and bared to take the brunt of this supernatural storm, it was not being shaken by the blasts of wind. In fact it barely stirred at all and no snow settled upon its thick, wooden top, or even atop the post from which it hung. It was a sign depicting a ship being dragged down towards a fiery blaze, with all of those on board destined for death, even if they did not yet know it. Mason had seen it somewhere before but was not sure whether it had been in a dream or waking life. Which one, indeed, was more real, and which was more bizarre? Which one had become more painful? Either way, he now knew where to go. He turned down the path that was obscured to the point of invisibility by the elements, merely knowing it was the right direction. It was time.

He stumbled into the familiar passageway, slamming the door shut behind him, and suddenly became aware of the extreme bestial bite of the cold outside now that he was thrust into warmer surroundings. He stood hunched over, his body shuddering as it adjusted to the shock of the new temperature. This temple of evil seemed warm and humid, the air smothered with that sickly, sweet smell, no matter how the world heaved outside. The snow from his suit fell to the floor and melted with resigned defeat, before soaking through the stones to the restless, raging sea beneath.

Minutes before, Mason had arrived at the small flight of steps, in the midst of the tempest, and descended them with difficulty, the wind ready to send him tumbling down as he tried to keep his footing on the icy stone. All around the building the sea had started to rise up. Vast depths of water were twirling, were twisting themselves with loud claps into the air, as high as they could conceivably lift themselves, before their strength left them and they sunk hopelessly back down to their pool of origin. Waves had been breaking along the pathway, threatening, with each step Mason took, to force him into the freezing water, the spray of their crash showering him as if in competition with the snow. As he had neared the building, he had borne witness to a contest of force between the water on either side of the walkway, both sides trying to push the other backwards, and they seemed to sway and teeter in this reverse tug-of-war. On any other occasion Mason would have deemed it an unwise idea to even consider descending the stairs, let alone entering this building, which lay under and in the midst of this howling body of water. However, tonight the natural world was far from the greatest danger and he felt sure that fate would not permit him to suffer injury until he had entered the demonic dungeon. He had knocked loudly upon the door before readying his pistol, but when no answer came he kicked it open himself, a feat he would have deemed impossible days ago, due to the sheer strength and weight of the door. Nonetheless it had swung open easily. Perhaps something had wanted him to enter. Perhaps, after all the entranceways he had unlawfully burst through in the days prior to this netherworld of night, he was being granted safe passage through one final portal.

With the door closed behind him and his body adjusting to the warmth, Mason slowly began to make his way along the corridor to the bar. So far the place was deathly silent, the tormented storm outside and the blasting crash of the waves against the exterior walls of this tunnel creating the only sounds. After a particularly loud crash a few drops of water would come trickling in through gaps in the stones of the wall, leaving Mason with the impression that the hallway was due to cave in on itself momentarily.

As he journeyed down the dark passageway, crawling ever closer to the core, the pungent smell assaulted his nostrils once more. For the first time Mason recognised it. He had smelt it a lot in recent times. He had tasted it. He had felt its smooth, warm caresses as it had trickled between his fingers and from his head. It had smeared his clothes a brutal, ruby red, painting him as a disturbing figure, a savage, remorseless warlord. The scent was warm and fresh. It saturated the air as though it had been used to make the wax of the candles that burned, emanating their vile odour, at the passage's end, as though it had been smeared, still moist, across the very face of the walls. Perhaps it was Sadler's. Perhaps Mason had known the smell all along.

He turned to enter the bar. Once again it was hushed and deserted. The loud waves still crashed around it but an uncomfortable quiet reigned within, as though the walls fought a battle with the beasts outside to keep this silent sanctuary just as it was, to forbid any sound within. The candles cast great, lurching shadows across the room and their light served to make the distant corners even darker. Their shimmering flames constituted the only movement in the room, besides Mason's heavy breathing, as they flickered in the wind, constantly threatening to surrender and abandon the room to blackness. The flicker made the shadows dance across the faces of the pillars, giving one who looked upon the scene a sensation similar to seasickness, as though the room itself was shaking, shifting, transforming before their gaze. Mason shook his head, ignoring this dazzlingly unstable wilderness, this element-fuelled illusion, and crossed the room to step through the next door.

Albright's office was similarly devoid of action or sound. No evil eyes waited to glare through Mason. No shark-like smile gleamed at him. No noise echoed from outside either. This room was silent, free from the thunderous roar of the sea, as though Albright had fortified this particular part of his stronghold, ensuring that the heart of his labyrinth could not be disturbed, even by the formidable powers of nature. The room's appearance was as it had been on his previous visits, but struck Mason with more overbearing power than usual. The ceiling seemed to climb to a more commanding altitude, allowing the foul scent from the candles outside to rise to an even loftier height, to taint heaven with its impurity. The lamps positioned in the four corners were switched off and the room was governed by a dark gloom, broken every few seconds by the bright blasts of lightning flashing through the panes of glass that dwelt about the summit of the ceiling. The only thing lacking in this vision of ungodly opulence was the master himself.

Mason's eyes examined the paintings above his head for the final time. They had seemingly changed again. The whale was now locked in a bloody final conflict with the ship's captain. The corpses of the crew drifted upon the ocean and the captain stood upon the only piece of the vessel still floating, harpoon ready to drive into the beast's brain, while the whale's jaws had already begun to close around him, trapping the two in a death pact. In the second painting, the crew lay scattered about the deck, skewered and butchered, their blood drenching the planks, while others hung from the masts by their necks. The boat was a mass grave, without a living soul in sight. In the third there was no longer any vessel visible at all, only a depiction of the sun rising as a storm subsided, after sucking all that had dared to tread the crests of its waves below. In the final painting a sole survivor, thinned to an unimaginable measure, feasted on the raw, rotting, disease-ridden flesh of his dead comrades' bodies. Mason scanned these jarring images, both in disbelief and resignation. He did not know how they could have changed and he did not know what the changes meant. He was unsure whether or not this was part of the on-going dream that had become intrinsic to his universe, or whether his madness had finally claimed a full and fatal victory over his senses. However, in whatever demented reality in which he currently resided, it mattered little what had happened. This was the path he had chosen, the world he now occupied, and he had no choice but to accept whatever it presented to him. His eyes now fixed themselves on the door behind Albright's desk, through which the villain had come and gone on the occasions of their interviews. A new bastille of intrigue. Mason crossed the room and readied himself for whatever waited on the other side.

Behind the darkened, oak door was another room, furnished as luxuriously as the previous one but far smaller. The same soft carpet slid across the floor and similar patterns climbed the walls up towards a high ceiling, while a table and a single chair were the sole occupants of the space. The room was little more than a junction, an office or reception of sorts, with three doors leading from it. These doors did not concern Mason. The object that immediately gripped his undivided attention sat upon the table. He approached slowly, his heavy footfall silenced by the carpet, and saw a small pile of photographs waiting.

The picture that resided on top displayed two familiar men in brown suits, sitting at a table in a familiar house. One of them was leaning backwards in his chair, somehow pulling off an incredible balancing act as he hovered inches above the floor. Albright stood threateningly over him, his arms twisted round due to the force of the blow he had just struck. Mason resumed the impatient scan he had started in the development laboratory days before, with no regard for where the pictures had come from or why they had been left lying upon this desk. Mason was only concerned with viewing the final photographs in this treasured, highly sought after series. What had been the cause of all this suffering?

The following photographs showed the other man rising from his chair and stepping forward, while the man on the ground struggled to return to his feet. Albright was standing still as they moved in stop motion, before withdrawing a pistol from his suit. The halting movements of the two men stopped and all three stood frozen as the photographs continued. Three other large men entered the room. Two of them positioned themselves behind the man in the brown suit who was standing, while the other restrained the one who had been knocked to the ground. One of the large men began taking something from his pocket, an object that appeared to be a roll of wire or cable. He unrolled a small length of it and raised his arms above the head of the man who was still standing. Suddenly a noticeable change came across the characters in the room. Everyone's attention turned towards the camera stationed outside. Albright looked up at the window that the photographer had been surveying through and the photograph at the bottom of the pile showed the weapon in his grasp flashing brightly. So Sadler, assuming it was Sadler who had taken these pictures, had been caught, had positioned himself too close to something big, something secret. Albright and his men had seen the eavesdropper outside, and running away had only been the futile delaying of a verdict which he had sentenced himself to on that very day. These people knew how to hunt. One look, one glimpse of a face, was sufficient for a man like Albright to track a person down, to make them regret every second of their life, to send someone like Mason after them. Mason wondered where the pictures had been. Had Sadler confessed under torture? Although it was too late to make any difference, he somehow felt a strange sense of satisfaction in knowing that the photographs had actually existed. They showed assault, at the very least, and also what appeared to be the intent and preparation to kill. If these two men had disappeared then this evidence could be considered condemning. Albright could see out the remainder of his life in an extremely unenviable position, with his wealth and power having abandoned him, if these photographs were revealed to the world. To somebody like Albright, they would seem worth murdering for.

"We found them in her apartment, before we snapped her pretty neck."

A voice behind Mason darted into the previously silent confines of the little office, a voice he vaguely recognised but could not precisely place. Mason turned around slowly. Three men stood in Albright's large chamber, glaring at him, one with a ridiculous, unsettling grin fixed upon his face.

Mason thought he recognised the man on the left. He was, more or less, of the same dimensions as the first person he had encountered in this whole venture, the man who had brought the assignment to his home a little over a week before, that had delivered this curse to his door. He wore the same suit, sunglasses and hat, but seemed somehow larger, more imposing and intimidating. His hands no longer displayed the complex network of burst veins and were now wrapped by smooth, white skin.

The right side of this trio consisted of the burly, corrupt detective, a brooding scowl his only expression. He continuously shifted his position with an obvious sense of discomfort. It was clear he did not want to be there. He was assisting in the completion of a dangerous job that he had accepted and had now been brought right to the hub of the ghastly tale. He wiped his perspiring forehead and waited to see what move the other men made.

In between them there stood a young man, the one with the eerie, lurid smile, who was staring at Mason. He was thin, but appeared both strong and powerful nonetheless, and he stood straight, confident in the force of his body. He looked far younger than the other two, as though he could be no more than thirty years of age. Neatly cropped hair of the darkest black was combed to run backwards along his scalp. His skin was darker than the others, shining with a healthy complexion, and his face lacked the natural wrinkles and creases of the other men. Despite his apparent youth, he exuded an air of power and confidence, a man used to being listened to, used to punishing those who disobeyed. The psychotic grin upon his face revealed a set of dazzlingly, white teeth, the perfect weapon for tearing through flesh.

He continued standing motionless, glaring at Mason mischievously, as though he laughed at Mason's naivety, his innocence at failing to understand a joke, as though the keeper of a secret, who enjoyed the slow descent of the guillotine upon another's body and mind. He wore a suit of the plushest, black velvet, as if it were designed for sole the purpose of lying beneath diamonds in a shop front window, and he seemed to draw the attention of the entire room upon him. Everyone and everything else seemed miniscule and insignificant in comparison. He swallowed up the sepulchral space with his stature, a fallen angel gloating in its midst, grinning at its own wicked power.

"Well Mr. Mason, I see that you must have gained the upper hand with my little pet. Though it would appear that he left some marks upon you, marks that you are not likely to forget."

It was then that Mason realised what had somehow managed to elude his fractured mind up until this point. That voice. It sounded younger. There was no more coughing or retching and that slight twinge of a foreign accent was now definitely audible, definitely pronounced. The graces of a gentleman in good company mixed with the power of a man devoid of scruples, a man who would stop short of nothing. The voice that echoed around the room, swallowing up the air that floated through its empty spaces, now more forcefully than he had ever heard it before, but with that same softness, that same barrelling power from a voice that never needed to raise its volume. Mason choked back a gasp of disbelief as he gazed into those familiar piercing eyes, eyes that marauded through the world, challenging anybody who dared to meet them and hold their gaze, that gaze that pierced like needles, enforcing an injection of malignance directly into the bloodstream. The changing paintings, the disfigured creature that had tried to kill him, the dreams or premonitions, depending on how one viewed them, the howling insanity of the entire charade, everything – he had attempted to dismiss it. He had assumed that he was losing his mind, that his suffering mental state, stretched beyond recovery had finally collapsed, that his paranoia and fear had created this grotesque pantomime of delusion and madness, of discomposing images and inexplicable hallucinations, through which he wandered. However, though he had finally fixed his focus upon a singular vision and was master of a decided purpose, he now stood staring at a man who, days before, had looked as though he had just barely managed to crawl from his open grave to rasp more commands of doom into the world, as though he had pulled himself out of the dirt by his skeletal nails, his evil smile and eyes undiminished by the decrepitude of the faces that had surrounded him in death. Now this man stood returning his awe-struck gaze of horror, without a blotch upon his skin, without of any of the inherent stains that a life of shameless sin should have sketched there, devoid of the maps of decay that should have been tattooed upon his body. Mason felt his pained mind overheating, his brain seizing up, giving in to this defiance of order and values. Although he had surrendered to the sacrifice of logic and reality some time ago, this act seemed a step too far. This seemed beyond personal injustice – it was unjust and blasphemous to the world, to the natural orders of life and death. This walking cadaver of chaos seemed destined, somehow, to live longer than was normal, than was natural, to prepare itself for another life of misdeeds inflicted upon the world. Nonetheless, Mason had come tonight with one goal in mind and, despite the terror that twirled its way about his insides, he was still determined to achieve it, regardless of whether the thing he murdered was fresh from the grip of the cradle or the grave. Mason breathed deeply, desperate to swallow fear and panic, before forcing the utterance of a single sombre word.

"Albright"

The grin twisted its way into a fully-fledged smile, those shark's teeth glittering in the darkened light. Their sharp points parted as Albright spoke.

"Good evening Mr. Mason. I was waiting eagerly to see which one of you would make it back here tonight. To be honest, I am quite impressed by you. Impressed and very surprised. How exactly did you manage to overpower my sentinel?"

Mason's conscious mind feverishly fought back fear and disbelief. If this was a warped nightmare or a plane of multiple possible dementias, then perhaps he could not be hurt. However, his body cried in pain from the wounds the dream had inflicted thus far. No, this was a reality with which he still had to reckon.

"You had her murdered Alright! You've killed innocent people!" he spat at the young man in front of him.

"Yes, Mr. Mason, I did. Alas, that was somewhat her fault for getting involved with Sadler and for remaining by his side until the end."

"It wasn't her fault. She was just his girlfriend, she hadn't seen him in weeks. Rachel had washed her hands of Sadler. She was just an innocent in this. In your own contaminated mind you had a reason for silencing Sadler, but she knew nothing! You didn't have to involve her!"

Another smile, slightly different in its nature, of a kind Mason had not yet been witness to, passed across Albright's face, full of even more despicable malice than before. A little laugh escaped his throat.

"Is that really what she told you? You believed it to be that simple?" Albright spoke between his disdainful laughs. "Oh, she had most certainly not washed her hands of Sadler. They still saw each other regularly, their conversations always arranged secretly and their meetings in busy public places where we were powerless to approach them. They still loved each other. Why do you think she was so distraught and of such a jaded physique? She was heartbroken. She was reduced to that shrivelled wreck that you saw by panic, stress and fear, not even for her own well-being, but fear for his."

Mason felt a new tremor stirring inside. A creeping sickness began to course its way quickly through his body.

"Furthermore, Mr. Mason, it was not me who involved her. I simply questioned her regarding his whereabouts. It was not until you began searching for the photographs that Sadler panicked and gave her copies to hide. An idiotic thing to do of course, endangering her life like that, making it necessary for us to dispose of her. If Sadler had been the only one that had known about the pictures then we would have killed him alone – it was your meddling in affairs that you were ordered to steer clear of that caused her death. If you had just gone after Sadler instead of attempting to wage a secret war against me, to discover more than you were entitled to know, Rachel Gaines would still be alive."

"You're lying," Mason managed to quietly and pitifully shout, even though he knew that this was the exact sort of finale that was tailored and fitted for this carnival of omnipotent sorrow.

"I am not lying and deep down you know it. That is what she told me herself. She told me all about how she had urged Sadler to give her the photographs, even though he insisted that it would mean her becoming further involved in the situation. She told me how she had promised him that she did not care, how she had just wanted the two of them to bring the photographs to the police and end their misery, so that they could be happy once again. They were going to get married once it was all over. She told me this between her screams as we tortured her. She confessed everything through her broken mouth. She shouted her love for him, with pathetic crying sobs, and she screamed his name when I told her what I had done to him, before we ended her life."

Mason's mind was spinning. On top of all the agony suffered by those involved thus far, this was too much for him to take. His thoughts flew back to all that she had told him, to the horrific state she had been in the one and only time they had spoken face to face. He remembered how she had appeared – desolate, drug addicted, hate-filled, with nothing left for her in life. He remembered the unnatural manner in which she had pronounced her words, words explaining where Sadler had been going and to whom he had owed money, and how these words had sounded recited. They had not been recited due to the sheer number of people she had been forced to explain Sadler's story to, but rather because she had been instructed to say it. She had rehearsed the misleading narrative, practiced it numerous times, perfecting her story to keep herself and Raymond safe. She had not been the jaded, shattered soul that he had simply accepted her as but a woman waiting for the person she loved, panic, fear and grief stricken over their fate, hoping that someday this whirlwind of deception and violence would be over and that they could be together again. Mason could only assume that Sadler had felt the same. Sadler's words, "it's over … for both of us", reverberated in Mason's memory once more, along with the realisation that he had been mistaken, that Sadler had been talking about himself and Rachel. Mason had brought one of them to death's door and left him there at the mercy of his enemies, whilst in doing so involving the other and making sure that her destiny was also perdition and brutality. Mason choked back a concoction of pain and traumatic sadness. The rage and fury of before still swam around inside him but there were no longer any logical thoughts of an aftermath to go with them, of how to explain his story if he survived, how to justify his actions to an unlistening, accusing world. He had lost himself. He had nothing left to live for other than the slaughter of Albright, to squeeze every evil drop from that morbid existence, before his own life was ended. Apart from this one deed which now wholly consumed his imagination, Mason's entire conception of being, there was nothing else he could do for this world. If he died in this final struggle it was of no consequence. He had become a monster like the others, like his enemies, and his last task on earth would be an attempt to remove this dark stain, to force Albright into departure along with him, to join each other in an incessant afterlife of persecution. Nothing mattered anymore. Everybody in this room would die tonight.

"All this for a collection of photographs," he muttered, his sanity spiralling, submerged beneath the showering sparks of violent thoughts.

Albright's laugh produced another uniquely demented sound.

"And you also believe that this is about nothing more than the photographs? You still have not worked out what really happened here? I know I deceived and framed you, made sure you did exactly what I wanted you to, but I still expected you to have discovered something of what was really happening all the while. Are you not curious about the changes that have taken place before your eyes – the pictures, the man who attacked you, my own formerly aged face, the dreams that I am sure you have been having?"

"What are you talking about?" Mason stammered, half in a daze, scarcely concerned as to what Albright's solution would be, having wandered far too deeply into these wicked, twisted tunnels of witchcraft to be bothered any longer by the hows and whys.

"The photographs were just our way of identifying a target. We had always needed to kill somebody, to bring them here and complete our ritual. Sadler incessantly hounded and harassed my business affairs, following me as I saw my deals through, as I pushed a few people hard. Some people too hard for his liking."

As he said this, Albright devilishly glanced at the photographs that

Mason still clutched in his hands.

"Sadler's involving himself only assisted me in deciding whom exactly I would kill. Once I knew what evidence Sadler had potentially procured it seemed that I could solve two of my problems by disposing of him. It also meant that once we had him, I was in possession of a justifiable reason to have some slight fun, rather than killing him immediately."

Outside the storm continued to roar, but was kept silent within, the frail, old building's exterior hiding the power of the structure within. The vibrations of a cacophonous clap of thunder could be felt rumbling through the ground underfoot.

"We are a certain, very particular, type of people, Mr. Mason, and we require an alternative set of necessities in order to survive. I had suspected that your search of Sadler's personal library would have yielded some clues as to this. This building is a temple of sorts, for the fortunate, for the gifted and the cursed, for everybody who is afflicted or blessed, with our gift of cyclical life."

Mason listened incredulously to Albright's speech, not knowing what to make of his crazed ravings.

"If we so choose, we will not die. Every so often we must simply find ourselves another victim, one with which to replenish our decaying lives, to use in the rejuvenation of our crippled youth. All of us except this gentleman here," he said nodding towards the detective, who continued shifting uneasily. "He is like me in other ways, fuelled by desires for money and power. If we had not acquired Sadler by the night of the 29th we would have been doomed – once we ritualistically pick our victim there is no altering it. You have helped ensure the continuation of our kind. As you yourself have witnessed, I have worn the body of a man with ownership of a multitude of different ages, time and again, revolving in my seasons as the earth does around the sun. I have lived far beyond the scope of your mortal conception of existence and I intend to live for far longer still."

Mason could not decide what to take from these revelations, whether to believe them as the most logical explanation for illogical, unbelievable and impossible circumstances or to disregard them as the ranting of an insane and evil megalomaniac exalted from control of his ego, the revelations' madness masqueraded by the flawed sensory perceptions of his own damaged mind.

"You won't live much longer Albright, I'm going to make sure of it," he mumbled.

Albright continued to laugh.

"I am afraid that what you intend to accomplish is impossible. You cannot kill us. Try your utmost, I beg you, but we will still triumph. Before tonight's end you will feel my wrath. You will realise the futility of your efforts, the foolishness of meddling in business that was not your own. Tonight you shall squeal and scream. The cries of your voice will be choked by your own blood and innards, as you beg me for mercy. But you shall receive none. You shall die a slow, agonising death at my hands and I will relish your howls with just as much joy and gleeful jubilation as I did those I was gifted during the torture of those two unfortunate lovers!"

Mason's mind snapped. Without thinking he pulled out the pistol and fired two shots straight into Albright's heart. The thing immediately fell to the ground, lifeless. Mason had read that time slowed down drastically in such situations, that one could hear their own heart beating with the steady, pitiless thump of a mechanical funeral march. However, it was the opposite. The nightmare reached a remarkable rapidity, speeding itself into a relentless blur, a maelstrom crashing and curling all in its path. The detective was reaching for his own weapon but Mason reacted too quickly for him, plunging several leaden cylinders into his body, which slumped into a mound upon the floor, the blood pooling around his corpse almost invisible against the heavy tone of the carpet.

Before Mason was afforded sufficient time to determine the exact condition of his two victims, the smaller man powered into him like a juggernaut, crashing into Mason's chest with an almighty momentum. They struggled on the ground, the man in the sunglasses atop Mason, allowing him no room to aim his weapon, clawing and biting with small, sharp teeth, spitting and screaming indecipherable noises of pure, animal rage. The man was small but attacked with such savagery that it took Mason, especially in his drastic state of battery, a significant effort to overpower him. He was able to fend off the fierce fiend for a few moments with his undamaged arm, suffering bites and scratches, the little creature tearing small pieces of skin and flesh from it, until Mason managed to weakly eye gouge it with the fingers of his other arm. The man screeched and tumbled backwards off him. Mason now fired the pistol until it declared that it was empty. The man staggered on the spot as Mason lunged across the room, using the full force of his body to knock him to the ground, before stamping upon the man's head with his heavy boots. In his blind, bloodthirsty passion of frantic ferocity, and his new-born desire for nothing in life other than death, he kept stamping frenziedly until the man's skull had been completely crushed, caved in beneath the pressure of his boot.

Mason caught his breath as he glanced at the other bodies. The detective lay on the ground, still as a coffin, his loathsome life having left the limitations of its confines. The shots had hit him about the stomach, tearing it open with remorseless wounds. Mason turned to fix his glare upon what had once been Albright, a craven pleading within contesting the logical arguments forwarded by his remaining reason, begging him not to look. Albright was slowly getting to his feet. Mason watched with difficulty, rendered paralytic with disgust and dread, sickened that this thing could still fight on, that it truly was coming back to haunt the world once more, to rectify its failures, to enact further foul deeds just as it had prophesised.

Albright rose. That body of consummate blight was revived to its full capacity for malevolent, morbid power, and stood surveying its kingdom before it. The bullet holes and blood still peered through his ripped, black suit but he did not heed them any more than he would have a fallen eyelash that lay upon his shoulder. Albright continued to cultivate that vicious shark's smile. He laughed manically with a lunatic's bellow that rose high towards the ceiling.

"I told you Mr. Mason, you cannot kill me. Soon my other minion will rise up again, despite your best efforts. As long as my church stands, we will live and you will die. Now it is time for your part in this affair to be brought to an end."

Albright reached into his jacket and withdrew a small piece of metal, the same silver handle that he had gripped in the photographs Mason had seen in Sadler's development laboratory, the ones taken from Sadler's perspective before he had been murdered, pictures that he could recall but that may not have ever existed. A small button, set into the grip, was pressed, and out flicked a sharp, cruel looking blade. The storm outside clapped loudly, its sounds finally bursting through the building's fortifications, as though the elements were applauding, demanding a climax to this cataclysm of calamity. Albright satisfied them. He approached Mason, nimbly stepping from side to side. The knife and his teeth both flickered in the flashes of lightning that rapidly and repeatedly illuminated the darkened chamber in spectacular fashion. Mason's eyes followed the twitching movements of the blade, whist simultaneously trying to meet the eyes of its master. It sliced forward, aimed at his waist. Mason managed to jump backwards, scarcely in time, narrowly avoiding the slashing motion of the harsh, dancing metal. Albright laughed again, adhering to the path of Mason's retreat across the room.

As Mason looked frantically about for a weapon, Albright leapt forward again, this time grabbing him by the wrist with his free hand. Mason instinctively lifted his limp right arm to try and defend his body from the knife's descent. Albright's blade plunged into Mason's already flagellated arm, sending shrieks of bristling pain hurtling through every muscle governed by Mason's imbalanced nervous system. Albright withdrew the blade and struck again. The tearing metal landed in Mason's left side, just above his waist. Mason screamed in pain as he felt his insides being punctured beyond recovery. This time Albright held the blade in its position for a moment, scowling scornfully at Mason, enjoying every moment, before he pulled it out once more. As the knife left his body Mason felt his life force being torn out with it, being drained from within, the soul of another victim for Albright.

Mason folded over onto the floor beside the slain detective. Blood poured from his side. He could feel his body growing weaker. The time for his end was at hand.

"Do not worry Mr. Mason," Albright was roaring, "I am not going to allow you to die this easily. You may think that you feel pain right now but you know nothing of its limitless potential. When my minion is revived we will temporarily heal up that little wound of yours and soon you will be begging me to kill you!"

Mason's senses were growing duller by the second. He had to act quickly, before he passed out and was condemned to Albright's sick designs of torture. As he lay upon the floor, his eyes fixed upon the detective's dead face, drooped, pale and placid, Mason remembered the detective reaching for a weapon before he had been killed. Despite the pleading of his body to remain still, he quickly pushed his arm under the large man's body and grasped the pistol. In one movement he pulled the weapon out from underneath the corpse and fired several shots, almost at point blank range, straight into Albright's chest. The thing fell to the ground as before. Mason painfully picked himself up, blood flowing freely from his wound, beyond all hope of recovery. He limped towards Albright's apparently deceased body and put the gun's barrel against the cold skin of its head before pulling the trigger once more. The interior of Albright's skull exploded across the carpet, a sudden shot of crimson, inhuman magma. Mason had no idea what effect this would have, whether or not Albright would return once more. Whatever happened, he had to act quickly.

A passage from the diary of Samuel Walters suddenly recalled itself to Mason's mind, the memory ignited by Albright's words –

"As long as my church stands, we will live and you will die."

Mason remembered the village people, watching the flames ascend to the sky, the words of their preacher, the common conjecture that the only way to rid their town of the evil was to destroy the demons' sanctuary, the one thing that kept them grounded in this reality, that kept their resurrected lifelines resonating over and over again, powered and propelled by the blood of their victims.

Mason staggered towards the door that led back to the bar, clutching his gaping side, almost keeling over with the effort of every step, his hand dripping as he weltered in his own pouring liquid. As he glanced behind, the flashes of light showed that the body of the small man was starting to shudder and shake. He counted the contents of the detective's pistol. There were only two bullets left. One would have to be saved in the event of a particular outcome, to ensure that this did not end Albright's way, no matter what came to pass. He would destroy this place or, failing that, take his own life.

Every slight movement caused agony to rupture throughout Mason's animated corpse. With each motion of forward momentum he came close to passing out, his vision constantly brightening to the point of blindness before returning to normal as the pain briefly subsided. He reached the deserted bar, the effects of the storm shaking its weak structure far more than that of Albright's room. Here there lay the possibility of destruction. The power of the storm had continued to escalate. The decayed pillars and columns quivered weakly each time a wave broke against the walls outside or overhead, sending fragments of dust, stone and wood falling to the floor. One could almost feel the sway of the buckling building above, as its old, wooden foundations lurched beneath the immense force of the apocalyptic crescendo outside. The building was ancient and fragile. It had not been built for conditions such as these – nothing in the city had been. Mason pictured buildings in the heart of the forsaken metropolis toppling over as the world disintegrated around them. The city had never before experienced such an unforgiving heat wave and its suffering, its punishment for what went on within its boundaries, was now being further compounded, as the heat was broken only by the destructive powers of ice, wind and water. The foundations groaned, crying out for help, for support, for mercy, as they vainly attempted to hold the building together.

Mason crawled behind the bar and began to toss bottles of spirits against these old wooden supports, the glass breaking and dribbling their contents down the wood, like diabolic sap bubbling from a cursed tree. Each action was one step closer to death. Mason knew that he was dying, that there was nothing to be done but to finish this saga his way. His body was fuelled to override a pain that in other circumstances would already have killed him, fuelled by the adrenaline of his hate, his anger, his sorrow, his guilt and his absolute need to feel that he had done something right before he exited this wicked world.

As Mason continued showering the room in alcohol and broken

glass, Albright's minion entered the bar. The condition of its body resembled Albright's, the bullet wounds and blood still there but seemingly neither paining nor affecting it. However, its head, which Mason had crushed beneath his boot, was a mess of blood and bone, with other unidentifiable parts bulging out from what was barely recognisable as a human crown.

It stumbled forward without direction. Mason crashed a large bottle over the remains of its head, repulsively spilling the contents upon its exposed inside, broken glass burying itself in places while the dripping liquid mixed with dark mucus. Mason repeatedly stabbed this walking carcass in the stomach with the jagged bottle edge before it stopped moving and sunk to the floor at his feet. Mason fired another bullet into it, hoping it might buy him some time. Now he had one bullet left, either for himself or for Albright.

Mason was slipping in and out of consciousness. He had to finish this monstrous fantasy immediately. Behind the bar he found several boxes of matches, and began lighting and tossing them across the floor, igniting the spilt alcohol. The room erupted into a volcano of flame, the fingers of fire fiercely grasping whatever lay before them, not allowing any object escape, greedily devouring their prey and converting them into useless, charred waste. The fingers crawled their ways up the old, wooden columns and the supports that were built into the wall, instantly causing them to shake even more hopelessly and helplessly than before, and subsequently start to crumble. The heat and the pain were too much for Mason and he fell atop a stool, propping himself up with his elbows upon the bar, trying to remain conscious, to stay alive long enough to see the place burn. The fire was now spreading down the hallway and into Albright's rooms, beyond control or reason. The walls shook more violently with each passing second as Mason's jaded eyes drearily drifted down, deep down towards an ever closer sleep. Finally one of the wooden beams collapsed completely and the stones that sat above and about it began to fall loose. Pools of icy water began to pour in, challenging the fire in a primordial battle of the elements. Another collapse in an opposite corner sent in further floods of water. The fire continued to lick its way across the ceiling, along the tops of the columns and supports that still feebly stood, as bitterly cold water began to pool upon the floor, rising steadily. Stones started to fall from the wall with greater frequency, almost at random now, allowing more passage to the floods, granting further entry to the forces of nature, to a storm that would wash all traces of this vile palace from the face of the earth.

A voracious scream forced itself into Mason's semi-conscious state. Albright stood at the door, a wild look of insanity assuming control of his features as he saw his empire burning and crumbling about him. His head and body had returned to their normal state, the bullet wounds having disappeared beneath the holes in his jacket. He watched the rocks crashing to the ground from the ceiling; his evil eyes drank in the water that would destroy his temple, that would possibly save the lives of so many. He waded through the water, now almost at waist height, determined that if all this should be destroyed then Mason would be too, that he himself would escape and forge another empire elsewhere.

Mason still sat upon the stool, by this stage almost fully submerged in freezing, cold water. A pool of red mingled with the water that immediately surrounded him as the hole in his body began its final release. He now watched passing events in a stop start fashion as he prepared to leave life, to sleep forever. His vision became like the reels of continuous photographs, still shots gradually changing but missing the vital seconds that linked them. He saw Albright standing above him, looking upon him with seething, tempestuous revulsion and relish. He felt the water rising above his mouth. He saw another corner of the ceiling collapse and watched water begin to flood into the room from down the blood-soaked corridor that led to the outside world. Albright lifted him up by the collar and Mason saw the knife reflect the few fires that remained burning in the farthest recesses of the ceiling.

Mason felt the knife being buried in his stomach and then the hand that held it twisting the blade in a vicious semi-circle. However, he hardly felt any pain at all, his body having already succumbed to an almost total, all-encompassing numbness. With the final act his body was capable of achieving, besides producing this broken vision for what little time was left to him, Mason put the gun to Albright's chest and fired the final shot. The photographs showed him Albright falling backwards. He heard a sound symbolic of pain, an unnaturally high-pitched scream, blended with the noise of retching blood. Between blackness, the pictures showed Albright, afloat in a lake of dark red, beginning to change. His hair was suddenly grey and his skin lightly marked, as when Mason had first met him. Next he was old and decrepit, his hair thin and his body stained by age, as he had been on the night that Mason had delivered Sadler to his end. Next he was a shrivelled wreck being drowned beneath the growing, growling force of the waves, rare strands of withered hair tenuously holding to a bruised scalp. His skin was wrinkled and his teeth, what remained of them between the cracks and gaps, were now yellow and putrid. The only features that retained their ever-present power were the eyes that glared at Mason as they sunk beneath the water, down to their damnation. The two men maintained eye contact, neither man moving nor aspiring to fight their respective fates any longer. They merely stared, their eyes finishing this duel in a similar fashion to how it had begun. Mason watched Albright disappear, his eyes still open, burning with their unique, furious fires, even as they became completely submerged.

Mason felt tidal waves sweeping in to feast upon his own body, as floods burst through the fallen wall behind the bar and the entire room became enveloped in this natural reckoning. He heard the building collapse, demolished forever, and felt himself being pulled downwards before he closed his eyes for the final time. The floor was now gone from underneath him and Mason was dragged far beneath the ruins of the building, joining Albright on his journey to the world below, to whatever abyss lay waiting for them. He had taken revenge for some of those who had not been able to take it for themselves. He had dealt out some kind of justice, the only kind of justice that had been left, and as he slipped into slumber he was satisfied that he had done the right thing, that he had at least attempted to make up for a life terribly spent. He had tried and perhaps that was all that he could have done. He had sacrificed himself and he hoped that he had accounted for his crimes, redeemed at least some small salvation for his sins. He did not feel strained by the lack of air but rather drifted off slowly into a languid sleep, a sleep in which he hoped there would be no nightmares, no blood or corpses, neither guilt nor pain. Alan sunk further beneath the storm.

CHAPTER 24

Mason found himself awakening achingly slowly. He had been asleep for what seemed an unparalleled period of time, sweating profusely, his white shirt soaked with the damp stamps of perspiration. He stood up with great effort and drank down a glass of warm water that sat beside him.

As he did so, he could not prevent his eyes from falling upon the daunting photographs that lay waiting upon the table beside him.

Mason crossed the room to the large window and watched the city outside. The smouldering sun was stationed high overhead, beating down upon the melting, molten brickwork of the city with an incredible, hitherto unknown heat. An announcement drifted across the expanse of immobile air from the radio in the next room. The city was experiencing the most brutal heat-wave in its sordid, recorded history. Water supplies were running low, with rivers and reservoirs drying up by the hour. Barbara Madsen, the eternally sunny weatherwoman, ended her exhausting forecast with the news that the temperature was only going to rise, that there was no end in sight, nothing to indicate that the heat was to break in the near future. Something about the report sounded unnatural, rehearsed, even laboured, as though the recital was merely the same report being repeated for the thousandth time, having long ago lost all of its meaning.

Mason rubbed sleep from his eyes as he listened to the report with a sense of impending disaster. Familiar disaster. He could not remember exactly what he had been dreaming about, though it had struck him inexplicably powerfully and he was sure that it had been related to the troublesome case in which he had become embroiled. He had no recollection of falling asleep and was faintly aware that the dream had impressed upon him something akin to distinct recognition, as though its events were both a repetition of his past while also premonitions of the acts that were destined to haunt his life. He shook his head. Clearly the disturbing nature of this case was getting to him. He decided that it was best to try and finish it as quickly as possible, for all concerned.

Mason looked out the window once more. For a reason which he himself could not explain, a particular car, parked amongst the row of vehicles constantly on guard outside, fearfully grabbed his attention. He was sure that he had seen it before but, try as he might, he could not remember where or when. As he stood observing the car, it pulled out from underneath the shade of the buildings and into the baking heat, driving away with a solemn, reserved speed.

A sharp, shrill noise shattered Mason's train of thought. He turned and, as he did so, his eyes once more passed over the images of the young man and woman in the frames of the photographs upon the table, sitting next to a mess of books, papers and folders.

An unsettling feeling of dread came over Mason and told him that things were going to get worse.

He rubbed the painful bruise that marked his forehead. Somehow he suspected that he already knew how all of this was going to end.

Mason focused on the noise.

The telephone was ringing.